VENGEANCE

Book Three of The Evolutioneers Series

By

Anna Alexander

AnnaAlexander.net
Newsletter
http://eepurl.com/Q0tsz

House of Rosenorn
Vengeance

Print Edition
Editing by Jessa Slade. Copy Editing by Eilis Flynn
Cover design by Dar Albert
Electronic book publication March 2020

What do you get when you cross a whip-welding, mask-wearing vigilante and a set of uber-wealthy telepathic twins, with a serial killer out for vengeance?

The end of the world.

Well, the end of the world as they know it.

After surviving a plane crash that left them with telepathic powers that bounds them together as one emotional collective, twins Ethan and Ronan Daniels have struggled with how to fit into their new reality. Especially Ethan, who relies on his brother to keep the voices in his head from driving him insane.

A brief stint with the crime-fighting group the Evolutioneers gave them hope that there was a place for them. And when a cry for help in the night brings them face to face with a mask-wearing woman dispensing her own version of justice, they find appearances can be deceptive, and they are eager to learn more about the avenging angel who is able to block her thoughts to them.

By day Jameson Alinari runs a women's shelter. By night she makes personal visits to those who have committed crimes against women. Having a pair of handsome twins bust in during a "teaching moment" was a complication she did not need. But when one of her former targets is murdered in a grisly fashion, she is now reliant on the hot twins to prove her innocence.

What she never expected was the chemistry that ignited with not one but both Daniels twins. Her future was on the line. She didn't have time indulge in night-time fantasies. Or did she?

As the body count rises, Jameson fights for independence in a relationship that feels too, too perfect, as Ethan and Ronan fight to prove what seems so wrong can be oh so right.

Dedication

For my family. Always.

And for those who are fighting the fight for silenced every day. To the woman who had their voiced silenced. The fight will continue.

A Note from the Author

What can I do? That is a question I've asked myself often since I became an adult. Since my eyes were truly opened to the horrors of the world. What can I do to help those in need? How can I help when I feel as if I don't have the knowledge, resources, or time? How I can help when there is *so much* to do. Too many in need.

It's overwhelming. I understand. But we can't *not* do anything at all. Everyone deserves happiness. Everyone deserves a decent quality of life. As long as there are those who will use their power to oppress others, the fight will not end.

Over the last ten years I have had the privilege of working on the Emerald City Writers Conference and the Passport to Romance reader event. With our efforts we were able to donate thousands to the Domestic Abuse Women's Network, an organization dedicate to helping women in need. If you attended either of those events, you had a hand in contributing to the cause. Continue that momentum. Support your local charities. Attend events they sponsor. Buy a raffle ticket. Share the information on social media. Every little bit counts. Every person counts.

Thank you.

Find Anna Online

Website

annaalexander.net

Facebook

facebook.com/pages/Anna-Alexander/282170065189471

Twitter

twitter.com/AnnaWriter

Newsletter

http://eepurl.com/Q0tsz

CHAPTER ONE

WOULD A BULLET between the eyes stop the incessant noise of the voices in his head, or would the racket follow him beyond death?

"Fuck, Ethan. Are you struggling that much?"

Ethan Daniels opened his eyes and peered across the dark interior of the limousine at his twin. "I'm fine," he muttered.

"Sure." Ronan settled deeper into his seat and popped open another button on his dress shirt. He always did prefer the relaxed and casual look over a tie. "That's why you're contemplating thoughts of suicide."

"I'm not—"

Don't bullshit me.

Ronan's harsh words sliced through the cacophony of his thoughts. Although they shared a telepathic ability, Ronan seemed to manage the relentless attack on the mind better than Ethan did. Maybe that was because Ronan himself was a bit scattered, with his thoughts zipping from one topic to the next with the speed of a hummingbird.

Ethan, however, struggled to maintain the walls he tried to erect between noise and sanity. The stress was easier to manage when he was at home or on the odd occasion he was forced to go into the office to take care of business. But on nights like this, when he was obligated to schmooze with their company's shareholders, then yes, perhaps he was more likely to consider extreme measures to silence the voices.

"I'm not contemplating suicide," he said and rested his head back against the seat. "There were a lot of double-talking assholes in that room, and I'm exhausted from trying to sort through the bullshit."

"I hear you." Ronan sighed and ran his hand through his hair. "But there must be a better alternative than death. Just the idea of…"

Ethan didn't need his powers to finish his brother's thought. They had lost enough family over the years. They were all each other had left. One more loss would break them.

"I'm sorry." Ethan tapped his brother on the leg. "No more maudlin thoughts. At least for now. And I *was* handling my powers better. Especially after that night Matthew Madden tried to stage a military coup over the country."

Ronan chuckled. "I've been feeling it too. The control, even amongst the chaos. Before we ran into Crystal that night, I thought your head was going to explode being near so many people. Then we met her and, *pow!* Clarity."

As soon as Ethan heard her pleas for help, it was as if the foundation of his own powers locked into place. He had a focus. He had a purpose. The brothers had been able to use their powers for something good as they worked with Max and his team, the Evolutioneers, to save Crystal in a flurry of activity.

And then it was over.

The good guys had won. The bad guys were disposed of. And Ethan and Ronan went back to running their company as the struggle to maintain control of Ethan's powers resumed.

"Maybe we should talk to Max about setting up a simulator of some kind," Ronan suggested. "Doc Kelly mentioned Network was working on a program to help the others hone their powers. It would be worth it to have something to help with ours."

"Perhaps. But first I'd like to have a moment with Network to see how vulnerable our new security software really is."

Ronan chuckled. "She'll probably charge us a pretty penny."

"For her skills? Totally worth it."

Arghhhhhhhh!

Both brothers sat upright as a cry in the night reverberated in their heads. The scream seemed to come from a male and it was laced with pain.

"Which direction was that from?" Ronan asked, shaking his head as if he just had his bell rung.

Ethan sat still, his attention focused inward as he concentrated.

Dear God, no. Please stop.

The anguished pleading made Ethan hurt as if an elephant were sitting on his chest. "Up ahead. To the left."

"Hey, Ted." Ronan knocked on the glass partition between them and their driver. "Turn left here. Someone's in distress."

"I'll call 911." Their trusted head of security reached for the call button on the steering column.

"No. We'll check it out first and call for emergency if needed."

In the rearview mirror, they saw Ted arch a dark brow in that way that Ethan envied. Somehow, he was able to raise just one thin eyebrow almost all the way up to his hairline as his lips flattened into a straight line.

"Why are we not contacting the appropriate authorities?" Ted asked, his heavy accent a mix of his Chinese origins and the several years he spent in the British Intelligence.

"Because we don't know what is going on yet," Ethan answered. "It could be a car accident or nothing more than a stubbed toe."

Ted grunted, clearly not convinced that they weren't walking into danger. But he guided the limo to where they directed and pulled to a stop.

The part of town they were in was a mix of old and new construction. The old construction consisted of charming Craftsman-style homes built in the 1920s and 1930s while the new, and supposedly improved, construction was composed of modern, multistoried townhomes that filled the same footprint as their more delightful neighbors. This less than brilliant strategy included no parking spaces for these new multifamily buildings, so the streets were filled bumper-to-bumper with cars.

"Four minutes," Ted said and tapped his forehead. "Tell me if anything is wrong and I will call the police."

"Ten minutes," Ronan replied, climbing out of the backseat while Ethan charged ahead, using his frontal lobe as if he were a basset hound following a scent. "Hopefully it will not take us longer than that and it will be nothing."

"Five minutes."

"Why do you do that? You know we're going to take as long as we'd like."

Ted grunted and relaxed back in his seat. "Someday you'll listen to me."

Ronan grinned. "That day is not today, my friend. We'll be back."

"Those screams seem to be coming from here." Ethan pointed to one of the newer condominium complexes.

The building looked as if a giant had stacked railroad cars on top of each other like toy blocks following the industrial/recycled look that was the latest architectural craze. The entrance was a glass and chrome door to the lobby with a call box off to the side.

Ethan turned to his brother, who shrugged, then reached out to Ted. *Could you give us a hand with the door?*

Through the driver's door window Ethan saw Ted's eyes open and his chest rise with a sigh. Getting out of the car, he stepped over to join them while reaching into his back pocket to pull out a business card–size case. He slid out a thin metal pick, then went to work on the lock, swinging the door opened in a matter of seconds.

He raised his fingers. "Nine minutes."

Ronan scowled as Ethan shot ahead of him through the door and up the staircase. Floor by floor they paused on the landing and reached out with their powers, trying to pinpoint where the distress call was coming from.

"All I hear are their screams. Can you make out anything coherent?" Ronan asked.

"Not really." Ethan closed his eyes. "Lots of 'Stop it' and 'Please God help me.' But that's it. Can you feel anything?"

While the twins both had telepathic and empathic abilities, Ethan was better at mind-reading while Ronan's ability to sense emotion was stronger.

Ronan shook his head, his brow furrowed. "All I feel is terror."

In unison, the brothers entered the hallway of the third

floor, where the signal grew stronger.

A few steps in, Ethan drew up short. He held Ronan back with his arm as if he were a driver protecting a passenger at a sudden stop. "Can you hear that? Is that in my head or an actual sound?"

"You mean that slapping sound?" Ronan covered and uncovered his ears. "That's in our heads."

Ethan's lips tightened. Yeah, they heard the same thing. "I think we're close. This way."

As they crept down the hall, Ethan homed in on the thoughts screaming in his head. The man's cries for help were now joined by another. A female, if he had to guess. A light, sweet tenor that was in direct opposition of the cruel nature of her thoughts.

Take it, big boy, she was saying. *Aren't you man enough? Or are you a fucking pussy?*

They approached the last door at the end of the hall, and Ethan laid his hands on the wood. Drawing in a breath, he paused to glance at his brother. "You don't think we're hearing a BDSM scene gone awry, do you?"

Ronan shrugged. "If we are, that would be funny as hell, but I don't think so. This guy's terror level is going through the roof. And the malice I am sensing from the person he's with is running just as high."

"That's what I was afraid of." He paused again. "Do we have a plan?"

"Bust in and save the day?"

"Are you serious? That's a horrible plan."

"Do you have a better one?" Ronan asked, knowing full well he didn't. "That's right. So let's do this thing."

"Okay. Right. We got this." Ethan shook his hands out and rolled his shoulders.

For shits and giggles, and because he really didn't want to ask Ted for more help, he tried the doorknob and was mildly surprised that the door opened without a hitch.

Huh. Do you think he let her in?

Or she picked the lock, like Ted did to the front door. Ronan chuckled. *Or she has skills like Spider-Man and climbed up the outside of the building to get in through a window.*

Ethan met his brother's gaze and watched the humor fade to a sickening realization. Just because the people they knew who also had special powers were good guys didn't mean there weren't others with similar abilities out there who engaged in criminal activities.

Now *that* was a sobering possibility. Ethan took another breath to steady his nerves.

The entrance of the unit was dark, with the only light coming in from the streetlamps shining through the windows. Leading the way, Ethan crept slowly into the living room that looked like any other living room in a contemporary city dwelling. There was the overstuffed sectional, matching armchair, and oversize television dominating the room. Kids' toys were stacked in the corner and spilled across the carpet like a pixelated rainbow.

Despite the evidence, he didn't sense any children in the house. Only the terrified man and the woman were near. Their emotions were running so high, Ethan couldn't latch onto their thoughts to envision a coherent sentence. It was as if he were climbing a rock wall at the gym that was on a conveyor belt that spun faster and faster. As soon as he was able to latch on, his grip would slip, and he'd be left scrambling.

For all they could tell, mom and dad were having a

cheeky evening in. Or perhaps the dad was engaging in some extracurricular activities while the kiddos were away. Of course, the mom could have found out about dad's extracurriculars and was taking it upon herself to settle the score. Ethan wasn't sure which scenario he preferred.

Careful of making a sound on the hardwood floor, the brothers edged closer to the smacking echo of against skin that was followed by a muffled scream. That was why they couldn't hear the man out loud. He had to be wearing a gag of some sort.

A bedroom door was open, allowing the light from inside the room to spill across the carpet. Their view from the dark hallway, in contrast to the light, illuminated the scene inside in Technicolor glory. Ethan rubbed his eyes to make certain he wasn't hallucinating.

A man in his mid-40s was tied spread-eagled to the bed, naked as all get out. The mattress was mostly stripped with the comforter and top sheet folded in tidy squares and placed on the floor. A lone lamp glowed on the nightstand, casting shadows over the man's body that was mottled with welts. His skin glistened with sweat as he writhed in his constraints, moaning around the ball gag in his mouth.

At the foot of the bed stood the source of his pain—a short, curvy woman with long dark hair pulled into a braid. She wore a top that looked like a combination of a corset and a bulletproof vest, and her toned legs were encased in black, painted-on pants that matched the boots on her feet. She also wore a mask that was somehow affixed to her face and did not require a tie of any kind.

At first glance she looked as Ethan expected a dominatrix to appear: powerful, sexy, in control of her movement and environment. A complete schoolboy fantasy. Well, if your fantasy sex goddess had full red lips curled into a menacing sneer and who used the entire force of her weight to slap a riding crop against the soles of your feet.

There was nothing sensual to her motions at all, which Ethan found odd. But what did he know about BDSM apart from what he'd picked up reading an occasional "Letters to *Penthouse*" or by watching an X-rated video? Sure, some people got off on that, but the man was screaming in agony, and the woman had only one thought on her mind. Vengeance. Whatever was happening at that moment was not consensual.

She pulled her hand back for another slap when Ronan bolted into action. He grabbed her wrist with one hand and pulled the crop out of her hand with the other.

With a startled gasp, she whirled to face him. "What the fuck? What are you doing?"

"That's what I was just thinking," he quipped. "What are *you* doing?"

She blinked at him once, then twice, and then it was as if she had been charged with electricity. In a flash she sprang, catching him with an uppercut right to his gut followed by a roundhouse kick that sent him sailing across the room into the dresser.

"Shit." Ethan straightened in alarm as she raced straight at him as he blocked the door. He raised his hands in defense, his muscles tensing for the impending fight.

When she didn't slow, he braced himself, ready for the collision—when she hit the floor, sliding across the hardwood on her backside between his legs, then jumped to her feet to race down the hall, her boots clicking like gunfire as she ran toward the front door.

Holy shit.

"Release him," Ethan said to Ronan, who was shaking his head and looked as though he was blinking away stars. "I'll go after her."

As he scrambled down the hallway after the woman, he sent a thought to Ted.

Call for medic. Someone is hurt. Apartment 312.

As he entered the hallway, he spotted the door to the stairs swinging shut. He chased after the tap-tap-tap of her boots racing up the staircase.

Up? Why would she go *up*? Did she have a helicopter parked on the roof he hadn't noticed? How the hell did she expect to escape?

With his longer legs, he was able to take the stairs two at a time and caught the door to the rooftop before it slammed shut. The woman was already halfway across the flat expanse when he emerged and was heading toward the door that led to another staircase that ran down the opposite side of the building.

"Stop," he shouted, not caring if the neighbors heard. His buttoned collar and tie choked his breathing, but he pushed on at top speed.

Even with her lead, he caught up to her quickly, the ends of her braid licking his fingers as he reached out. She burst through the door and quickly spun around, knocking his hand away and following up with another one of her uppercuts. Having seen that move before, he dodged her fist and the accompanying kick.

This guy just won't give up.

He cracked a smile at her aggravated thought. No. He was not going to give up. In her mind he saw that the man tied to the bed was not her first. There were other men who had met her cruel hand. Others she had made suffer. Until he figured out what it was he and Ronan had stumbled upon, she needed to be stopped.

The slick soles of his Ferragamos slipped on the steps as they grappled down another flight of stairs. He wasn't out to hurt her, just detain her until the authorities finally arrived. Clearly, she wasn't going to give him the chance to take her down, kicking and punching with an expertise he wasn't expecting. Thank God they had stepped up their training with Ted when the Evolutioneers had entered their lives. Otherwise, she would have laid him out flat at first contact.

Will you knock it off? He used his considerable height to back her into the corner where the two sides of the retaining wall met. *Stop!* he shouted into her mind.

"How did you…" She stilled and gasped, then her eyes widened. "Oh, no."

He caught a fleeting image in her mind. A fair-haired woman with damp wavy hair and a motorcycle helmet tucked under her arm. A backpack was slung over her shoulder and she wore a sheepish grin.

Ethan rocked back on his heels, stunned by the amazing turn of events. The first surprise was why she would think of this particular woman at that moment in time. The second was the fact that he had a passing acquaintance with the same woman.

But what topped them all was the black curtain that stole over the image in the next heartbeat. Curtain—*ha!* It was more like a steel-enforced barricade. No matter how hard he pushed, he could not break through the wall.

She had blocked her thoughts—to *him*.

All this time that he had had his telepathic ability, it was only his powers of concentration that had kept the thoughts of others from invading his mind. This was the first time anybody, except for his brother, willingly blocked their thoughts from him. It was as if she had flipped the switch on the television and *pow*, the evening's broadcast was done.

How was she doing that? And how did she even *know* to do that?

His surprise caught him off-guard for that split second it took for her to take advantage and ram her knee up between his legs.

"Shit!" He shifted his hips to avoid catastrophe, but she still managed to jam her knee hard into the inside of his thigh.

Permanent damage was averted, but it was still painful as hell as the stars sprung to his eyes and he doubled over. She shoved him away then reached for the whip at her hip. The accessory enhanced her dominatrix costume, yet she wielded the instrument as if she were Indiana Jones, lassoing the end to the railing of the stairs before she swung down the remaining stories to ground level. With a flick of her wrist, she unleashed the end from the railing and disappeared.

"What the fuck just happened?" he muttered and wiped his hand over his face. "Fuck."

Gingerly, he put his weight on his bruised leg and hobbled around, testing the use of his limb.

She got away, he told Ted and his brother. *She ran out the north entrance.*

Medics are arriving now, Ted replied. *Would you like me to try to track her?*

No. Let's make sure our guy's okay. Besides, I may have an idea of where to find her. There's no rush.

He limped down the stairs to the third floor and returned to the apartment. He shuffled to the bedroom, where he saw his brother applying ice and wet cloths to the man's legs.

"She got away," Ethan said. "That one's a fighter. Friend of yours?"

The man shook his head. "Never met her before." Shivers racked his body and he readjusted the blanket over his nakedness.

"Shouldn't the medics be here by now?" Ethan asked his brother.

"No. No medics," the man grunted and shifted his legs away. "No."

Is he for real?

Ronan shook his head. *Who knows. He said she appeared at his door and told him that a friend of his sent her. Apparently, he is going through a divorce and thought a buddy was being generous and sent him a hooker.*

Friend? Sounds like an enemy to me.

"Are you sure you don't want any medical or police help?" Ethan asked the man.

"I just want to forget the whole night happened. Thanks for stopping her," he said through his teeth as they were chattering. "You can leave now. If you don't, I'll call the police myself and tell them you're trespassing."

Idiot move, but if he wanted to be left alone, that was fine by them. When the medics arrived, they could deal with him.

"Glad to be of service," Ronan said. "We'll let ourselves out."

They made sure all the doors were shut as they left the apartment and elected to use the elevator to get down.

"That was an…interesting turn of events," Ronan said.

Ethan nodded with a grunt but remained silent.

The elevators slid open with a ding. "You're not going to let this go, are you?" Ronan asked.

"And you can?" Ethan replied incredulously.

"Yes."

"Seriously? Where were you the last fifteen minutes? That was insane. How can you just walk away from that?"

"Because when it comes down to it, what went on here really isn't any of our business. Besides, what's his name up there—uh, what did I pick up? Gerald?—Gerald said to butt out. Therefore, we butt out and have an interesting story the next time we meet up with Max and the gang. Vigilante crimefighting is more their style anyway."

"Maybe. But I saw something in her thoughts that was very intriguing."

They climbed into the limo and settled back into their seats. Ted didn't waste a moment before driving them off into the night.

"You're not going to share?" Ronan asked, waving an impatient hand when Ethan remained silent. "You're blocking your thoughts from me, you ass."

"That's right. And she blocked her thoughts from me."

"What?" Ronan stared at him. "That's not possible."

Ethan leaned back and grinned. His heart was still thumping wildly, but he savored the excitement. It wasn't often that he had one up on his brother. Especially when the bastard was lying through his teeth. Ronan was intrigued. Intrigued and aroused about the events that just transpired. Sure, the arousal part was rather distasteful in the grander scheme, but it was rare to be stimulated both mentally and physically in such a provocative fashion. He could claim to consider the matter closed, but Ronan was as eager for more information as he was.

"We don't even know where to find her," he said.

"*We* don't. But we know someone who does."

CHAPTER TWO

JAMESON DUCKED BEHIND the dumpster and covered her mouth and nose with her hands. She did so in part to block the stench of the trash, but mostly to muffle the sound of her trying to gain control of her breathing. The twenty minutes a day she spent jogging on the treadmill did not match the intensity of a fight to the death, racing down the stairs, and running eight blocks away from a bad guy.

Bad *guys*. There had been two of them.

What the hell had happened back there? Seriously. What the hell? There was always the risk that someone would interrupt one of her rehabilitation missions, but never did she imagine that twins would appear on the scene. Twins!

Two tall, dark, Mediterranean gods dressed as if they had just come from a fancy dinner party just wandered into the bedroom as if they had every right to be there. Gerald Mulvaney lived alone. She was positive. Who were they? Neighbors?

Perhaps she should have double-checked that Mulvaney had locked the door behind him after he let her into his apartment. At the time she was thinking it would make for an easier escape if it remained unlocked, and although it had, it wasn't quite the escape she had envisioned.

She slunk down farther into the chilly pit of darkness behind the garbage container and tried to focus. The most disturbing part of the entire encounter wasn't that these strangers caught her in the act of disciplining another asshole. But one of them had spoken to her directly into her mind. Didn't use his mouth in any way, shape, or form. At all.

Was he telepathic? A mind reader? Did they both have the abilities? Even more concerning, were they members of the Evolutioneers?

Fuck. The answer to all of those questions was a good solid maybe. And that was enough to make her worry for her safety for the first time since she was a kid.

Curse words blistered where they sat on her tongue, but she shut it all down and forced herself to think of mundane things such as a grocery list or the recipe for chocolate chip cookies. She had no idea how the guy's powers worked. How far was his mental reach? Was it best to think of blackness or try to blend into her surroundings by thinking of normal, everyday nonsense that could be from anyone in the neighborhood?

A black, two-door Honda Accord pulled up alongside the sidewalk with a screech. The headlights flashed twice. Jameson hit the flashlight icon on her cell phone, emitting a bright light with the same single. She carefully unfolded from her squatting position and waited for the blood flow to her legs to return to normal.

One. Two. Three. Four. She slapped at her pockets and belt. Mask, whip, knife, phone. Jameson never went anywhere without making sure the esstentials were still on her. Once she had the feeling back, she dashed from her hiding place and wrenched open the passenger door.

"Go, go, go," she instructed the driver.

Trini gave her a once-over, her dark eyes narrowed.

"What's going on, chica?"

"Just go." Jameson scanned the area around them, searching for law enforcement or one of the gorgeous twins. "I'll tell you on the way. Just go."

Trini pulled the seen-better-days Honda out onto the street. The old girl might not have been pretty to look at, but the car had an engine built for racing. Every extra dollar Trini scraped together she put into her baby.

"What happened to you, girl? Did he recognize you? Get away? What happened?"

Jameson took off her black mask and hunkered down low in her seat. "I don't know. Things started out fine. The dumbass let me into his apartment, no problem. He didn't even stop to question which of his friends would've sent a girl to his place."

"Pervert," Trini interjected.

"Uh-huh. I had him tied and was just getting into the groove when two—ah, I mean a man burst into the apartment. I have no idea who he was or where they—he came from. Maybe he was a friend or neighbor. I didn't ask. I skipped out of there as fast as I could."

"Damn." Trini glanced around before switching lanes and speeding onto the freeway on-ramp. "Do you think he made you?"

Trini's guess was as good as hers. If one or both of those men were mind readers, she shuddered to think what they might have picked up. How long had they been in the apartment before they made themselves known?

"I'm pretty sure he didn't. I just want to stay low, in case." No need for both of them to worry about the what-ifs. Besides, if Trini knew it wasn't a "he" but a "them," and one of them at least spoke directly into her mind, then the rest of the team would find out and they'd all be up her ass. Yeah. Too much of a mess to go there. "How did your night go?"

Trini's smile flashed bright in the shadows. "Did all right. Found two girls working the streets. Got them into the shelter on Maple Avenue."

"Young?"

"Nineteen, twenty. Too young to be hooking because they want to. Apparently they were fosters who ended up on the street as soon as they aged out of the system."

Damn. Jameson shook her head. For years she had been trying to work with the mayor's office and the bigwigs at DSHS on implementing a system that would give kids a solid foundation for adulthood instead of throwing them out on the street. So far, they had been mostly successful on getting the word to teens who were about to age out that they had options such as trade schools and grants for housing and school. The days of a backpack, some cash, and a hearty handshake were gone in most areas, but a few kids still fell through the cracks due to misinformation.

"Good job, Trini. I'm glad you found them. We'll save this world one person at a time. Or we'll die trying."

"True that, sister." She reached across the console with her hand opened wide. "Fly or die."

Jameson locked her thumb around Trini's, so their joined hands looked like wings, then as one they raised and lowered their hands. "Fly or die."

Trini's devotion to their cause was solid, as she had once been one of those kids on the street. Not because she had been a product of the foster system, but because being on the street was better than being sequestered in a two-bedroom apartment with her father, his girlfriend of the week, and nine brothers and sisters who had to fight for everything.

Jameson would never forget the rainy night years ago when her mother had opened the door of the shelter, revealing the petite Latina girl standing at the threshold saying, "I just need a towel. I can take care of myself, but I'm done with this rain."

After a few nights of sleeping in a warm bed of her own and some belly-warming Italian cooking, Jameson's mother was able to convince Trini to stick around and work for her GED. Of course, it hadn't been easy, but the struggle made Trini appreciate the rewards all the more.

The Evergreen Domestic Abuse Shelter was the place of hope for so many, and never failed to bring Jameson comfort seeing the front gate. Especially at that moment when Trini guided the sedan into the parking lot. The adrenaline pumping through Jameson's system since almost getting pinched finally began to ebb, leaving her as limp as a soggy French fry.

From the outside the shelter looked like a massive office building tucked away on the outskirt of the city's industrial area. And that was the point.

The building wasn't a shelter for only homeless women. It housed women and children who had fled the most desperate of situations. Women like Emily Mulvaney and her two children, who a week prior had to flee the house after her husband got drunk and put a knife to their four-year-old's throat when Emily told him she was leaving.

For the safety of the shelter's occupants, its location was kept as private as possible. No one wanted an enraged spouse showing up on their doorstep, so the location was known to only those select few in the police department who worked in the domestic violence divisions. Even then,

Jameson made sure the shelter was protected with several levels of safety protocol, including cameras, motion sensors, and coded door locks.

With Jameson's due diligence, her wards could sleep in comfort and peace. Especially Emily and her children, who weren't going to have to worry about her piece of shit husband anymore. Before Jameson was interrupted by the gorgeous twins, good ol' Gerald was agreeing to anything she asked of him.

She hoped.

God she hoped. Those twins couldn't have arrived at the worst time. She had been just about to seal the deal.

Trini parked in the garage under the shelter near a door marked "Engineering." The lot was semi-full of residents' vehicles and quiet with almost everyone in their beds for the night. Only the soft tread of their shoes on the concrete broke through the peaceful silence.

Jameson knocked twice on the marked door and paused for a moment before knocking three more times. She then inserted her key into the lock and pushed it open. Apparently, they were the last ones in, as the rest of her crew were already waiting inside.

A simple card table and four folding chairs took up the center of the room with a few surplus desk chairs added for extra seating. The main power supply and furnace for the building took up the rest of the space, as well as the shelter's computer server that had been added in recent years. A whiteboard covered the single bare wall in the room with a rack of keys hanging underneath. The team had stashes of provisions from extra blankets to backpacks full of toiletries in different storage lockers in the area.

Fluorescent lights overhead tinged everything in green,

which was fitting as she still felt sick about the twins.

Lucinda sat in one of the folding chairs with her foot popped on another. A giant tub of Red Vines rested on her lap, probably pilfered from the shelter's pantry. The red candy disappeared between her red-stained lips at a quick pace. Across the table from her sat Ashley, her ever-present notebook opened. They were both wearing black in various ensembles of dress that provided comfort and protection ranging from hooded sweatshirts to leather jackets.

"Took you long enough," Jules said when they entered. Her girlfriend Bryn was stuck to her side like Velcro, and they were cuddling as close as the desk chairs allowed. Rarely did you see one without the other, and they usually were touching in some way.

"The boss got popped," Trini replied and swiped a few vines from Lucinda's bucket.

"What?" the others exclaimed.

Jameson turned in horror at her friend and gave her the stink-eye. "Dude. Why would you say that? Besides, I told you it was probably no big deal."

"Who popped you and how?" Ash asked, her features pinched tight and her entire demeanor on guard.

"No one." Jameson waved her hands around as if to clear the room of the stench of Trini's statement. "Just a neighbor who came into the apartment while I was finishing up. I made a quick getaway and he was none the wiser of who I am. It's fine. He'll have a helluva story to tell his friends in the morning, and they'll all probably think he hallucinated. The most important thing to take away from tonight is..."

She strolled to the whiteboard and used the eraser to remove an address that had been written in blue ink.

"Gerald Mulvaney has been dealt with and should not be bothering Emily and her children anymore," she announced triumphantly.

"Should not or will not?" Ashley asked.

"What?" Damn it. She should've known Ashley was going to catch that slip. She was always so meticulous with her notes. But the truth was, anything was possible. They did their part and hoped some sense, or the fear of a reprisal, set these fools straight. "Oh, uh, will. Will. He will not be bothering them. Who else?"

"Scratch off the address on Jones Avenue," Lucinda said, blowing on her scarlet red nails then rubbing them on the lapel of her leather jacket. "That little bitch cried for his mama. Can you believe that? After the way he beat on his wife, that fool had the nerve to beg for mercy."

"Nice job, Lulu." Jameson removed the address from the list.

"The Buckwalter home was vacant," Jules said. "But Bryn and I gave out about ten backpacks and found shelters for a vanload of teens who had been sleeping under the Carrington Bridge."

"Nice."

"110 8th Street is cleared," Ashley added. "And 25th Place. And I did all of that and managed not to get nicked."

"Ha-ha, smartass. But good work. Now for an unrelated topic." Jameson reached for the bucket of vines and nabbed one for herself as she puzzled out how to broach the next subject.

"You guys kick so much ass, but we're going to have to take things down a thousand over the next day or two. We may have a member or two of the Evolutioneers sniffing around the shelter."

"The Evolutioneers?" Bryn bolted upright. "You mean those people that have strange powers?"

"Why would they be here?" Ash asked, her tone a mix of steel and wariness.

"Some of you may remember Alisia. She stopped by earlier tonight for supplies and is on the run from them. Trouble with her father. It's all bullshit, but here we are. She wasn't here long, but apparently one of the Evolutioneers has a really good sense of smell. Stands to reason they may pay a call."

"Was this the friend who rang the bell earlier this evening?" Trini asked. As one of the shelter's administrators, one of her tasks was door detail and watching the security monitors.

"Alisia is on the run from the Evolutioneers? Fuck." Ash sat back with her arms folded over her chest. "I thought she cleaned up and went straight."

"Who's Alisia?" Lucinda asked.

"A friend. A friend that goes back, way back. A sister and an original Crimson Angel who I would die and kill for. And she did go straight, Ash. Look, it's a long story and she's totally innocent, but she's on her own and needed help. But that also means that we may have people we were not expecting encroaching on our circle." She reached into a duffel bag that she had stashed in the corner earlier in the evening and pulled out some blouses, T-shirts, and pants. "If you all can take one or two of these with you on your way out and drop them in the donation bins in your shelters tomorrow, that would be great."

Jameson and Lucinda weren't the only ones running a charity. Ashley also worked part-time at a shelter for homeless and runaway teens while Jules worked for a food bank. Their little network had a line on the who and where of the dregs of the city. They also had the best opportunity of taking Alisia's clothes with her scent and scattering it across town.

There was an agitated boot tap from underneath the table and Ash's lips tightened. "I don't like the thought of the Evolutioneers being anywhere near here. We don't know what their agenda is."

"Trust me," Jameson said. "They are not here for any of us. They know nothing about us. It will all blow over in a day or two and then we can kick back up again."

Ashley swept her things up into her arms, and Jameson was glad to note she took a shirt too. "We shall see. But I'm going to strengthen my defenses and take extra patrols around here. I'll talk to you all later."

Defenses. Jameson shook her head. Once an Army grunt, always an Army grunt.

Lucinda got to her feet as well. "Hey, Ash. Give me a ride home?"

"Fine," came the terse reply.

Lucinda gave Jameson a high-five on the way out then paused to say over her shoulder to the couple cuddling in the corner, "Good luck with the move tomorrow, girls."

Jameson turned to Jules and Bryn with a big smile. "Oh yeah. Tomorrow is moving day."

The two girls shared smiles that were brighter than ten suns. Jules brought their clasped hands together to her lips. "I never thought Section 8 would approve us. Feels like it's been forever. Now I finally get to make a home with my favorite girl."

Bryn blushed a pretty shade of pink and pressed a kiss to her girlfriend's cheek. "I love you so much."

"Love you too, baby."

The Jules who sat basking in the glow of love was so different than the shy woman who had entered the shelter the year before. She too had served in the military like Ash, only she had served in the Navy.

Unfortunately, both women had suffered at the hands of their country and fellow servicemen. Jules had struggled to acclimate to civilian life once she returned home to the Indian reservation and the family who battled with alcohol and drug problems. Without the structure of the military, she had fallen into a deep well that was piled high with guilt over not being able to save family members who succumbed to their addictions.

Her tribe had supported her, knowing she wasn't to blame for her family's breakdown, but the military failed her with limited access to jobs and medical care. The shame of not being able to provide sent her to the street. She was supposed to have been the one who escaped the cycle. Instead, she had her feet kicked from under her, that was until the day she showed up at Evergreen and started to turn her life around.

The journey had not been easy, but now she had her happily ever after, with Bryn. The quiet Asian girl had befriended Jules when she had spotted her eating in the commissary by herself. For weeks Bryn just sat by the tall woman's side, not saying anything more but a simple hello or good morning. There were no questions, no judgments. Nothing but companionship until pleasantries turned into conversations, and conversations gave way to love.

"I'll bring gnocchi to the housewarming party," Jameson said and gave the two women a hug.

"Deal." Jules and Bryn left with one last fist bump and a

flying angel and strolled off into the shadows of the garage.

Jameson slung her empty bag over her shoulder and called out to the group climbing into their cars. "Good night, y'all."

As she made her way to the elevator, Trini followed. "I still think you should have told them about what really went down with that hombre at the condo."

"There's no need," Jameson replied with a grunt. "We're fine. It's not like I'm ever going to see that guy again. Really, we're fine."

CHAPTER THREE

ETHAN FLOPPED DOWN on the green-velvet upholstered sofa and pressed an icy bottle of water to his throbbing temple. He couldn't wait until he was back in his own bed or swimming laps in his pool. This little portion of Western Washington would be fine to visit for a day, but after almost a week, the endless expanse of brown rolling hills and being sequestered within the confines of a religious cult, the environment was getting to him. His body ached as if he had been hiking around the base of Mt. Rainier, even though he had been sitting on his ass all day, sorting through the thoughts of hundreds of people.

When he and Ronan gained their powers, they had made a moral decision to not intrude into a person's mind for shits and giggles. A task easier said than done when most people tended to live their thoughts and emotions on their sleeve, shouting their intent to the world as if they were using a loudspeaker. Over the last few years, he had gotten better at blocking most of the noise. His control was still far from perfect, but at least he managed to function like a normal human being.

But now he had purposely put himself in a room with a congregation of people who just had their world swept out from underneath them with the sole purpose of reading their thoughts. He was amazed he could stumble back to the main house and not collapse the moment he stepped into the sun.

Why did he subject himself to such torture? Because Max Madden had called to ask if one of the twins could assist the Evolutioneers on a mission. He wanted to have both of them onsite, but twins of any kind attracted attention. With only one of them present, they would have an easier time protecting their identity.

Unbeknownst to Max, the mission in question was the perfect opportunity for Ethan to tackle several of his projects, including testing his powers. As a bonus, he was able to score a set of the sweet high-tech sunglasses Max designed for all of the team members.

"Will this help?"

Ethan opened his eyes to see a blonde woman standing by his side, holding out a glass filled with amber liquid. Her smile was warm, but in her eyes she looked every bit as exhausted as he felt.

"I'm not sure, but I won't turn it down." He took the glass, holding it between his hands as if the liquid would flow straight into his bloodstream and bring him back to life.

"Enjoy," she said. "It's my father's best."

Ethan took a sip and regarded the woman as she flopped into the armchair across from him. Alisia Caldwell was the main reason he agreed to go on this mission to help unweave the tangle of chaos her father had created in his community.

Besides him and Alisia, Doc and Chase were part of the Evolutioneers team Max sent while he was dealing with other issues on his front door, including taking care of his pregnant wife.

The team was staying at Alisia's father's house, along

with her younger sister, using the elegant Georgian-style home as their base of operation. The décor was 1990s homespun country, complete with cinnamon-scented potpourri filling brown wicker baskets and green-checked gingham pillows. A den of false security that hid the nefarious acts of its owner.

Ethan's previous interactions with Alisia had been few since he and Ronan met the Evolutioneers. Alisia was special to the group as she didn't have any powers of her own, but she had been a colleague and friend of Doc Kelly's and was brought into the team to assist Doc in her research in determining why and how they had developed their superpowers.

From what Ethan had been told, the research suggested that a combination of pollutants in the water, the air, and in the earth created a potential powder keg inside each individual. When someone who had the right elemental makeup experienced a tragedy, the spike of adrenaline would ignite the chemicals in their body and give them an enhanced talent. For Ethan and his brother, it took their innate twin communication and expanded it to the ability to read minds and sense others' emotions.

Doc Kelly had asked if they would be so kind as to help contribute to her research. If it meant understanding what had happened to them and possibly lead to a way to lessen or remove their powers, the brothers agreed, which meant that on occasion they had worked with Alisia as well. He didn't know much about her from their earlier interactions except that she was funny, quick-witted, and extremely competent at her job, but for the most part kept to herself.

Everyone's perception of her changed when the group recently discovered she had been running from a very painful past. The truth came out when her father, the head of a megachurch, had hired the Evolutioneers to track down his daughter, not knowing she worked for them.

It had been a rough week for Max and his team as they worked to discover who the real villain was after finding out that their friend had been hiding her true identity from them. After Alisia went on the run to clear her name, she delivered evidence that her father had a side business of drugging his parishioners and was about to embark on a launch of that designer drug to the public. Alisia had been a loose thread he needed cut, which was why he wanted her found.

With Alisia's father soon to be going to jail, there was now the impossible task of finding out who exactly within the church knew and aided with the operation. They also had a compound of parishioners who were suddenly without a spiritual leader. That was why Max had called on Ethan or Ronan to lend a hand in signaling out the innocent from the guilty.

Of course Ethan couldn't point to a person and announce that they were thinking how to cover up their crimes, but he could observe and signal to the others when someone was lying or was nervous about being caught. From then on it was up to the authorities to find the evidence to convict the person. His task was just to narrow down the search.

And it was also an excellent opportunity to talk to Alisia, who had become a surprising piece of a puzzle he had been working on that had started to become an obsession. Now he just had to find the right time to broach the subject with her. They had been so busy on the church's compound, they had been going non-stop since he arrived. Until now.

Doc and one of the other team members, Chase, were out in the compound assisting medical staff with those who had been personally affected by the drugs and going through withdrawal. At the moment it was just him and Alisia in the house, along with her sister, Mary Beth.

After his initial arrival he hadn't seen much of the teenager. She spent most of her time alone dealing with her own feelings of learning that her entire life and what she had known about her mother, father, and half-sister had been a horrendous lie.

The events of the last few days had also taken their toll on Alisia. Even with all the shit she went through to clear her name, Ethan could tell by her actions that it was her relationship with her sister that concerned her the most.

"She is doing better, you know," he said. "Your sister."

Alisia's gaze traveled to the second floor, where her sister had been holed up in her room for the last few days.

"Did you read her mind?" she asked.

"Not after that first day to see what she knew about your father's operation. But I can sense her emotions a bit. Ronan's better at that, but I can feel her fear. She's scared and uncertain. Now that the drug is out of her system, she's thinking more logically too. I feel her slowly resigning herself to the truth. I can sense that need to trust you. But fear is blocking her. She needs time."

"I'm willing to give her that." Alisia sighed. "I *want* to give her that. But it's obvious the community does not like me being here. They don't like either of us being here. They think the entire family betrayed them, and they want us gone. I don't blame them. We both need a fresh start, but I would really like to have her trust before I take her away from the only home she's ever known."

"I think she'll be ready to understand that soon."

Alisia sighed again and leaned back in her seat. Her eyes became unfocused and she began to chew on her lower lip.

Ethan tapped the side of his glass with his ring finger, contemplating just how to proceed with the real reason why he had been so eager to accept Max's invitation to go on this mission.

Fuck it. Just do it.

"Alisia. There is something I've been wanting to talk to you about."

"I'm fine." She waved her hand as if clearing the air. "Whatever is going on between me and Ripley, I am fine."

He chuckled. Right. That entire relationship between Alisia and the shape-shifter was something he had no desire to dive into. The heat he had seen burning between them was enough to melt a glacier, but that was nothing compared to the tension that was as thick as the walls to Fort Knox.

"I wasn't going to ask you about Ripley. Whatever is going on between you two is complicated. Obviously, you both have thoughts in that regard, and I have no interest in being privy to that discussion. Actually, I wanted to talk to you about something unrelated. Something I'm not exactly sure of… Yeah. I don't know."

"Okay…" Her brow furrowed as her grip tightened on her glass.

"The other night my brother and I met a woman. Well, stumbled upon her would be a more accurate description. We didn't catch her name, so I'm hoping you can help me identify her."

"Me?"

"Yes. You." He leaned forward. "I'm going to send you a

thought. A picture. Ready? Do you know who she is?" He drew in a breath and projected a picture of the mystery woman looking as she had the moment he entered that bedroom. Braid flicking, a smirk on her lips as she taunted her captive.

Jameson.

Alisia gasped, then sat upright. A black veil dropped on her thoughts for a second before being ripped away, and then it was as if her thoughts had been a ball of glass that fell to the floor, scattering jagged shards across the floor. There were so many images: darkness, blood, nights spent on the street, in the backseat of someone's car. Ethan grew so dizzy with the speed, he had to close his eyes to steady himself.

"Why would you think I knew her?" she asked, taking a healthy sip of whiskey. She might be acting cool and collected, but her hand trembled.

"She projected a thought. One of you, before she dropped the veil on her thoughts." Much like Alisia just tried to do, although not nearly as well. "Please. Can you tell me who she is? It's important."

Alisia's eyes darted around the room as if she were looking for the means to escape. The muscles along her jaw bunched as she swallowed. "She is an acquaintance. From way back. That's all I can say."

"Can say or will say?"

"Both."

Her staunch loyalty was a trait he had heard mentioned often in the last week, so he wasn't altogether surprised she wouldn't reveal the much-needed info about her friend. But Alisia was his only lead, so he had to keep pressing.

"Please? We found her torturing a man. Full-on torture, Alisia. Whatever she was doing needs an explanation. What if she's out there torturing more people? Shouldn't she be stopped?"

She shook her head and pressed the heel of her hand to her brow. "I can't tell you what she was doing or what that was about. We lost track of each other a few years ago."

"How about a name?"

"No." Her lips went back into a firm line. "I can't."

"But—"

"Ethan. No."

She was done. He saw it in the press of her lips and the steel in her eyes. He felt it in his bones. She wasn't going to give.

A flare of frustration ignited in his chest then died a quick death. She was protecting her friend. He understood that, but it still sucked.

However, the conversation wasn't a total loss. Little did Alisia know that she had already given him a name. The first clue in the puzzle he was desperate to solve.

As to why he was desperate, he hadn't the foggiest idea. But the fire in his gut would not leave him be. Even Ronan's thoughts drifted to the events of that night on a regular basis. This woman was important to him. Or at least was going to be. To both him and his brother. He was absolutely certain of it.

This mystery woman closed her thoughts to him. Solidly shut, closed up tight. Why had she been able to do that and no one else? He had to know why.

He took another sip of his drink and pictured the mystery woman. No. Not just the mystery woman.

Jameson.

CHAPTER FOUR

"I DON'T CARE who they are," Jameson snapped into her phone. "Even if they want to pull up to the gates with truckloads of cash, no one gets details of the location without my permission."

"Jameson," groaned Shepard Samuels, president of the board of the Evergreen Women's Center. "I know how protective you are of the center's location, but this sponsor wants to give us big bucks. Big! They want a tour of the facility to see how their funds could best be used."

The shelter she ran was part of a larger charitable organization that offered humanitarian services to people in need. The administrative offices of the charity occupied the entire top floor of an office building located just south of the city. They shared the building with a data security firm, a temp agency, and the deli on the first floor that served the best baguette sandwiches she ever had. Not only were their neighbors friendly, they also provided excellent opportunities for the shelter's patrons to find employment.

And the office was far enough away from the shelter to keep their location private—a fact that Shepard was well aware of.

She was tempted to tell Shepard that his sponsor could best use their funds right up their ass. Some of the women and children in her facility were on the run for their lives from ex-significant others, abusive parents, and predators who had driven them from their homes in often traumatic ways. They came to her facility for safety, and by God she would give them that safety and protect it with her life. Not even Shepard knew the exact location of the shelter.

And it was going to stay that way.

"No tours. Period."

Whatever he said next was muffled as he was probably running his hand over his face. An action he did often when they were at a board meeting, charity event, lunch dates, basically any time they butted heads.

Shepard was a necessary evil in her world. He believed in their cause and understood their mission. Awesome. He was also a successful white businessman who was very good at getting other white businessmen to part with their charitable funds. Also awesome. But he loved to play with the numbers. If there was a way to stretch a dollar or gain one more contribution, Shepard could kiss ass with the best of them.

"No tours," she repeated in her firmest tone. "I will go to my grave defending that policy. But I understand the importance of funding. This is my offer: I will meet you at your office. If they really want to donate, they will agree to meet me there. Take it or leave it."

Shepherd's grumble reminded her of the grind of a broken blender. Then he sighed. "Your fierce protectiveness is why you are so great at your job, Jameson. Even if it does make me want to pull my hair out. Fine. Meet me at the office. One hour."

"One hour. Promise. I may even show some teeth when I smile this time."

"Just be your charming self," he said, not able to keep the chuckle out of his voice.

"Always."

One hour turned into an hour and thirty minutes with a baseball game snarling the afternoon traffic. Shepard was pacing outside the closed door of his office with his hands behind his back. His fingers flexed and twisted, displaying his agitation. At least his graying hair was still neat and tidy, and his suit jacket buttoned. Apparently, he hadn't gotten annoyed with her enough yet to start running his hands through his perfect hair or tugging on his tie.

"Geez, Jameson," Shepard exclaimed when he spotted her. "Could you take any longer?"

"Yes, I can. But you can blame out-of-town sports fans who don't understand one-way streets for my delay."

"These men are not used to waiting. Their time is incredibly valuable."

"Everyone's time is valuable, Shepard. Why are you so nervous?" She paused to look at her reflection in the glass of the picture of a seascape hanging on the wall. It was one of those generic home-store finds, but the dark background made for an excellent mirror in times of need. She ran her fingertips underneath her eyes to capture the escaping eyeliner that was making her look like a raccoon, which wasn't going to do. "Who do you have in there anyway? Bill Gates? He has donated to our cause before. He and his wife are lovely people."

"No. Someone new. Come on, let's go."

"Okay, okay. Sheesh."

Shepard opened his office door with a flourish and waved for her to enter first. Jameson drew in a breath and put on her congenial, most welcoming, why yes, we would love to accept your money smile, and entered the office.

"Thank you for waiting. You know how game-day traffic—gah—" Her words caught in her throat as if she were still wading through the commute and the car in front of her slammed on its brakes.

"Jameson, let me introduce you to our guests," Shepard said.

At least that was what she thought he said. She didn't know. She hadn't a clue because suddenly Shepard sounded as if he were an adult in a Charlie Brown cartoon. *Wha-wha-whawha-whawha*, as her brain went off the rails.

The two gentlemen, who had gotten to their feet when she entered, stared back at her with identical sets of dark brown eyes. Even the grins they wore matched and grew wider the longer she gaped at them.

Fucking hell. It was the twins from the week before.

And if she had to guess from their shit-eating grins, both of them could read minds.

Double shit.

Thank God for her reflexes that had been sharpened from traumas from the past, for they kicked in and made her mind a blank slate, closing herself off from the sights and sounds around her. It was a skill she had learned when she and her mother lived in a shabby little apartment after her father walked out on them.

She had no idea why they were called apartments when the walls were so thin it was as if you were living in the same room. All day long the noise had been non-stop. The cries of the children next door who had gone another day without food. The upstairs neighbor who beat on his wife, or the lady down the hall who sold her body for another hit of crack. Jameson caught on quickly how to block out the world, and she used those skills to block anything the two brothers might see in her mind.

"Jameson?" Shepard asked. "Are you all right?"

"What?" Jameson started. Right. Business meeting. They were here to discuss business. Their presence did not mean they recognized her from the night before. It was a slim chance they didn't, but a chance nonetheless. "Sorry. I was just taken a bit aback. I wasn't expecting you to be twins."

Her inner self smacked her forehead. Could she sound more lame?

"I had been telling Mr. and Mr. Daniels here about the extraordinary job you have been doing as the shelter's director after you took over for your mother when she retired," Shepard said.

Daniels. Crap. She was so busy freaking out that she had totally missed their names when Shepard introduced them.

"Oh. Thank you?" she muttered.

"It's a pleasure to meet you, Ms. Alinari. I'm Ronan." The Greek god-like of a man who reminded her of a playboy who spent most of his time on his Mediterranean yacht held out a well-manicured hand as amusement twinkled in his eyes.

Her gaze bounced between his offered hand and those dark brown eyes. How did his powers work? Was it just close proximity, or did he have a greater reach into her thoughts through physical contact?

The corner of his mouth lifted higher. Almost as if he were daring her to touch him.

"It's a pleasure," she mumbled back and attempted what could be technically called a handshake. A tap on his fingers was more like it, which irked every fiber of her being.

A handshake was a marker of your worth and indicated your level of confidence. Too firm and you could be taken for a blowhard. Too weak and you might as well roll onto your back and expose your vulnerable underbelly for the kill. She had spent weeks as a teenager practicing the perfect handshake, and now when she needed to exert her dominance the most, she was relegated to limp-wristed weakness.

Ronan's smile widened, and she tried to ignore a flutter of attraction to his wildly good looks. He was lean and muscled like a runner or someone who had a semiweekly tennis match. And his skin had the healthy golden glow of someone who could afford to eat daily with the freshest of ingredients. He was tall, but not so much taller that she injured her neck to look up at him. A very nice package indeed.

Of the two of them, Ronan appeared to be the more jovial twin with his button-down shirt opened at the collar and a ready grin. His brother appeared to be the more reserved of the two, dressed in a black suit and tie as though he had just come from a board meeting or funeral.

Although he seemed to share a similar physique as his brother, he was a bit paler. He stood with his feet braced apart and his arms folded as he frowned at her with an intensity that punched her right in the chest. This must be the brother she had sparred with the other night.

Funny thing, though—it wasn't a frown of disapproval, but rather one of consideration. His brow furrowed as if she were a puzzle he was trying to figure out and having no luck in doing so.

Well, he could puzzle all he wanted to. If the two of them wanted to donate to the center, excellent. But they had no business with her on a personal level. The sooner she concluded this meeting, the sooner she could return to her work. Which meant she needed to hurry up and get her head out of her ass and focus on the task at hand.

"Thank you so much for meeting me here," she said as she took a seat in the chair by Shepard's desk. She crossed her stocking-clad legs at the knee and rested her hands in her lap. "Sorry for the delay. Game-day traffic is always tricky. Now, I understand you are interested in making a donation to the women's shelter but had some questions. How can I assist?"

Ronan sat on the sofa, settling back into the corner and stretching his arm along the top. The gesture caused the fabric of his shirt to stretch across his pectorals and threaten the integrity of the top-clasped buttons. "Mr. Samuels was filling us in on the basics of your organization. Our company, Daniels Software, has always been about inclusivity and diversity, but since the beginning of the Me-Too movement, our company is making a pledge that we take harassment and abuse seriously, not only within our workplace but outside as well. You see, Daniels Software is in a unique position to be an advocate for anti-harassment and bullying. We are in the IT field, which is still predominantly male, as well as a software producer of video games, which is far behind the times in counting women within its ranks. Right, Ethan?" He glanced up at his brother, who had remained standing. "Ethan?"

His brother started then blinked hard. "Yes. That's right." He sat on the edge on the other end of the couch. "From the research we've done on your organization, the Evergreen Women's Center is more than just a shelter. We've seen it also provides resources and classes for those in need of not only a home, but also work. We don't want to throw a bunch of money your way and claim that our civic responsibility has been satisfied. We want to make a true difference, whether that's providing cash or new surveillance systems for the shelter, or training opportunities for those who wish to go into the technology fields."

Damn it. They were exactly the type of sponsor the shelter needed. A frickin' dream come true. There was a catch. There had to be a catch.

"And what would you want from the organization in return?"

"Your undying praise and eternal gratitude?" Ronan replied with a chuckle. Great. He was charming too. "I'm joking. What we really want is an opportunity, Ms. Alinari. An opportunity to make a real difference in this crazy world."

"We are so excited to give you that opportunity, gentlemen," Shepard gushed. "How are you planning on proceeding?"

"To begin, we would need to know what the different divisions are within the organization," Ethan answered. "We also would like to know what your goals are regarding what you need and what you want for each division. We also need to know the layout of the shelter itself and the physical capabilities of the building there. A tour of the facility would be the best before we make a decision."

"Mr. Daniels, thank you for the offer of your assistance, and you can tour this office to your heart's content. But not the shelter. I will be happy to provide you with a list of our current equipment and the building's dimensions, electrical, and HVAC capabilities, but no one gets into the actual facility unless absolutely necessary and with extensive background checks. I am not being melodramatic by saying lives are at stake. I will do everything in my power to prevent an abuser from showing up on my doorstep."

"We appreciate your concern and steadfastness, Ms. Alinari," Ethan said. "And we do not mean to disrupt or cause strife for those who are calling the shelter home. Once the work is approved, we'll set up a system to keep your people safe. Our aim is to do what's best for both you and those who need the services the shelter provides. We want your people to succeed."

He was good, she'd give him that. Guilt was always an excellent motivator.

Shepard was probably already counting their donation money, but Jameson was far more cautious. She trusted that he did his homework on the brothers and their company to confirm that they were legit and would follow promises with cash. However, she was not going to discount that they had more than the motive of wanting to benefit the organization on their agenda. The timing of their meeting was too convenient.

"Shepard speaks very highly of you, Ms. Alinari," Ronan added. "Though he did admit that sometimes you could be a bit…ferocious when it comes to protecting those who are in your care."

"I'll take that as a compliment," she said. "The women and children who seek our services have often been bounced around from one organization to another, leaving horrors you cannot imagine. They need an advocate, and I am willing and happy to be that for them. Don't be deluded by the notion that we are a charity. We do charitable work, yes. But we try not to give handouts. Many who come to the center don't want a free ride. They want a chance, an opportunity for something better. They didn't ask to be put in their situations, so I do my damnedest to assist them any way I can. And those who will push them down or try to do harm—" her smile widened with malicious intent—"I will do everything in my power to stop them."

"I think I'm beginning to understand you more and more," Ronan said, his eyes narrowed.

"We can start with the basics," Ethan said. "I'm sure you missed your lunch or had to cut it short by meeting us. Why don't we grab a bite now and discuss more about the infrastructure and the layout of the organization? Any site visits, if needed, can be discussed at a future date."

"That sounds perfect," Shepard said, clapping his hands. "Unfortunately, I have a meeting with the IRS in a few minutes—they do love to keep track of how we are spending our funds—but Jameson would love to attend. Besides, she's the best person to talk to about the center and its needs."

Pretty sneaky, sis. How convenient for Shepard to be unavailable at this very moment and leave her at the mercy of the gorgeous twins.

"Who says this needs to be done today?" she asked. "I'm sure you gentlemen wouldn't mind postponing a more in-depth meeting for a day or two. Shepard knows our financials much better than I do. This will give us some time to gather any information you may need."

Ethan stood up and buttoned his blazer. "Why can't we do both? We would love to talk to you more about your vision for the center and how we may be able to assist. We can meet again in a few days or week to discuss more of the particulars before we finalize a plan."

Damn it. If they had been any other donor, she would be ecstatic and jump at the chance to talk about her passion for the organization and the shelter, but there was more than lunch and talk of charitable work on their minds. She just knew it. Suspicion ran straight to her bones and vibrated as if she had touched her tongue to the end of a battery.

"Well." She stood and brushed at her skirt to ensure the fabric fell to her knees. "I guess I can spare one hour of my time. There is a pie shop around the corner. They serve more than just pie, and it's run by a woman who used to live at the shelter. I always try to support those who have been through our program in any way I can."

And the fact that it was a wide-open room was a bonus as well. If she was going to be pressured into this meeting, it was going to be on her turf.

Ronan's eyes sparkled. "Pie? I love pie," he said, and the tip of his tongue flicked along his lower lip as if the pie he was thinking of was not of the fruit or chocolate variety.

Oh yes. They were dangerous, all right. And on more than one level. Just how much trouble was she going to get into spending time with these two?

"Let's—uh." She cleared her throat. Did the air conditioning turn off all of a sudden? "Just, ah, follow me, please. Shepard, I'll talk to you later."

He waved them out of his office with a cheery, "Can't wait to hear the details."

"Do you get visits from the IRS often?" Ronan asked as they entered the elevator.

"It feels that way." She pressed her back as close to the wall as possible to distance herself from the brothers. Their manliness was extra potent in the enclosed space. Despite her mind flashing constant warnings to keep away, her curious libido was like a cat catching a whiff of some high-quality nip.

Were her standards so low that all a man needed to

push her sexual awareness buttons was to dress well and smell nice? Ugh. Maybe she needed to follow Trini's advice and get laid every once in a while.

Wait. What had they been talking about? She blinked hard and shifted her gaze from admiring the fit of Ethan's coat on his shoulders. Right. The IRS. Definitely not sex.

"Uh, about once a month I'm asked to provide financial records on one item or another. I guess it does cause questions when our weekly grocery receipts look like we're throwing parties all the time. Sodas, snacks, birthday cakes, because someone is always having a birthday. Things like that." The doors to the elevator whooshed open. "Oh. Look at that sun. It turned into such a lovely day, didn't it?"

She continued to prattle on about innocuous things like the weather and traffic on the short, two-block walk to the restaurant. The brothers chatted on in kind, but underneath the pleasantries she felt an underlining need that they wanted to question her on personal matters scratching against her skin like a Brillo pad.

"Here we are. Welcome to the Pie Place." Jameson rushed a step ahead to open the door. The welcoming scent of fresh-baked apple pies surrounded her in a familiar cinnamon hug, bolstering her confidence.

Much to her disappointment, the Pie Place was between meal rushes and relatively empty when they entered. Darn it. She was hoping for a good-size crowd sitting nearby in the hopes that potential eavesdroppers would force their conversation to remain strictly business.

"Hello, Ms. Jameson. It's good to see you again." A young girl of about sixteen greeted her at the door.

"Tiffany. What a surprise." She reached for a hug, the soft pom-pom of the girl's ultra-curly hair tickling Jameson's nose as she squeezed her tight. "What are you doing here? Why aren't you in school?"

"It's a teacher in-service day. And Mama can always use an extra hand." She did a double take at the twins standing behind Jameson and her smile widened as her dark lashes fluttered. "Are you here for business or pleasure today?"

"Business," she snapped and frowned at the girl with a "knock it off" glare. "It's always business."

"I wouldn't necessarily say that," Ronan interjected. "It smells fantastic in here. I think it will end up being more about pleasure than business by the time we're through."

Tiffany giggled and reached for a set of menus. "Table or booth?"

"Is that booth in the corner available?" Ethan pointed to the far back of the room.

"Absolutely," Tiffany replied before Jameson could voice an objection. "Follow me."

Of course, he would pick a location the farthest away from anybody else in the restaurant.

Ethan gestured for her to slide into the booth first, and to her relief, they had the decency to sit together on the opposite side of her.

"Do y'all know what you want to drink?" Tiffany asked.

"Lemonade," Jameson answered.

"That sounds good," Ethan replied.

Ronan added, "We'll take one too."

"Excellent. I'll be back soon."

It wouldn't be soon enough for Jameson.

"She's a nice girl," Ronan said.

"Yes. She is." Jameson futzed with her menu, even though she ordered the same thing every time she was there. "She's a good kid who works hard. So does her mother."

"You've known them long?"

"About three years." Banter and small talk was a necessary skill she learned to schmooze potential donors, and she could converse with the best of them. But this tête-à-tête was killing her. "They've come a long way since then. But that's about all I'm willing to tell you. If you want more of their story, you'll have to ask them yourself."

Ronan broke out in laughter as his brother continued to gaze at her with puzzlement.

Tiffany's arrival put a hold on their conversation as she delivered their beverages. "Are you ready to order?"

"Ladies first." Ethan gestured in her direction.

"Oh, I already know what Jameson wants, shepherd's pie with a side of gravy," Tiffany said with a chuckle. "What about for you gentlemen?"

"The chicken pot pie, with extra peas on the side, thank you," they said in unison. Then they each picked up their glasses with their left hand, took a sip, and placed it back on the tabletop with a syncopated pop.

The ladies froze for a moment before sharing a "what the hell was that" glance.

"Oh…kay. Excellent choice." Tiffany stepped away. "I'll get that fired up for you."

Well, that was creepy. Wonder if that was some weird twin thing from birth or a mind reading trick, Jameson mused as she withdrew a notepad and a pen from her purse. Opening the book to a blank page, she set it on the table and squared her shoulders, preparing to stick to business.

"So, what did Shepard tell you about the Evergreen Women's Center? I'll fill in what he may have missed. Shepard likes to focus on the numbers, but I'd like to make sure you have more details about the demographic of who actually uses our services."

"He gave us a good idea of what your organization does for the community and what it needs." Ethan sat back and placed his folded hands on the table. "But let's cut to the chase. What we would really like to ask you about is what you were doing in the bedroom of Gerald Mulvaney the other week."

Tha fuck?

Well. That was certainly cutting right to the quick now, wasn't it? Talk about trying to throw a girl off balance. What made them so positive that it was her that they saw that night? And even more pressing, how did they find her so quickly?

Focus, James, focus. Tony Stark their asses. Don't confirm anything.

"Gerald Mulvaney?" She gave them her best startled and confused expression. "I'm not sure I'm following."

"Let me help you," Ethan said and projected an image of her taking a riding crop to the bottom of Mulvaney's feet.

Hot damn. Now that was a striking image, wasn't it? Is that what she really looked like? Hmm. Maybe she needed to rethink her wardrobe. From Ethan's point of view, she looked more like a porn star dominatrix than avenging angel.

Wait. He put that image directly into her mind. Double fuck.

"I'm sorry. What is going to help me?" How long could she continue to play dumb?

Not very long.

She jumped with a high-pitched squeak as if her seat had been electrocuted as the unspoken words reverberated in her mind.

"Ronan, knock it off." Ethan frowned at his brother. "No need to be coy, Ms. Alinari. You were there, we were there. And yes, we can read your mind. We try not to intrude on another person's thoughts, but if projected loudly and directly at us, no matter how much we wish it, we can still hear you. For now, though, your thoughts are safe. If you answer our questions."

Right. No point in putting up pretenses anymore. The jig was up.

She took her time picking up her glass and taking a slow sip on the straw. The tart lemonade added more pinch to her lips. "Blackmail is not an attractive quality in a man, Mr. Daniels."

Ronan chuckled. "This isn't blackmail, wildcat."

Wildcat? Please. "Only an inquisition into a subject you have no business in."

"It became our business when we heard Mr. Mulvaney and his terror," Ethan replied, as somber as ever.

Saved by the lunch plate. Tiffany appeared at their table with their orders and Jameson was tempted to slide out of the booth, using the young girl as a barricade to escape. Before she could make a move, Ethan reached out and placed his fingers over her clenched fist. The heat of his palm against her cold fingers made her heart race. How were they doing that?

You said you wouldn't read my thoughts, she projected at him with a glare.

I'm not reading them. The look in your eyes was enough of a warning. And I know you're smart. I would've made the same move if I was on your side of the table.

As Tiffany placed the dishes before them, Jameson stared at the hand covering hers. His fingers were long, the nails manicured, but not feminine. His grip was in no way menacing but did convey a warning. He wasn't going to let her go easily.

Even as her stomach clenched with dread, a warmth settled over her shoulders and oozed down her back like warm honey. What was *happening* to her?

"This looks divine," Ronan said and picked up his fork, ready to dig into his meal. He swiped her pot of gravy and poured a generous helping over his mashed potatoes.

Seriously? The man was going to eat at a time like this? *And* steal her gravy?

"Eat," Ethan ordered, releasing her hand and digging into the flaky pastry crust with steam rising from the vent on top that revealed the creamy inside. "This meeting was not meant to be confrontational, but rather informational."

"Is it now?" she asked, not believing him for a moment. She folded her arms under her breasts. "What does Mulvaney mean to you?"

"Nothing," Ethan replied. "What does he mean to you?"

"If you have never met or had any dealings with Gerald Mulvaney, why do you care?"

"Curiosity, maybe," Ethan answered. "Or the need to see justice prevail. Without all the facts, it's hard to determine what that justice is."

"Justice," she scoffed.

"Yes, justice. We cannot let what we saw pass by without a second thought. Someone was being targeted. At first glance it looked like Mulvaney was the victim, but after what we've discovered over the last few days, now we're not so certain. We would like to know what the truth is."

"The truth?" Geez. These two were a trip. She glanced around the restaurant to see if anyone was paying attention to them, but the few patrons appeared to be focused on their own lunches. "And what have you discovered? What difference is it to you what I do?"

"Either we witnessed a man being assaulted and didn't try hard enough to catch his assailant, or there was more to the situation than met the eye. We don't like not knowing which one it was."

"Still doesn't answer why it matters to you."

Ronan gestured with his fork. "It matters because we are human beings and have compassion for others. With our—talent—we understand more than most people about what goes on inside the human mind. It's sad and joyous, extraordinary and depraved. Everything and nothing at the same time. We want to help people in need, if they let us."

Ethan wiped his mouth with his napkin and leaned back in his seat. "How about we tell you what we *do* know, and you fill in the rest? Gerald Mulvaney, age forty-four, college graduate, works as a branch manager for a bank downtown. He's been residing at the condominium for the last five years with his wife and daughter. However, despite the presence of the toys we found in the living room, there seems to be no indication of the aforementioned wife and daughter currently living with him. We know we saw you at his residence engaging in what might have been construed as a bit of BDSM play, but in actuality was a form of torture. You do not have a criminal record, but there appears to be a juvenile record that is sealed. We also know that when it comes to the women and children in your shelter, you are, as you said before, a fierce protector. How are we doing so far?"

Interesting, Jameson mused as she contemplated the brothers with another slow sip of lemonade. Observant fellows.

"We also know that Mrs. Mulvaney has a long list of visits to the emergency room for assorted cuts and bruises. Four times this year alone," Ethan continued. "So, what are we missing?"

She sat upright with a start. "And how would you know medical information about Mrs. Mulvaney?"

Ronan's grin stretched from ear to ear. "Software guys. Remember? We have ways with a computer."

Very interesting. The brothers claimed to not read minds for privacy reasons but had no compunction about hacking a few systems to gain information if they decided to. Where would they draw the line? And how could she get that to work in her favor?

With their ability to gain information at their whim, what did they already know about her? And if they knew what they thought they knew and about her visit to Mulvaney's, why confront her in person and not go to the authorities? What did they want from her?

Very, very, very interesting indeed.

She twirled her fork into her pie, mixing up the buttery potatoes with the silky gravy. She took her time scooping up a forkful and blowing off the steam before placing the delicious morsel in her mouth and chewing. Slowly. Oh, so slowly.

After she finished her bite, she went in for another forkful. "You may be missing the part about Gerald Mulvaney being a grade-A asshole and wife beater. Also, the fact that he threatened his wife that if she left him, he would murder their child."

"Where is Mrs. Mulvaney now?" Ethan asked.

"I haven't a clue," Jameson replied with wide eyes as she

took another bite of her lunch.

"Do you know what finally convinced her to leave?" Ronan asked.

"I don't know why you think I would have that information. However, in my experience with situations such as these, tensions probably escalated. Lines were crossed. For example...a husband starts to sexually molest their child. That might be the event that encourages a woman to flee for the safety of herself and her daughter, besides the death threats. Again, just an example." She fluttered her lashes and went back to her meal.

"Jesus," Ronan muttered, looking a little nauseated. "What is wrong with people?"

"If you stepped out of your penthouse and spent some time on the streets, you'll find out exactly what is wrong with people. You'll find out more than you ever wanted to know. Besides, aren't you the mind reader? You should know first-hand what assholes people are."

"So you took it upon yourself to teach Mulvaney a lesson?" Ethan asked.

"Ha. Men like Gerald Mulvaney never learn. They are spoiled, entitled men who believe the world revolves around them and they are special just for breathing. They are takers, abusers. They do not learn. But they may heed a warning."

"There must be another way. Why haven't the police stepped in?" Ethan asked.

"Police do what they can, but it's ineffectual and the equivalent of moving one piece of straw from a two-ton bale of hay. On average, only a small percentage of domestic abuse cases reach court, and of those only a smaller percent actually see a conviction. It's the abusers' word against the abused. It's up to the victim to decide if the risk is worth the potential hell of testifying and threats from their abuser. You've seen what happens when a victim tries to speak out. They get inundated with abuse of public opinion. Often they find it easier to stay and keep being abused."

Ronan tossed his napkin on top of his empty plate. "That's one of the most depressing things I've ever heard."

"Now imagine living it. It is a battle that has to be fought every day. These people need assistance. They need an advocate."

"And that's you."

"Maybe. Depends on what you're going to tell the police."

Ethan sighed. "We told you. We're not going to the police. We just wanted to find out why, as well as…" A question hovered in his gaze. No, it was more like a need, a longing of a heart's desire that brought her to the edge of her seat that longer the end of his sentence hovered. Then in a blink it was gone and the corners of his lips turned down in a sad frown. "Never mind. The why was the main reason."

As well as…what? Whatever was on his mind must have been important, for Ronan reached over and patted his brother's arm as if he understood. Now she wished she was the one who could read minds.

What was happening? The conversation was going way off the rails and needed to come to an end. They were getting all the information from her she was willing to give. She was a busy girl with a lot on her plate. Two hunky guys did not fit into her world, no matter how intrigued she was about their powers. Or their relationship with each other. Or just them, period.

Fuck. Maybe she did need a hobby.

"Thank you for lunch, gentlemen. Now, if this little meeting was a ruse to ask me about a chance encounter you had with someone that might have possibly looked a little bit like me, then this conversation is over. If you truly meant what you told Shepard and wish to donate money and services to the shelter, I'll be happy to get you the information you need and arrange an appointment with you for another day."

"Don't go." Ethan reached across the table and grasped her hand again. This time his grip was stronger, almost desperate. "We meant what we said earlier. You're right, the people in your care do need support. And advocates. We want to help in any way we can. Money, equipment. Whatever you need."

Until that moment she used to believe Shepard had the softest hands of any man she ever knew. Hands that had seen very little manual labor except for the constant glad-handing of people with money and power.

The texture of Ethan's hands was just as soft. Maybe more so. But beneath that suppleness was a strength that made her breath catch. In his grip she didn't feel menace. She felt his sincerity, his conviction. With a simple touch she felt his need to have her trust. And when she met his gaze, that plea was multiplied tenfold, drowning her with the need to connect.

She didn't mean to, but she gave his fingers a squeeze before pulling free from his hold. The longer she was with them, the more she wanted to stay. "Talk is cheap. Let's see what you really bring to the table."

Ronan chuckled and reached for the dessert menu. "I like you. I like you a lot."

"Hold that thought, Sparky. You don't know me yet."

"I have a feeling we will get to know each other very well over the next few days," Ethan said. "And we won't need to read your mind to do so."

Was that a promise or a threat?

Even more distressing, which one did she want it to be?

CHAPTER FIVE

RONAN GAZED AT his brother and wasn't certain which was more absurd: Ethan's penchant for standing at the floor-to-ceiling windows of their high-rise office, staring out into the horizon with his hands behind his back and perpetual frown on his forehead, or him standing in his usual spot just inside the doorway watching his brother ruminate.

There had once been a time when Ethan had attacked life and the challenges therein with an enthusiasm and vigor some would deem as reckless. But that was before the plane crash that killed their parents and ignited their telepathic powers. Since then, Ethan had turned into a version of a man that at times even Ronan didn't recognize. It hurt his heart to see his brother with the constant weight of stress on his shoulders.

They were starting to understand the how and why they received their powers, but both were utterly clueless as to what part of their lifestyle had governed how those abilities were determined.

According to Dr. Kelly, the trauma they went through in the plane crash caused the spike of adrenaline to trigger the emergence of their powers. If they shared the same DNA, wouldn't it stand to reason they would inherit their powers equally? Yet somehow Ronan possessed a greater gift for empathy and could not only sense emotions, but sometimes alter what another person was feeling while Ethan was as telepathic as a hacker exploiting an unguarded internet connection. If Ethan relaxed his guard for one moment, he would be inundated with the thoughts of every person within a hundred-yard radius. The constant struggle to keep out as many of those thoughts as possible had him living on the edge of exhaustion.

Ronan did what he could to shoulder some of that burden and project a sense of calmness and serenity before Ethan neared a breaking point. It was the only way to keep them both sane.

"I'd offer you a penny for your thoughts," Ronan said, finally breaking the silence. "But I'd be buried alive. Let me guess the major one at the forefront of your mind. Jameson Alinari."

"That one is easy," Ethan replied, turning away from the stunning view. "She's been the one at the front of your mind as well."

"I won't deny it. She's incredibly interesting. Not to mention very attractive."

Ethan shrugged, although there was no hiding the tiny flick of desire Ronan felt rush through his brother's body. "I'm not dead."

No, he wasn't. Far from it, actually. Thank God.

"What exactly are your intentions toward Ms. Alinari?"

"At this point, I'm still trying to sort out..." Ethan paused with a sigh. "Everything. She's going to be important to us. I can feel it."

"Are you adding psychic to your abilities? Maybe we should ask Crystal about the future."

"Don't be silly." His gaze darted away. "Even if she did know, she wouldn't tell us."

Ronan snorted. "She refused to tell you, didn't she?"

"Covered her thoughts by singing 'The Macarena.' She doesn't know the words, so it was mostly mumbling to the rhythm."

"Figures."

The song "Freak on a Leash" by Korn erupted from the pocket of Ethan's sport coat. He reached inside to withdraw his phone. As he scrolled through items on the screen, his frown deepened and nostrils flared. Whatever Ethan had read made him anxious enough that his anxiety reached across the room to slap Ronan in the face. "And the plot thickens."

"What's going on?"

"Gerald Mulvaney is dead." He punched a few buttons on his phone. "Ted, bring the car around."

"What? He's dead?" he called out as Ethan rushed past him and down the hall to the elevator. "How do you know?"

"With Network's help, I set an alert on my phone for any online transmission containing Jameson's name, Gerald Mulvaney, his wife's and daughter's names, the shelter, everything I could think of. A police report of a 911 call to his home just hit my box. Housekeeper discovered his body."

"When was this?"

"This morning."

"This morning? That doesn't make sense. He was alive when we saw him last. Does it say what the cause of death was?"

"Not yet. Once we get in the car I'll see if any new reports have posted. The last notice was that the medical examiner was on their way."

The snap of their footsteps on the parking lot floor were

drowned out by the screech of tires as Ted pulled the Cadillac in front of them. With barely a pause, they climbed into the backseat and were on their way.

"An alert on Jameson. A little extreme, don't you think, brother?" Ronan asked. "Seriously. What is the endgame here? Your interest in her is almost an obsession."

"I don't know," Ethan said. He ran his fingers through his hair and pressed them into the base of his skull. "There's something about her, it's beyond attraction. When we were on that rooftop, she sensed I could read her thoughts. Then she shut them down. Bam. No matter how hard I pushed, I couldn't get through. I've never met anyone who could close themselves off completely. How is she able to do that? Is she the only one who can? There are just so many questions."

"I get it. She's intriguing. But don't forget you're not the only one involved here. And neither is she."

At least Ethan had the grace to look away with a guilty pinch to his lips.

Yeah. That's right. The challenges of being telepathically and empathetically linked to your twin. While they were able to control the thoughts they shared with each other, what one felt, so did the other. They experienced everything together. *Everything.* Wherever Ethan's emotions were heading, Ronan had to follow in some capacity. Which meant Ethan's obsession with Jameson Alinari would soon become his.

Even if their emotions and thoughts weren't coiled together in the same unbreakable rope, Ronan could not lose Ethan. His brother was the only family he had left, and his closest friend. As children they had joked that they were meant to be together forever. From womb to tomb, they'd say. After the crash, they were certain that their lifespans were destined to be lived as one.

Doc said there was no physiological proof that they had merged into one entity, but they knew it was true. Whether it was death or madness, where one went, the other would follow.

Which made Ethan's behavior of late a curiosity. For the first time in years Ronan sensed within his brother an emotion that had been fleeting at best.

Hope.

"I can't believe you got Network to tag her. Aren't you worried she'll tell Alisia?" Ronan asked.

"No. Yes." Ethan blew out a breath. "Didn't think about that, really."

"Jesus. What happened to the good old-fashioned method of asking a girl on a date?"

"We don't have the luxury, remember? Besides, I don't want to date her."

"Oh really?" Ronan asked with an incredulous raise of his brows. He was all for cultivating Ethan's newfound energy, but it had to be for the right reasons. "Then it's sex you're after? Or her ability to shut you out."

Ethan grimaced. "I didn't mean it like that. I'm interested, but I don't know how I feel. Wait. Do *you* want to date her?"

The tinge of hurt and fear in that question made Ronan want to burst out laughing. His brother was smitten. There was no denying that. And the question was plain dumb. If Ethan was going to date her, Ronan was going to date her. That was how their powers worked.

"I find her interesting and wouldn't mind drinks or a nice dinner out for conversation. However, let's just make sure she's not a murderer first, okay?"

"Agreed," Ethan said, not making eye contact but his posture eased, ever so slightly.

Ronan bit back a grin. If it made Ethan breathe more easily to take the lead on the topic of Jameson, let him. He could be patient.

The bustle and congestion of downtown high-rises eased into the gray and gloomy anonymity of the industrial district where the Evergreen Women's Center was located. The shelter looked just as they had imagined yet was completely different. Large and boxy, yes. Those boxes were ticked. But they hadn't expected it to blend in so seamlessly with the other warehouses in the vicinity. They would have guessed that this specific building was some sort of warehouse if they had not done their research.

Ted pulled up to the gated entrance and pushed the call button. There was a soft whir as the lens of the camera focused on the car.

"Can I help you, sir?" asked a feminine voice through the speaker.

"Ethan and Ronan Daniels here to see Ms. Alinari," Ted replied.

There was silence for a good solid minute before the reply came, "I do not see an appointment under that name. Have a nice day."

Ethan nodded at Ted, who then pushed the call button again. "May you please check again? It is of great importance."

"No appointment, no entry. Good-bye."

"I've got this, Ted," Ronan said.

He climbed out of the car and walked up to the call box and pressed the button. After receiving no response, he pressed it again. Then again and again and again until the box squawked.

"No appointment, no interest. Do I need to call the authorities on you?"

"Tell Jameson we are here on a life-or-death situation. You can also tell her that it will take us no time to get the passcode to the gate and be at the front door whenever we wish."

He strode back to the car with a confident swagger and came back to his seat. A few seconds later the gates opened and Ted drove them to the entrance of the building.

A five-foot nothing bundle of spitfire wearing three-inch heels, a brown suede jacket, and a death glare stood at the top step, blocking the front door.

Ronan got out of the car with his hand raised as Jameson's lips parted with what he was certain was the beginning of a blistering tirade. "Before you start, we've known the location of the center for a while. We researched public records of properties owned by the Evergreen Women's Collective and associated members. Satellite pictures from Google Earth confirmed the rest. It really wasn't that hard to find where you were."

Her frown deepened and her fists came to rest on her hips. "You promised never to read my mind."

"I didn't. It was logical that would be your first question. We need to talk."

"That's what phones are for."

"This is too important," Ethan replied. He gestured up to the security cameras filming the entrance. "We can do this out here if you wish, but I don't think you want to have this conversation with who knows who watching or listening. It's about a mutual acquaintance of ours."

She pursed her lips and growled with frustration. The

effect was more cute than menacing. She nodded at Ted. "Your chauffeur?"

"Yes."

Her lips pursed harder as she grunted. "Sir. Would you mind getting out of the car and standing over there, please?" She pointed to the corner of the parking lot.

Is she being serious? Ted asked with a confused glance to the brothers.

I'm going to say yes. She's been a straight shooter, Ronan replied with a shrug.

Ted took a few steps to the side of the car.

"No." Jameson pointed again. "All the way over there. And place the car keys on the ground where you are, please."

Both brothers shrugged again in unison and nodded for Ted to keep going. When he was a good fifty yards away, he stopped.

"Thank you," she said. "You two, follow me."

To their surprise she did not turn to reenter the building. Instead, she marched past them down the stairs and picked up the car keys. She then slipped into the backseat of their town car.

Ronan turned to Ethan with a grin of surprise. Neither of them saw that coming.

The brothers joined Jameson in the car. The expansive backseat became snug and intimate with the three of them, and her gentle berry and cashmere scent filled the space with warmth.

As soon as the door shut she launched into it. "What's this all about?"

Ethan did not bother to mince words. "Gerald Mulvaney is dead."

She sucked in a breath and her eyes widened. Her shock rolled through her body and spread out to encompass the brothers. "Dead? As in dead dead?"

Her genuine surprise hit Ronan in the gut and eased his mind as to whether she might have had anything to do with Mulvaney's demise.

"Dead dead. Otherwise we wouldn't be here. What do you know, Jameson?" Ethan asked.

"Me?" This time her shock was tense with a flare of disgust. "What makes you think I had anything to do with this? He might've dropped dead from a heart attack for all we know. Or ran his car into a pole in some drunken accident."

"Sorry, sweetheart." Ethan reached down and pulled a tablet from the console hidden in the seat. "He was murdered. I had a friend do some research and she sent me the police files. I'll spare you some of the more gruesome photos."

It did pay to have friends who were vigilante crime-fighters. Network was able to use her skills to hack into the police mainframe and forward them records of the current investigation. Included in those files were photos from the medical examiner of Mulvaney tied to his bed in a similar fashion as when they had found him with Jameson the week prior. Only this time he had welts all over his body as if he had been beaten with a thin cane. On his inner thigh the word "ABUSER" had been carved with a sharp object.

The ME hadn't come back yet with an official cause of death, and although there was the slightest chance the man had taken his own life, Ronan would bet his left nut that the man had been murdered.

"If you didn't know anything about this," Ethan said,

"do you know who would?"

The breath hissed out from between Jameson's lips as she leaned back and rubbed her hands over her silk-clad belly as if she were going to be sick. "I don't understand. I don't understand at all," she muttered.

"Do you think his wife would have done something like this?" Ronan asked. His arm tingled, desperate to offer comfort and bring against his side for a hug, but he hadn't yet earned the right to touch her in such a way.

She shook her head. "Violence is not in Mrs. Mulvaney's nature. Which was why she allowed her husband to abuse her for so long. It took her forever to realize what was happening in her world, then when she did, she was afraid to fight back. Besides, the family was permanently relocated up north two days ago. I found her a good lawyer to help her with her divorce. She had no need to go back."

Ethan shifted in his seat, leaning forward to rest his hands on his knees. "Did he have any other enemies? Who else knew about his behavior?"

"Actually, I'm surprised the police haven't approached you for information," Ronan said. "If his wife filed for divorce based on spousal abuse, they would want to question everyone she's connected with."

"I wouldn't be surprised if they did call you any minute," Ethan added.

Jameson shook her head, still lost in thought. "I know the hospital called the police at least once when she went to the emergency room after fainting at the grocery store. She had a concussion from being hit in the head the night before. Any family members or close friends who might have been paying attention to their relationship would know, or at least suspect what was happening in that household. And then there's…"

"And then there's who?" Ronan prompted.

Her eyes darted back and forth before she shook her head again. "Nothing. I'm just trying to get a handle on the situation. I've had spouses and significant others turn up dead before. They either committed suicide, or were involved with gangs or drugs. But that…" She gestured to the images on the tablet. "That is a first."

A blare of a cell phone interrupted their conversation. Jameson patted her jacket for the opening to her pocket and withdrew her phone, glancing at the display.

"Jesus. I thought you guys weren't the physic ones. I better take this. Hello. Yes, *Detective Sanchez.*" She looked at them, her eyes wild. "What was that about Emily Mulvaney? Is there something wrong with her case?" There was a long pause before she replied, "Of course. I understand. I am in the middle of a meeting right now, but I could be there in just over an hour. Yes. Will do, Detective." She ended the call and tapped the corner of her phone against her chin.

"That was the detective in charge of the domestic violence division with the police department. Homicide is asking for information on Mrs. Mulvaney and wants to meet with me. He knows how protective we are of the center's location. The homicide detective is willing to have me meet with them at the station. Otherwise, they'll have no choice but to bring that detective here to question me."

"Do you want us to go with you?" Ethan asked.

Jameson shook her head. "That'll just look odd. I can do this."

"Just make sure you look surprised if they tell you that Mulvaney is dead," Ronan suggested.

The glare she threw him conveyed that she did not find

him funny in the slightest. She sighed and reached for the handle of the door. "I guess we're finished here. If you'll excuse me."

Ethan reached out and placed his hand over hers. Just as at the restaurant, something seemed to pass between the two of them whenever they touched. Ronan sensed it then and it blazed now. There was a connection, an understanding of some sort. It was a sensation that seemed to bring peace to Ethan. Since Ronan had no good reason to touch Jameson to test the theory, it made him wonder if he would experience that same sensation if he were to have contact.

And if he didn't feel that same electricity?

The possibility that he wouldn't share the same spark with Jameson was too terrible to contemplate.

"We're not finished," Ethan said to her. "We are far from finished. The man you tortured has been murdered. If you didn't do it, we need to find out who did."

"Why us?" Jameson asked, her brows raised. "Isn't that the police's job?"

"Yes. But if somebody knows what you've been up to, they might try to pin it on you. How do you know you won't be a suspect?"

She pulled her hand away and crossed her arms over her chest. "What makes you so sure I didn't do it?"

"You're not a murderer, Jameson. You are a fighter. You're a warrior. But not a murderer."

The stiffness in her posture did not ease and her gaze darted to everywhere but them. "I'll be fine."

"Let us do some digging around. You know we have connections," Ronan offered. "We can at least see if this was an isolated murder or if someone is trying to get your attention by copying what you had started." He sat back in his seat and smiled. "Just so we're clear, we are going to investigate this with or without your help. If I were you, I'd want to be involved."

Those full lips of hers pinched together and she scowled. "Why are you doing this? Don't you have a mega-conglomerate to run?"

"We have one company, not a conglomerate. And reliable employees. As for why we're concerned?" Ronan shrugged. "We like you. We like what you do and what you believe in. This whole situation may be a big coincidence, or it could be someone targeting you. We don't like uncertainties."

For several long seconds she leveled an intense stare at him then switched that look to Ethan. It seemed as if she were trying to stare into their souls, weighing, judging.

Ronan couldn't help himself and sent a tentative probe to her mind, not to read her thoughts, but to get a sense of the speed and workings of her mind. Much to his shock, but not surprise, he found a black barrier to her thoughts. How *did* she do that?

After what felt like an eternity, she sighed again and reached for the handle of the door. "Meet me tonight. Ten o'clock."

She glanced at each of them again before turning away. *6969 Mapplethorpe Ave SW.*

The brothers gasped in surprise as she chuckled and opened the door. "Let's see if you can remember that."

They watched her hips twitch in her formfitting skirt as she walked away and strode up the stairs in her heels as if she were walking on a fashion runway. As one the brothers turned to each other with the same look of amazement.

She projected to them on purpose! Did she do it as a

joke? Or maybe she was beginning to trust them, even if it was just a little bit. Nevertheless, they had a date for that night.

Well, sort of a date. However, it was another opportunity to spend time with the enigmatic Jameson Alinari.

Ronan still didn't have an idea as to how she was going to fit into their lives. Professionally or personally. And at the moment it was a coin toss for him as to which prospect he was more excited about. But based on the vibes Ethan was projecting, his brother was ready to get up close and personal with Jameson Alinari.

CHAPTER SIX

"WHAT DO YOU mean, you won't be there tonight?" Ashley asked Jameson over the phone as she was climbing into her car.

"I have to meet with these big-time donors that Shepard wants me to wine and dine."

"At ten o'clock at night?"

"I know, weird, huh? Millionaires. What are you gonna do, am I right?" She shifted her cell phone to her other ear and pinned it with her shoulder as she locked in her seatbelt.

"That fucking sucks. I was hoping to get some updates on a few of those cases I've been working."

"About that," Jameson said. "I think we should suspend confronting these lowlife significant others for a little bit longer."

"Why would we do that?" Ashley asked sharply. "You said the Evolutioneer threat was over and we were good to go."

"I think Gerald Mulvaney went to the police about what happened the other night. Detective Sanchez wanted to get in contact with Emily. Maybe I'm just being paranoid, but I don't want to give the police any more reason to look into our business than necessary."

"Sanchez said Mulvaney went to the police?"

"He wouldn't give me specifics. He was just asking me

where to find Emily. Again, I may just be paranoid, but I'd feel a lot better if we just dialed it back. Track these fuckers down and keep an eye on them, but not confront them. At least for now."

Was Jameson purposely being obtuse and not telling Ashley the truth? Hell, yeah. Somebody had gone after Gerald Mulvaney. Someone who knew what he did to his family. For all she knew, it was one of her girls who had gone after him and killed him. God, she hoped that wasn't the case. Until she was certain who she could rule out, it was best to keep as much information to herself as possible.

"All right," Ash conceded, her disappointment clanging over the line like a heavy bell. "I'll see if I can find out any information and lay low, for now."

"Thanks. And it's only temporary. You can take the night off and be up early to head to Cougar Mountain. You've been saying how much you like watching the skydivers. Besides, there are so many other things we can be doing. Tell the girls I'll catch up with them later and see what they need. Be safe."

"You too," Ashley said with a distracted tone in her voice.

Grrr. Jameson turned off her phone and set it in the center console. That went about as well as she had expected. Hopefully Ash didn't suspect anything was amiss. Jameson never missed a night out with the girls. Well, except that one time when she had a horrible sinus infection and the temperature of 104. And even then, she had stayed up until they all returned to get the details of their night.

Well, what was done was done. She had bigger issues to deal with.

Turning the satillite radio to the spa/yoga music station,

she headed downtown and allowed the soothing strings of a violin to seep into her muscles and ease the tension that had been riding her shoulders all day. Whenever she went out to lay down some bare-knuckled education, she'd blare the loudest, angriest alternative rock, but that type of energy would not do going head-to-head with the Daniels twins. Those boys were going to require her to remain at her tip-top, headstrong shape.

Despite being a big city, most of the downtown area was quiet at this time of night, except for the three-block strip of bars and nightclubs that catered to the late-night crowd, no matter the day of the week.

Jameson approached the building with the longest line extending from the entrance and turned into the driveway. She pressed the button to open the gate to the parking garage underneath the five-story high-rise and waited.

The upper levels of the building held apartments and offices, with the lower floors dedicated to the hottest nightclub in town. From what she had heard about the place, things got pretty kinky inside. If she had a moment in her day when she thought about anything other than the shelter, she might be tempted to see the goings-on for herself. But since spending time on anything other than her calling seemed ridiculous, she never bothered to check it out. The building's owner was a total sweetheart, however, and was more than happy to give the women's center ample office space as well as set aside a few apartment units for their use at a reasonable fee.

A familiar black town car was parked in the garage with its nose pointing toward the exit. She parked a few spots away and climbed out of her car.

The driver's door to the town car opened and the chauffeur jumped out to open the passenger door, except the twins climbed out of the car before he could reach the latch. Ronan was dressed for relaxation in faded jeans, black T-shirt, and a leather sport jacket, while Ethan was dressed in slacks, white button-down, and a tie. No jacket? she wanted to ask, but she wondered if that was as casual as he ever dressed.

"Do you three travel everywhere together?" Jameson asked.

"Yes." The brothers answered as if it were obvious. Ethan added, "Believe me, it's safer for everyone on the road to not have a driver distracted by a random thought crashing your concentration."

"Huh. Guess that's something I never thought about," Jameson replied.

Ethan gestured to the driver. "Jameson, meet Ted."

"Pleasure to meet you." Jameson held out her hand for her go-to handshake.

Ted took her hand, turning her wrist so her fingers pointed down, and bowed slightly. "Pleasure is all mine," he said with a British accent.

Her brows rose. "Why do I get the feeling that your skill set involves more than driving a car?"

"Because you have excellent instincts," he said, schooling his grin. He leaned back against the side of the car and pulled out a cell phone from his pocket. "Call me if you need me."

"Where to?" Ronan asked her, settling the messenger bag he carried on his shoulder.

"This way." Jameson turned on her heel and marched toward the elevator.

Two sets of footsteps followed closely behind her.

"How was the visit with the detective?" Ethan asked.

"Fine. Told them what I knew about Emily. They gave me their card and told me to call them if I were to hear from her. Not too bad."

"Lucky girl."

Luck, schmuck. She knew how to answer questions. Keep it simple and only answer the question being asked, not the one you thought was asked. Never give more detail than necessary.

As they waited for the elevator, the brothers seemed to grow restless with each second that passed, swaying as if their skin was growing too tight for their frames.

"Did you have to pick a location that was so crowded?" Ethan asked with a hint of strain in his voice.

"It's convenient, and more private than you think." She entered the elevator as the doors opened and paused with her fingers hovering over the button for the fourth floor. "Are you getting too many thoughts from the people here?"

"It's normally not so bad," he said and dug his fingers into the back of his neck. "But these are not normal people. Do you have any idea what is going on in that nightclub?"

"I've heard things," she replied. Tales of the sexcapades that happened on the upper floor were legendary.

"Whatever you've heard pales in comparison to what's actually going on." Ronan shifted his feet and stood with his hands covering his groin. "There are some seriously naughty, dirty people upstairs."

Jameson sucked in a laugh as a bit of guilt made her chest tight.

She hadn't thought about how the lust-filled thoughts of a couple hundred people might affect a telepath. As it was, the brothers both looked as if they had front-row center seats to the sexy action. Sweat had broken out on their foreheads and their cheeks were flushed a becoming pink. If Ronan had his teeth clenched any tighter, the muscles in his jaw were going to burst out of his skin.

Seeing the two of them turned on was hot, so hot that Jameson felt the lick of heat herself deep in her belly as she wondered if that was how they looked in full-out sexual congress.

No, sis, the angel on her shoulder warned. You don't want to know that.

Why not? A girl can fantasize, right?

Sure. But not them. They'll learn things about you no one else will know. Not even yourself.

True. Too true. Thank you, angel, for keeping me focused.

You're going to take a long bath tomorrow, aren't you?

Maybe. Probably. Odds are rolling in that favor.

I warned you.

She jabbed at the button for the apartment level and tried to silence her conscience. "Hopefully if we get above them, we'll be far enough away."

"I hope to God that's true," Ethan muttered.

"What is the range on your powers?"

"We can go a couple hundred miles and still hear each other." Ethan paused to pant. He reached behind him to grab the handrail. "With other people, about fifty, a hundred yards. If they have no filter and we've dropped our barriers."

As the elevator passed the first and second floors, Ronan let loose with a low groan while Ethan's fingers tightened on the railing.

"Are you two going to be all right?" she asked.

"Fine," Ethan muttered, his eyes shut tight. "You'll be fine. It will be fine. We'll all be fine."

Holy shit. Those two looked as if they were about to come on the spot. And damn if she didn't want to see them do it. They needed to get out of here fast. She pushed the door open button several times when they reach their floor and blew a lock of hair off her sticky forehead.

"Just down here," she said and raced down the hall. Her hand shook as she worked the key into the deadbolt and opened the door.

She flipped on the entry light to the cozy two-bedroom apartment and tossed her bag on the kitchen counter. "There are some bottles of water in the refrigerator if you're thirsty. And there may be some granola bars in the cupboard."

Oh, how she wished they had a bit of liquor in the cupboards. But since the apartment was sometimes used by someone escaping a situation where excessive drinking was involved, they didn't store any on the premises.

She moved to turn on the lamp near the couch in the attached living room. The master bedroom and en suite was on the right, and a second bedroom and bathroom were to the left. She firmly shut both doors, blocking the sight of comfy beds and mounds of pillows. There would be no need to enter either bedroom with any of the brothers that evening.

Or any evening, her angel reminded her.

Oh, shut up, her devil answered back. Let the girl relieve some stress, why don't you? She could do worse. Way worse. In fact, she has—

Stop it. Both of you.

Geez. That's what she needed at this moment in time.

Her conscience arguing about her sex life.

She cleared her throat, pulled the hem of her sweater down over her hips, and stepped back to the kitchen to open her bag. The brothers set themselves up at the kitchen table, with several laptops set before them. Whoa. The boys came prepared. She leaned against the counter.

"You need the wi-fi password?" she asked.

"No need. We travel with our own network. More secure that way," Ronan answered with a wink. His cheeks were still pink, but the earlier strain of lust seemed to have dissipated.

"Give me a moment to get some files sorted," Ethan said, typing away at his keyboard. He paused for a moment to unbutton the cuffs of his dress shirt then rolled up his sleeves.

Jameson about swallowed her tongue as he exposed the golden skin and fine muscles of his forearms. Damn. What the hell was up with that? How did a man go from hot to sizzling with just the simple roll of a cuff? Stupidest thing ever. But damn, he looked mighty fine.

Ronan chuckled, low in his throat, as Ethan gasped and the pink returned to his cheeks.

She growled in frustration. She was not attracted to them, she was not attracted to them, she was not attracted to them.

Ronan's chuckle deepened and his eyes sparkled.

"What?" she snapped.

The huge grin he tried to contain broke free. "Nothing."

"You sound as if I'm amusing you somehow."

"You *are* amusing. You are perfectly delightful. Don't you want me to be amused by you?"

"Of course not. This is serious business. Me just standing here is not amusing in the slightest."

He raised a brow at that. "Wildcat, you are doing much more than just standing there."

Knock it off. She projected at him and sent an image of a cleaver flying, a definitive arc in the air.

Ronan's chuckle returned and he leaned back in his chair, folding his arms over his chest with that sexy smirk still on his lips.

Ethan cleared his throat. "If we could get down to business. Our friend with access to police files sent us updated information. The autopsy report hasn't been completed yet, but it appears that Mr. Mulvaney was found Tuesday evening by a housekeeper he had hired a few weeks ago. It was only her second time at the apartment."

"Poor lady," Ronan added.

"The reports we have been able to get our hands on shows that the last time anyone saw Mulvaney alive before the housekeeper was when he left work on Monday evening. The housekeeper appeared Wednesday morning. That's a day and a half where his whereabouts are unknown," Ethan said.

"Do we have any footage from security or traffic cameras in the area?" Ronan asked.

"There are some shots of the street entrance, but nothing unusual. Everyone entering has a key."

"It is not a complete picture," Jameson interjected. "Someone can come in from the backside and the roof. There aren't any cameras there."

"And you know this how?" Ronan asked with a raised brow.

"I did *my* research before I paid Mr. Mulvaney a visit. How do you think I got into the building last time?"

Ethan rested his elbows on the table and clasped his hands together, peering at her from over his knuckles. "Speaking of last time, who else knew about your visit?"

Jameson swallowed and took a step back until her butt hit the back of the couch. She'd had a feeling this was coming. That she would have to reveal more details about her mission and those who assisted. Could she do it?

Should she do it?

"You said you wanted to help," she said in a low tone. "That you believed in my mission. I don't know how much information I can trust you two with. There is more than me and my life at stake. More than just me who can be affected."

"Fair enough," Ethan said. "We do believe you, Jameson. We believe you didn't kill Gerald Mulvaney. But we want to make sure you will not be implicated in his murder in any way, and to do that, we'll need details. I'm not exactly sure what we can do to prove that you can trust us, except for us to try and understand what it is that you do."

He did have a point. And if he really wanted to, he could go back on his word and delve into her mind and find all her secrets anyway, although it would be a really shitty thing to do.

She drew in a breath and folded her arms, settling back against the couch. "I lead a group. We've all been in the system one way or the other, either as runaways or we were homeless, so we know what a person who is in trouble looks like."

"You were homeless?" Ronan asked, his eyes holding concern.

"What makes you jump right to homeless?"

"From what we've heard about your mother, it sounded

as if you were close, so I didn't think you were a runaway. That would leave homelessness."

"Right." She shifted her weight from one hip to the other as her chest grew tight. "We were without a home for a bit when I was younger."

"Is that when you accrued a juvenile record?" Ethan asked.

"Accrued." She snorted. That was one way to call it. "No. That happened when we had a place to live."

"What did you do to get a record?" Ronan asked.

She sat up straighter. "That is none of your business and has nothing to do with what is happening now or my team. Thank you very much."

"Do you have a name?" Ethan asked.

"What?" Damn, it was hard to keep track of their train of thought.

"Every team has a name." Ronan shrugged. "What is it?"

"Crimson Angels," she murmured.

"Good name," they replied in unison.

Jameson bit back a smile. "We've been together for years. We started out patrolling the streets. We had a van full of supplies, blankets, backpacks of food and toiletries. Anyone we found on the streets, we would try to get them into a shelter, or just do what we could to make them more comfortable. The longer we patrolled, the more we found women and families put on the street by an abusive significant other. It was too many. And the number of families coming to my shelter, and other shelters, kept growing. That's when we decided the abusers needed to be stopped since the police weren't doing anything about it."

"You got into vigilantism," Ethan stated.

"Somebody had to. The patriarchy is doing nothing to

police themselves. Anytime a woman speaks out, it's a congratulatory handshake to the abuser and the boys-will-be-boys shrug. Still. Now! That's bullshit. They have to be held accountable. And we're the ones who are going to do it."

"I understand your reason, Jameson," Ethan said even as he shook his head. "But there has to be another way. Besides being illegal, vigilantism leads to chaos. And as we are experiencing now, chaos is not the answer."

"We have to fight fire with fire."

"It needs to be fought judiciously. In court. With law enforcement."

She rolled her eyes and shifted her weight. "Spoken like a man with money. These women are left with nothing. They escape with barely the clothes on their back. They can't afford lawyers. And the shelter and center can't afford to help with all those legal fees, even though we do get a lot of pro bono help. There's just too many in need. A bandage isn't the answer. Being reactive isn't the answer. We have to be proactive and stop the problem at the source. We need to shut these abusers down for good." She punctuated her statement with a smack of her fist against her open palm.

"But murder isn't the answer. It will not do your cause any good."

"I did not kill that man!" She rubbed the space between her eyes until spots began to form in her vision. "Look, these men, men like Mulvaney, they only understand two things: money and power. Since we're short on funds, we're fighting them with power. Until there is a significant shift in society structure, which we all know is never going to happen in our lifetime, this is the only way we have to fight."

"I'm sorry, Jameson," Ethan said. Beside him, Ronan had a matching sad light in his eyes.

"Sorry for what?"

"For whatever happened to you," Ronan answered. "For whatever made you distrust the system and made you feel as if violence is the only answer."

"Don't do that." Her arms tightened across her chest with restrained anger. "You don't owe me an apology. Do men in general owe me an apology? Perhaps. Does the government? Sure as hell they do. Do those bastards that allow predators to roam freely on the street? Yeah, those fuckers for certain do. But don't patronize me by apologizing for mankind at large. I don't need it."

Ethan stood and crossed the short distance to her side. Pure stubbornness kept her feet planted on the floor. The closer he drew, the farther her chin tipped up to stare him right in the eye.

"You're tired," he said.

"I'm fine. I'm used to being up late at night."

"No. You're tired." He tapped the center of his chest. "Here."

She snapped her teeth together and looked away, her eyes darting everywhere except at the brothers.

She wasn't tired. She was exhausted. For so many years she had been fighting. Fighting the system, fighting the establishment. So many roadblocks, so many obstacles, and all she wanted was to make a change in the world. To make the world better. Why did people make it so difficult?

"Jameson," Ethan murmured and took another step closer. His heat buffered the chills skipping over her skin. "You don't have to do it on your own anymore."

"I'm not on my own. I told you. I have my team."

"Your team can only do so much. Let us help you."

"I'm trying. I'm here, aren't I?"

"That's not what I mean." As he swayed closer, the heat of his body flourished, reaching out as if it were a physical entity. "You've been a champion for others for so long. Who's been a champion for you? Who do you get to lean on, or just be allowed to exist in the same space with no expectations of anything but companionship? Everyone needs someone, Jameson. Let us be there for you."

Jameson didn't want to, but she was helpless to resist the pull of the sincerity in his voice. She looked up into his face. His too, too handsome face and dark eyes swimming with longing. Just what exactly was he asking from her? Did she want to give whatever that was to him?

Ethan took another micro step closer, his torso brushing her arm. She didn't stop him, but she didn't move away either as he slowly, oh so slowly wrapped his arms around her and drew her against his body.

She wanted to resist, purely on principle that she was a strong, independent woman, but then he encouraged her to lay her head on his chest and she melted. His arms felt so good. When was the last time she had been held like this? By a virtual stranger. With nothing but kindness and compassion. Never, as far as she could remember.

Ethan stood there, silent, providing some comfort after a long, long, long struggle.

Maybe it was the lateness of the hour, or the stress of the last week—*ha!*—decade. But she felt a shift in the wall she kept up between herself and others. Fine cracks began to form, and to her horror, tears began to slip down her cheeks. She bit her lower lip, absolutely refusing to sob out loud, but the tears refused to stop. Before she knew it, she had her arms wrapped tight around Ethan's waist and she was soaking the front of his shirt.

Despite the awesomeness of Ethan's hug, and her absolute embarrassment of falling apart, a prickle tapped at her conscience that something wasn't quite right. As if something was missing, but she couldn't think of what.

And then she felt it. A second source of heat approached her from behind, coming ever closer until she felt a brush against her hand.

She opened her eyes to see a tissue being pressed into her palm.

Ronan.

Ronan and his strong, capable-looking hand stood beside her, not quite embracing her as Ethan was, but still a steady and supportive force. Somehow, she was certain that if she leaned a little bit backward, he would be right there waiting to embrace her.

Had she lost her ever-loving mind? Of all the times to indulge in a fantasy about a hot twin threesome, this was not how she imagined it.

"Thank you," she murmured, taking the tissue and wiping at her cheeks. She untangled herself from Ethan's embrace. "Sorry. Don't know what came over me."

"We do," Ronan said and brushed the back of his fingers along her cheek. "It was what you needed."

Needs. He thought he knew what she needed? Hell, at that moment she had no idea what she needed. World peace was always good, but what she was afraid of was that what she needed was more hugs. Long, warm, strong hugs that lasted all through the night.

She stepped away from the cozy enclosure of their bodies and went to retrieve a bottle of water from the refrigerator. They were getting wildly off topic. Taking a seat at the table, she cleared her throat. "Where were we? Right. We were making a list of who might have known I made a visit to Mulvaney."

The brothers shared a glance then stared at her for several moments before they sighed in unison. Their eyebrows and the corners of their mouths twitched as if to say, "this is not over" before Ethan resumed his seat in front of his laptop.

"You said your friends would know—your Angels," he said.

"Yes. Mostly we patrol for anyone on the street needing housing assistance or a care package. If there is a person abusing their family, or making it difficult to leave, Ashley, Lucinda, and I are the ones who will make personal contact. But it's not like we go out looking for fights or jump people in the dark." She drummed her fingertips on the tabletop. "At least I don't. Ashley might, because she finds that shit funny as hell."

"What exactly does 'personal contact' mean?" Ronan asked. "What do you girls do?"

She smiled. "We sit down the abuser and have a chat. Sometimes all it takes is for that person to realize that their target is not on their own and has an ally. When they see that they no longer hold the power, they'll leave the person alone. Other times, it takes a…deeper conversation to convince them to change their ways."

"And by 'deeper' you mean torture."

"Like responds to like," she said before she took a swig of her water. "If it takes the fear of God to make them understand, then I'm happy to be the messenger."

"What if Mulvaney had taken a swing at you?" Ronan

asked with worry in his eyes.

"By the time he realized what was going on, he was already tied up. But I have had guys try to fight me."

"Good God," he exclaimed.

"Assholes like that aren't used to anyone fighting back. The minute I knock them on their ass, they're ready to listen." Her grin widened. "Plus, I'm pretty good with my whip."

Ronan dropped his head in his hands and his shoulders shuddered. He peeked a glance at his brother who shared a similar look of horror.

"But what if—That's so..." Ethan stuttered. He might have kept his thoughts about her activities to himself, but his feelings were stamped all over his face. He sucked in a breath and then another. "Okay. Who was next on your list?"

She shrugged. "We haven't had anyone who's made quite a fuss about disrupting their significant other's life like Mulvaney did."

"No one at all? If so, we could have them tailed and see if they're attacked like Mulvaney was."

"You want me to go after someone?" she asked in surprise. "I thought that was opposite of what you wanted."

"No, no. Of course we don't want you to go after anyone," Ethan said. "I was thinking that whoever that was could be targeted in the same way as Mulvaney. If so, then we know whoever the killer is knows about you and is using you to get to their victims."

She chuckled grimly and leaned back in her seat, resting her arm on the back of the chair. "You don't want me to get my knuckles all bloody?"

"No. No, we don't," Ronan replied with a groan. "Personally, I don't want you anywhere near danger." He held up a finger before she could sputter. "But I know it's not my place to tell you what to do. Regardless, I still don't like it."

"Fair enough." Watching him admit he had no control over her was incredibly attractive. "I can make someone up. Say I'm doing research and see if anyone follows."

And if so, that would mean whoever the killer was, it was somebody on her team.

Fuck. Even as the thought entered her mind, her heart vehemently rejected it. The possibility was ludicrous. Wasn't it?

"This is all making me very, very tired," she said. Her eyes were growing heavy and she rubbed at the ache that bloomed in her chest at the thought that someone close to her could be a murderer.

Ethan reached out and patted the back of her hand. "Let's take a look at the police report and start brainstorming ideas of who else might have had it out for Mulvaney."

For the next several hours they worked together, looking for a clue or a link as to who the killer might be. The list was short, unfortunately, and Jameson was afraid it meant nothing in the long run. As soon as a name cropped up, there seemed to be a police report or activity that struck the possibility down.

"You're exhausted," Ethan said. "Let's call it a night and see what happens tomorrow. We can give you a ride home."

"No need." She stood and slipped her jacket on. "I drove, remember?"

Ronan stood as well, closing his laptop as Ethan did the same. "We don't like the thought of you going home alone. It doesn't feel right."

We. She smiled. Did Ronan even realize he was speaking for him *and* his brother, or was the inclusion a natural with them?

"That's called 'uncertainty' because you are dealing with a strong, independent woman and don't know what to do with yourself. I shudder to think of the type of women you two date. Entitled socialites? Do they have Mummy or Daddy or the butler on speed dial?"

The brothers exchanged curious glances.

"You have no idea," Ronan muttered.

Actually, once the words came out of her mouth, she realized she didn't want to think about their dating life in any capacity. If she spent a moment thinking about the women they did date and how she didn't measure up in the status department, then somehow her subconscious would think that deep down inside she wanted to measure up. To speculate for just a nanosecond that she was lacking in any capacity was foolishness she did not have the time to entertain.

"Can we see you tomorrow?" Ethan asked as they went to the door, shutting off lights as they went.

"Uh, I have work to do tomorrow." She kept her focus on locking the apartment door behind them.

"How about Friday? There's a fundraiser at the art museum. The Gateses are hosting. Imagine the contacts you can make there for the center."

Gah! The man was an assassin, tempting her with what she valued most.

"I'll see if I can work it into my schedule. I'll keep you posted."

They rode the elevator down to the garage in silence. She watched in amusement as their cheeks turned pink once again and their bodies tensed as they passed through the levels occupied by the nightclub. She hadn't a clue as to what they were picking up, but if it was anything like the throb of the bass from the music rolling up her spine and tickling her nipples, they must be in an excruciating state.

When the doors opened, they rushed out into the cool confines of the garage, and the boys escorted her to her car. After she pushed the fob to unlock the doors, Ronan bounded ahead and opened the driver-side door for her.

"Thank you," she said.

Ethan stopped her with a touch on her arm. "Be careful, Jameson. Call us if you need anything. Promise me."

"I will," she eased past her suddenly dry lips.

Ethan lifted his hand higher and ran the back of his fingers over her cheek. His touch was warm, comforting. Slowly, ever so slowly he leaned closer and pressed his lips to her forehead. A blanket of warmth engulfed her, squeezing and shaping around her in all the right places, soothing her weary body. As he stepped away, the warmth eased but did not disappear altogether. She turned away from the hunger blazing in his eyes, not ready to face her own needs—and ran nose-first into Ronan's chest.

He chuckled and lifted her chin with the tip of his finger. "Have a good night, wildcat."

Ronan was much more daring and placed a kiss to her cheek, brushing the corner of her lips. If she were braver, she would have indulged her curiosity of the spark of his touch and turned a fraction of an inch to lay her lips on his.

Stop the train. She was tired, definitely tired. The brothers were invading her senses, and if she wasn't careful, she'd want to stay between them forever.

"That looks good on you," Ronan said.

"What?" She blinked in confusion.

He gestured in a circle as if to encompass her. "Your walls coming down."

Oh, for fuck's sake.

She mumbled her good-nights and climbed into her car, ignoring the sight of both of them breaking into a grin at her thoughts as she sped away.

Damn it. They promised not to read her mind.

Get over yourself, sis. You know they didn't have to work hard to know you're curious to be the filling in that sandwich.

Perhaps. But they didn't need to look happy she was having those thoughts. Thinking about doing something and taking action were two different things. Everyone knew that.

Do you, sis? Do you? Because you could probably fuck them both with only your mind and everyone would be left satisfied.

Holy shit. That was probably true.

"No. No, no," she shouted out loud, rubbing her fingers in her ears as if to wipe away the thought. "I didn't need to know that!"

But now that she did, how in the hell was she ever going to forget?

CHAPTER SEVEN

"JAMESON MARIE ALINARI. What have you done?" Alisia's voice snapped across the phone line.

"Ah. So the fugitive has returned." Jameson tucked her cell phone between her ear and shoulder and continued to flip through the papers on her desk. Between the investigation into Mulvaney's death and her other duties, she had been running behind on completing her administrative tasks for the shelter. "I saw the headlines about your father. I tried to call you, but I figured you had ditched the burner phone I gave you. How are you doing, sis? Big bad dad is vanquished. Yay?"

Alisia sighed, and Jameson swore she could see her friend in the distance, flopping onto a couch and throwing her hand over her eyes. "Yeah. Sure. Yay. The man who betrayed his family and his church will now go to jail and will never speak again because my shape-shifting boyfriend ripped out his vocal cords and almost killed him. So yeah, yay. Everything is just grand."

"Boyfriend? The shape-shifter is your boyfriend? Ha ha! I knew it."

"No. He's not, really. I mean. It's complicated. And that's not why I called you."

"I'm sorry." The poor woman sounded beyond exhausted. "I can't imagine what you've been through. I wish I could have been there for you."

"You helped me plenty. Really. I so appreciated it. Besides," Alisia chuckled. "It sounds like you've been having troubles of your own lately."

"What do you mean?"

"Ethan Daniels came to help at the church last week. He asked me about a woman he found engaged in some…interesting activities. The image he projected into my mind looked an awful lot like how I saw you on the night I came for help. Now I find out one of the Evolutioneers is assisting the Daniels brothers in investigating a case involving a certain female vigilante. James. Sis. What is going on?"

Ah. Fucknut. "To use your words, it's complicated."

"Jameson, are you in trouble?"

"Not any more than usual." Sad, but true. From the day she was born, trouble seemed to stick to her like flypaper. "It's no big deal, really."

"Look, I know my world has pretty much burned around me in Mount Vesuvius fashion, but I'm here for you. I would've called sooner, but this is the first time I've had access to a telephone and in a place that is not surrounded by angry cult members or the police. Come on. What's going on with you?"

Jameson set aside her stack of papers, her attention now completely obliterated. Even if she managed to somehow organize the mess, she couldn't trust that the task was complete.

She blew at the strands of hair that had escaped her braid and were sticking to her cheek. "Let's just say that the objectives of the Crimson Angels have expanded a bit since you were a part of the team."

Alisia chuckled without humor, and her tone sounded

as if she were pinching the bridge of her nose. "Expanded how?"

"Expanded as in we're taking a more direct approach in helping the women in our shelter."

"Meaning…?"

"You hurt my girls, I'm gonna hurt you."

"Shit, Jameson. You're going around town like the Girl with the Dragon Tattoo and the other night you had the nerve to lecture me?"

"I wouldn't say we've gone to that extreme. Seriously, it's nothing. The Daniels twins and I crossed paths the other night while I was…working. Now we've joined forces. They're going to donate some money to the shelter and help me with other projects. It's no big deal."

"Right. But they're getting the Evolutioneers involved. It *is* a big deal."

"Are the twins Evolutioneers?" Shit. She never did confirm that little tidbit.

"Not really. They act more like consultants. Ethan was asked to come help at the church because things were crazy. We needed to know who was loyal to my father and who was just an unfortunate victim in the church's crimes. Also, everyone was freaking the fuck out as they were coming down from the drugs they had ingested. He helped to soothe some of the raw emotions."

"Jesus, Alisia. That sounds awful. How are you holding up? Really."

The weight of her sigh sounded as if she had a skyscraper on her shoulders. "I'm fine. My sister, Mary Beth, is finally coming around to me being back in her life. She seems to like the new house we're able to rent, but she's apprehensive about life outside the compound's walls. I am in no hurry for her to rush into embracing a new existence, but she at least deserves the chance to start over. I can't wait for things to finally settle down."

"And your shifter boyfriend?"

"Not an issue. Right now, my sole focus is on my sister."

"So why are you on the phone with me? Go take care of your sister."

"You're my sister too, Jameson. I'm going to worry about you. Especially if you're hanging with the Daniels brothers."

"Why? Is there something dubious about them I should know about?"

Alisia was silent for several moments. "No. They're actually pretty cool. Smart. Funny. Super hot. But I know they are tight with my boss. If you're trying to lay low, it's not going to happen with those two up in your business."

"I got this. Besides, nobody takes better care of me than me."

There was a knock on her office door a second before it swung open and one of the devils themselves poked his head inside. "We need to talk, now," Ronan said.

"Who is that?" Alisia asked, her voice on high alert. "Is that one of the twins?"

"No," Jameson lied. What the hell? Not only did she not have an appointment with either of them, how did they get into the building? "Someone who sounds similar. Look, I have to go. I have a meeting. And you need to get back to your sister. I'll keep you posted if anything major happens. And you do the same for me."

"Jameson."

" 'Kay—love you—'bye." She disconnected the call as Ronan entered her office.

His clothes were fresh from the 1980s with a Ghostbusters T-shirt under his navy sport jacket with the sleeves pushed up to his elbow, black jeans, and white trainers. A fun ensemble that was in direct contrast to the solemn pinch to his lips and the same worry in his eyes as the last time he showed up at the shelter from out of the blue.

"Please don't tell me someone died," she said. "Please, please, please don't tell me someone died."

"Sorry, wildcat," he said, shutting the door behind him. He leaned against it with his arms folded. "Wish I had better news."

"What?" It was as if she had been doused in a bucket of ice water after being set on fire. "I was joking. Somebody died? Who?"

"Does the name Travis Fitzherbert mean anything to you?"

"No. And with a name like that, I think I would remember."

His eyes narrowed and he nodded. "He was found dead this morning in his home. His body was in a similar condition as Mulvaney's, so that's why we're alarmed. Where have you been all day, anyway? We've been trying to call you."

She gestured to indicate the disaster that was her office. "I've been here, working. Besides, you couldn't have called me. You don't have my number."

"We do. Wasn't hard to grease the right networks to find it." Ronan grinned as if he were in on some secret joke.

She picked up her phone and scrolled through the notifications. "Oh. You must have been the joker I've been ignoring all day. You might have had my number, but I don't have yours. I don't answer unknown calls."

"What about texts?"

"Block those, too. There are a lot of weirdos and scammers in the world."

He shook his head. "When I want you to be a little careless… Anyway, grab your bag. We're leaving."

"Uh, no. You don't get to order me around. And remember." She waved her hands around. "Working."

"Right. Sorry. Let me rephrase that." He straightened and adjusted his sport coat. "My dear Jameson. Will you please do me the honor of coming with me so we can ensure that this murder is not connected to the other murder that you may become implicated with? I would hate to see you land in jail forever. Thanks ever so much."

She leaned back in her and gave him the same narrow-eyed treatment he had given her earlier. "You do make a good point."

"I've been told I'm a smart guy."

"Smartass is more like it."

Damn. This bombshell was not welcomed at all.

The possibility that the two murders were related could be a good thing, right? Especially if she had no idea who this Fitz-whatever dude was. She'd be in the clear. But what if the murders weren't related? And what if she somehow became tied to his murder as well?

"Fuck," she grunted then reached to open her desk drawer. "Let me grab my purse."

"I knew you'd see reason." He opened her office door, revealing Trini lounging against the wall, blocking their path.

"Hey, handsome," she said. "Who are you?"

"Trini," Jameson said. "This is Ronan Daniels. Ronan, this is Trini. She's supposed to head up security here.

Apparently, she's sleeping on the job if you got in."

"Oh, no. I allowed him to be granted access. Recognized him from the other day." She rubbed the tops of her red lacquered nails over her shirt.

"I should fire you," Jameson said with a shake of her head.

"But you won't." She grinned. "You love me too much."

"Pleasure to meet you," he said with his most charming smile and reached out to clasp her hand between the two of his.

"Hmm. Manners. So far I like. So, where do you think you're going, sis? You said to not allow you to leave your office until your desk was clear. It don't look clear to me."

"Sorry. That would be my fault." Ronan stuck his hands in his jeans pockets and shrugged with a boyish grin. "I need to borrow your boss for a few hours. I'm certain you can hold down the fort without her."

Trini smirked. "We'll manage all right."

Gah! She did not have time for this banter. "I'll be available by phone and text if you need me. Hopefully I won't be gone long." Jameson locked her office door behind her—not that Trini couldn't get in with her master key; still, security first.

"Have fun," Trini called out after them. "Don't do anything I would do."

"Why does that sound like she would do a lot?" Ronan asked.

"Because she would."

Trini liked to self-medicate with adrenaline rushes. Not the best form of treatment, but it wasn't the worst.

"I take it she's one of your Crimson Angels," Ronan said as they exited the building.

"What makes you say that?" she asked suspiciously.

"The angel wings she had tattooed on the inside of her wrist. They were red."

"Ah. Well. Some of the crew got inked after their first mission."

"Really? Where's your tattoo?" He glanced at her up and down as if he'd be able to see through her clothing.

"What makes you think I have a tattoo?"

He rubbed at his chin and chuckled. "You are a woman who carries your emotions and life experiences not only on your soul but with every action you do and everything you say. I'm surprised you don't have your entire life story tattooed on every inch of your body."

How very astute of him. "You are right *and* wrong. I would have every experience tattooed on my body. Which is why I don't have any. Once I got the first one, I wouldn't know when to stop."

Ted was waiting for them by the side of the car, a big black SUV this time, and smoothly opened the back door for Jameson as they approached. Ethan was waiting inside with a tablet on his lap, typing furiously at a separate keyboard.

"Anything new?" Ronan asked as he slid into the front seat.

"I'm getting more specifics from Network." He paused from his work to look over at Jameson. The lines bracketing his mouth were deep with concern. "It's always a pleasure to see you. I just wish it was never because a dead body was discovered."

"I've got to say, if this is your way of trying to ask me out, your technique needs some work."

The corner of his lips twitched and he turned the tablet

to face her. “Does this man look familiar?”

Hmm… Typical thirty- to forty-something-year-old white dude with buzzed sandy hair and bushy eyebrows, wearing an oversized T-shirt with the logo of a sporting goods store across the chest. Looked like another bro to her.

“Not at all. Am I supposed to know him?”

“This is Travis Fitzherbert. His body was found this morning at his house by his brother. They were supposed to go to the football game today. The brother made a call to 911 just under two hours ago.”

“Wait. How do you know all this already?”

“The same way we found out about Mulvaney. We have an associate who is practically a computer herself. She set up a program for me to scan police calls and 911 entries for certain search words. As soon as a call comes through with the right keywords, it sends the data to me.”

“In other words, you know someone who has hacked into the police system. I take it this is one of your Evolutioneer friends?”

Ethan laughed and shook his head as if to say wouldn’t you like to know. “According to the initial call, Fitzherbert was found laid out in the same way as Mulvaney. Tied to a bed, nude, bruises and abrasions on the body, and the word ‘RAPIST’ carved into his thigh.”

So Ethan wasn’t going to give up his contact, huh? Cool. Cool. Cool. No matter. She knew it had to be an Evolutioneer. Based on what Alisia told her, they were the only people she knew of with those kinds of resources.

“If you’re looking for keywords, yeah, that’s enough of a match to Mulvaney to catch my interest. So where are we going?” she asked, as Ted headed toward the outskirt of town.

"To the scene of the crime, of course."

Her initial laughter died a swift death as she realized he was serious. "We can't just go to a crime scene and start poking around. Are you insane?"

"I guess I should've been more specific. We're going to go *near* the crime scene. We're going to get close enough so Ronan and I can read the minds of those investigating and get more information."

"Okay. And what am I supposed to do?"

"Try to see if what we find lends more of a connection between Mulvaney and Fitzherbert besides the way they were killed."

Right. Like she was going to figure out anything off the top of her head. Everything was happening in such a whirlwind fashion, they could be taking her back to the shelter for all she knew.

But they didn't, of course. Ted drove them into one of those cookie-cutter developments. The kind of neighborhood where all the houses looked the same except for a slight variation of exterior paint color. The houses were built far too big for their lot size and took up the entire plot, sitting so close to each other that you could stick your hand out the kitchen window and slap the forehead of your neighbor next door.

As they passed through an intersection, Jameson spotted police vehicles and an aid car stationed on the street outside of a house. To her surprise, Ted drove past it down to the next block and turned the corner.

"Park in front of that house right there," Ethan instructed. "I don't sense anyone inside, and it's right behind the Fitzherbert home."

As Ethan set aside his tablet, Ted rolled down the windows on the side of the car closest to their target. Both Ethan and Ronan sat back in their seats and closed their eyes. The more relaxed they appeared, the tenser Ted became. Although he barely seemed to move a muscle, Jameson sensed his body go on full alert.

With her heartbeat outracing the hum of the car's engine, sweat began to bead on her forehead.

"I'm still not sure why I'm here," Jameson whispered. "I can't read minds."

"Close your eyes," Ethan said. "Ronan and I are going to funnel you the information being seen by the investigators. Hopefully you'll see if there's anything that triggers a memory or perhaps a clue if this is the same person that killed Mulvaney or if we're here on a wild goose chase."

And while they were sending her these images, what images would they see in her mind?

Stop it, James. The brothers promised they would not read her mind without permission, and so far they had kept their promise. At least as much as she could tell. If they had read her mind, they would have way, way more questions about her. Plus, she was beginning to trust them.

Ethan told her she was the only person he had met who could lock him out of her thoughts. If she stayed diligent, perhaps she could control what they had access to.

She nodded and settled deeper in her seat. Folding her hands and resting them in her lap, she closed her eyes.

"Here we go," Ethan said and suddenly she felt as if she were in a bubble.

The sensation was so weird. It was as if she were holding the hand of one of the brothers as they floated in a warm cloud. Which brother carried her she wasn't certain, but she definitely felt connected.

A part of her wanted to open her eyes and see if the connection severed, but the floating was too pleasant to let go.

Is this what it feels like to read someone's mind? she asked. *This is nice.*

Trust me, wildcat, Ronan replied. *Ethan is keeping you from the worst of it.*

Snippets of voices filtered through her thoughts until one crystallized into a coherent set of thoughts. It must've been the lead detective, for they were giving orders about what pictures to take and where the evidence that was being collected should be sent. The investigation was still in full swing, and it sounded as if there was plenty more of the house to go through.

Every now and again a flash of an image would flutter through her mind. A closed but unlocked bedroom window. A bloodstained shirt crumpled on the floor. And then there was the body.

It was a flash. Only a flash, but it was enough to make her gasp and all her muscles tighten in alarm. The victim had been stretched out on the bed much in the same fashion as Mulvaney, but complete with a ball gag in his mouth. He too was naked with his pale body covered with a pelt of hair that had been matted with sweat. And on the inside of his thigh was carved the word "RAPIST" with fine droplets of blood running down his leg and into the mattress beneath him.

Two sources of heat enveloped her at once. Ethan's hand reached across the distance of the backseat to envelop hers as the cloud around her intensified like a hug. That must've been Ronan trying to offer her comfort in some way from his place in the front seat.

"What are we not seeing, what are we not seeing?" the detective was thinking, clear as day.

The world shifted and more voices filtered through her head. Ethan had to be the one leading the charge, for she felt the deliberate stride of his actions as surely as if he were leading her on foot.

Now they were in the mind of one of the officers who was sorting through the list of household items he must've been looking at, wondering what might have been missed. Was it a photo of family members on the mantle? Or the military photo of the victim proudly displayed in the center? Furniture did not appear to be moved; the couch cushions were all in place.

Switch. They were now with another officer, more searching. The victim's children were adults and out of the house. Touches of a wife or a female significant other were all over the home, unless Fitzherbert was a fan of floral print couch cushions and bud vases with daisies on the kitchen table.

Switch. Now they were outside looking for footprints under the shrubbery by the bedroom windows.

Around and around, they traveled. From the detective to the medical examiner, they looked for a connection to Mulvaney.

"I'm not finding any direct link between Fitzherbert and Mulvaney," Ethan said with a sigh. He reached for the tablet and began to type. "The only thing is that they died the same way."

"They were *found* the same way," Ronan corrected. "Until the autopsy reports come in, we can't say how they died."

"Technicality," Ethan replied with a wave of his hand.

"My gut says they were murdered the same way. And thank you, Jameson." He looked up at her with wonder in his eyes. "For some reason, funneling images to you made it easier for me to concentrate. I wish I knew why," he finished with a confused mutter.

"What information have we been sent about Fitzherbert?" Ronan asked.

Ethan stared at her in deep consideration for a moment longer before he blinked hard and turned his attention to the tablet. "Let's see. All the initial data on him appears to be clean. Father of two, sells insurance. Former sergeant in the Army, stationed out of Joint Base Lewis-McChord."

"Fort Lewis? Maybe Ash knows him," Jameson blurted without thinking.

"Who?"

Ah crap.

"A friend of mine. She was in the Army too. Stationed and discharged from Fort Lewis about five years ago. Maybe she's heard of him." Please don't ask me to elaborate anymore.

"It wouldn't hurt to ask," Ethan said with a sigh and put down the tablet.

"You know, the whole serial killing theory seems weird to me," Jameson said. "There's no known link between the two victims, so why kill them the same way? I never understood that. Why leave a trail by murdering people in the exact same way? Wouldn't you be more likely to get away with murder if you changed up your MO?"

Ronan turned to stare at her with a slightly horrified expression on his face. "I knew you were dangerous, but that's downright frightening logic."

Jameson rolled her eyes. "I'm not a serial killer. However, if I were, I personally would not leave an identifiable trail."

"Unless you wanted people to know it was you," Ethan murmured and drummed his fingers on the top of his thigh. "That's part of the thrill, isn't it? Leaving clues for the police, the game of cat and mouse, how many people can you kill before you're caught? Maybe the killer is making a statement."

"Check out his associates."

Jameson started. It took her several seconds to realize it had been Ted who had spoken. He was usually so quiet.

"What did you say?" she asked.

"Check his associates," he repeated. "If it is a serial killer who is making a statement, perhaps Mulvaney and Fitzherbert are more connected than you think. Look to Fitzherbert's military associates. Check his background. If his wife had never called him in on abuse, perhaps there was a former girlfriend? Or colleague? Especially if he was in the military. He may have former Army friends who could be possible targets. Or assailants."

"Good thinking, Ted." Ethan flipped on the tablet and began typing the moment the screen booted up.

"This is all…this is all getting to be too much." Jameson rubbed her temples. "I'd like to go home now. I still have a long night ahead of me."

"You said you were going to stop doing vigilante work," Ronan said.

"I said I would take a pause. And I'm not doing vigilante work, not that it's any of your business."

Ethan gasped and turned toward her with disappointment in his eyes. "You have a date."

"Date? Who said date? I didn't say anything about a

date."

"I saw an image of the cocktail dresses you're deciding to wear. The red one is hot, by the way, so you should definitely *not* wear that one."

"You promised not to read my mind," she growled and shoved her finger in front of his face.

"I didn't. You projected. And I can't help it if you jam an image into my mind."

"This power of yours is kinda wishy-washy. It seems to come and go when it's convenient for you."

"It doesn't," Ethan barked, then pinched his lips together, huffing a breath out his nose. He leaned his head back against the seat and closed his eyes. "It doesn't. It's always on. If I don't have my walls up, it's constant noise. Like I'm at a symphony and they're tuning their instruments all at once. I have to keep constant guard or else I would go insane." He turned to face her with a look of wonder mixed with confusion pulling at his brow. "Except with you. Most of the time," he amended with a grin tugging at the corner of his mouth. "I guess it's the reverse with you. Your walls are always up, but when you're tired or stressed they fall, allowing your thoughts to scream out."

"Maybe," she murmured. She folded her arms across her belly and shrank back in her seat.

"I hope you'll teach me that trick someday," Ethan said softly.

Trick? If she was able to close off her thoughts, she certainly wasn't aware of it. And if she wasn't aware of it, she had no idea how to tell him how she accomplished the feat.

"I'll take you back now, Ms. Alinari," Ted said, pulling away from the curb.

"Thank you, Ted."

They traveled in silence for a few blocks until Ronan coughed. "So…"

"So what?" she asked when she realized he had directed his comment at her.

"If it's not a date, then…"

"Geez." She grabbed the end of her braid and pulled in an attempt to relieve the tension on her brain. "It's business. The chamber of commerce is having a summer ball and all the big business owners are to be in attendance. Shepard and I always go to try to woo some of those businesses to sponsor or give funds to the shelter and its charities. Again, not that it's any of your business."

"Sounds interesting." Ronan turned to face her. "We'd be delighted to escort you."

She sat up in her seat with alarm. "What? No. No way."

"Why not? We're business owners."

"The hub of Daniels Software is across the lake in another town. You don't qualify for an invitation."

Ronan chuckled. "I have a checkbook with a spot to write lots of numbers. That's all the invitation we'll need."

Damn it. Why were they determined to barge into every aspect of her life? And what would it take to make them understand not now, not ever?

Fire and pepper blistered her tongue as she gathered steam to lay into them to keep to themselves when Ethan's hand closed over the top of hers. That gentleness, that warmth stole right to her soul and stopped her mid-breath.

She glanced over at him and her tirade died at the need she saw in his dark eyes.

"Please," he whispered. "Let us take you, Jameson. There are strange things going on. What if someone is targeting you somehow? I'd hate it if you were out there with no backup."

Dammit all to hell. How could she refuse a man who looked at her as if his world would go dark without her?

It was her turn to rest her head back against the seat and close her eyes. "You two have been a pain in the ass since the moment I met you."

"That's a yes then?"

"Fine," she gritted out. "It's a yes. But I will meet you there. Shepard already arranged to pick me up."

"Thank you." He picked up her hand and pressed his lips to her knuckles. The tingle from the contact made her breath catch.

"Don't thank me yet." She slowly withdrew her hand, longing to stay in his warm hold but desperate to maintain her independence. "I said you could meet me there. I didn't say I would get you in or even converse with you."

Ronan laughed. "Watching you from across the room working rich people over for money will be entertainment enough. I'm looking forward to it."

Strangely enough, she was looking forward to it too.

CHAPTER EIGHT

USING THE BRIEF bursts of illumination from the streetlights as they passed, Ethan checked out his reflection in the window and adjusted his tie for the umpteenth time.

"Knock it off," Ronan said from the seat across from him. "You look good. We look good. It's a good thing we're attractive, because who would want to see the same ugly twice?"

"You're not funny."

"I'm trying to be. The tension running through you is going to make my back snap. Why are you so nervous?"

"I just want to make a good impression for Jameson."

"And?" Ronan drew out, clearly not buying that as being the only reason for his brother's nerves.

Ethan wilted in his seat. "I'm worried. About everything. About these murders, if and how Jameson is involved. And what about afterward? What happens when the killer is caught? Will she go back to her vigilantism? Will she even want...?" He blew out a breath and pulled at the end of his tie. "There is something about her that makes me want to give her everything she didn't have as a child. Security. Comfort. Keep her somewhere safe where nothing bad can touch her."

Ronan chuckled. "And she'd kick your ass for even thinking that."

That was an understatement. She'd probably strike him dead. "Without a doubt."

"Don't fret. It would be two of us she'd be fighting then. I'm right there with you, bro. She's fascinating. She swings on this pendulum of sweet and mothering to cutthroat and dangerous on a dime. I find the extremes charming as hell. I want to learn all there is to know." He sighed. "Don't worry. We have to have faith that it'll all work itself out somehow."

Ethan hummed in agreement then fell silent.

Ronan burst out laughing. "You tried asking Crystal about the future again."

"Maybe," Ethan muttered as heat rushed to his cheeks.

"And what did she say?" he asked with a knowing smile.

"Laughed in my ear when I called her. Then she hung up."

"That means it can't be bad, right? If she was laughing?"

Ethan smoothed his palms over his thighs. "It was more of a 'you dumb schmuck' laugh than an 'everything is going to be hunky-dory' chortle."

Despite his wish for the contrary, it was probably for the best they didn't know what was to be. According to Crystal—also known as Prism—the gift of a psychic was a double-edged sword. Yes, you knew the future and could prepare, but one teeny-tiny change of anything—a thought, a breath, a stiff breeze—at any time could change the outcome for good or ill. Sometimes the "more you know" adage did more harm than good. The stress of the ever-changing outcomes was unbearable for her at times.

Still… it would be nice to know what the future held for them and Jameson.

Unless it is bad. Ronan's thought drifted on the air between them.

Right. Guess Prism was right in withholding information.

Ted pulled the limo under the porte cochere of the hotel, and a valet rushed to open the car door.

Ethan and Ronan climbed out and paused to stand side by side on the sidewalk, staring at the entrance's revolving door as if it held the answer to their futures. Ethan checked the barriers in his mind, probing for weak spots. If his focus was going to be on Jameson, he needed his powers firmly in control.

Together, they drew a collective breath, held it, then let it out slowly between their lips before striding in unison through the front doors. The snap of the soles of their shoes on the marble floor was drowned out by the gasps of the lobby's patrons as they passed.

The brothers knew they made a striking pair. Tall, squared jaws, well dressed. One on their own was eye-catching. Two made people stop in their tracks. Their identical looks were the main reason Max wouldn't allow them to be officially part of the Evolutioneers. Even with a disguise, they wouldn't be able to hide their identities for very long, and to Max, privacy was everything.

They paused just inside the entrance to the ballroom. Ethan unfocused his vision and let his mind drift from person to person until he picked up a familiar vibration.

How much trouble would I get in if I punched these jokers in the throat?

"Catch that?" Ronan asked with amusement.

"Yep. That way." Ethan nodded to the left and weaved between the groupings of people toward the energy of Jameson's thoughts.

Ronan's chuckle echoed in his head. *What happened to*

observing her from afar?

She doesn't know what those men were thinking about her. Trust me, she'll thank us later.

Sorry to burst your bubble, brother. But I think she does know. And I don't think she's going to thank you for interfering.

✧ ✧ ✧

MOTHERFUCKERS.

How much trouble would she get in if she punched these jokers in the throat?

Jameson took a slow, slow sip of her ginger ale and contemplated the fate of the two bozos talking *at* her and not *to* her.

Well, Shepard would frown upon such behavior, that was for certain. But that was because as a cis white man, he'd probably never been dismissed out of turn, especially by chuckleheads like these. The only reason she approached them at all was because Frick and Frack here were the district managers of two of the biggest grocery chains in the state. Otherwise, she would've steered clear from the dude-bro vibes they were throwing.

There had been no reason at all for them to laugh in her face at her suggestion of having the shelter receive a discount for supplies. They were a non-profit organization, for pete's sake. Other companies had given them a discount on goods and services. And if possible, she sent qualified people to apply for any available job postings those companies had. The way they had reacted seemed as if she had asked them to open the stores for a free-for-all.

Fine. She ran her tongue over her teeth and sucked back the need to call bullshit. So they didn't want to lend a hand to those in need. In her book that meant the conversation was over, right?

Oh, no. In fact, twice now she had made the effort to walk away, and both times they shifted to block her path. As if she were interested in listening to their prattle about crazy two-in-the-morning customers and stock-boy antics.

"Isn't that hysterical, Jamie?" Tweedle Dee asked her, chortling at a joke she hadn't even bothered paying attention to.

Jamie? For real? It was getting close to the light turning green on busting open a can of whupass on these two. "Not really. Now, if you'll excuse me." She sidestepped to her left and Tweedle Dum torqued his hips, blocking her way again.

She tightened her grip on her wine glass before she slammed it on the bar top behind her with more force than was probably necessary.

That's it. The light was green. This punk was going down.

"Jameson, darling. There you are."

Behind her captors she spotted the Daniels twins striding her way in a syncopated gait. Numbness set in from the top of her head to the bottom of her toes as her extremities tingled. She swore that time slowed down and ZZ Top's "Sharp Dressed Man" played over the sound system.

The brothers cleaned up *good.* Really, really good. If someone snapped a photo of her at that moment, she wouldn't have been one bit surprised if her tongue was hanging out of her mouth.

Ronan wore a brown suede blazer over his crisp white shirt that was open at the collar. Dark jeans encased his legs down to his brown leather boots. As usual, Ethan was dressed more formally in a dark blue suit with matching silk tie.

Yes, she knew exactly what they wore, because her gaze scanned their bodies up and down many times as they drew closer. Ooo la la indeed.

"Ms. Alinari," Ethan greeted and reached toward her, drawing her away from the numbnuts who had blocked her way. "We've been looking all over for you. We'd love to talk more about your idea that would bring in millions of free advertising dollars to Daniels Software. I can't believe we're so lucky to catch you standing here all by yourself."

Before she realized it, Ethan had slipped her away and guided her across the ballroom.

"What was all that about?" she asked when they were out of earshot.

"I was just giving you a polite way of removing yourself from what was about to become an uncomfortable situation."

"You were saving me? I'm not a damsel in distress who needs saving. Besides, I was about to take my leave of them."

"How?"

"I was going to shoulder past them and if either of them blocked my way again, I was going to knee them in the balls and call them out for being predatory asshats."

The brothers shared a glance and a laugh. "No, you weren't," Ronan said.

"Sure I was."

Ethan shook his head. "You wouldn't. You would've stood there still smiling, although it would pain you, because it's the polite thing to do. And because you know that those men are someone you may need something from in the future, so unless it was absolutely necessary, you would put up with their crap as long as possible."

She frowned and the little crease in her forehead he was about to dub the Daniels wrinkle appeared. "You suck."

He patted her hand where it rested in the crook of his elbow. "I'm sorry."

"If it makes you feel any better," Ronan added, "if they had finished the thoughts they had going while staring at your cleavage, I would've pounded them into the ground for you. I have no need for their business."

Jameson rolled her eyes. "I was afraid that was going on. I even wore the black dress because Ethan said the red dress was sexy. I don't want to be sexy. This is not the event to be sexy."

"Wildcat, you can wear a potato sack and be sexy."

An image flashed in her mind of what she looked like at that moment as seen through Ronan's eyes. The skirt of her black dress fell just below her knees, and the three-quarter length sleeves covered her arms. She wore her dark hair down that evening, the thick waves falling to her shoulders.

The image of herself switched to that of one of a young Sophia Loren in the 1960s in her Italian, movie star glory. The images switched back and forth between her and Sophia and were accompanied by a wolf whistle.

"You are incorrigible." She hip-checked Ronan and gave him a small grin.

"But honest."

"Perhaps."

"And that wasn't me. That was Ethan."

She turned to Ethan in surprise and found him looking deliberately ahead with a devilish twinkle curling his lips.

A stocky man with apparent Pacific Islander origins whose toothy smile was almost as wide as his large shoulders jumped in front of them as if they were visiting a haunted house and he was part of the entertainment. The amber hotel lighting glinted off the blue in his black hair that was swept back into a helmet-styled pompadour, and his dark suit hung square around his middle, hiding his paunch.

"Mr. Daniels. Mr. Daniels," he exclaimed, exuberantly shaking both brothers' hands. "I'm so glad to see you here tonight."

"Mayor Tuputala." Ethan shook the cramp out of his fingers. "A pleasure as always."

"I hope that you are here because you are planning on leaving your offices across the lake and moving to the city. Huh? Huh?" He waggled his thick eyebrows and his body appeared to vibrate with anticipation. "I can get the council to make it very appealing for you. We will have some excellent real estate right next to the new train stop. Waterfront view."

"We have no plans to move, Mayor," Ronan said, denying the mayor with a gentle smile.

"That's because we have not had a proper meeting. Come, come see me. We'll talk." He bounced on his heels and licked his lips, practically salivating at the thought of having the Daniels name contributing to the city's finances. He swept his hand out, gesturing to the room. "As you can see, we love our business owners. These are my people creating jobs for my people. I love them. And I will love you."

"I'm sure you will," Ronan said with a chuckle. "But we're here for Jameson tonight."

"Jameson?" He finally glanced in her direction.

"Jameson Alinari, sir," she added, shaking his hand with a firm grip. "We've met before."

His eyes lit up. "Ah, yes. You are with the women's shelter."

"Yes, sir. And I'm eagerly looking forward to when the city council will vote on the proposition granting humanitarian businesses and shelters the same benefits on real estate as they do for corporations, such as Daniels Software. Will that be on next month's agenda?"

"What? Oh." A nervous titter edged his chuckle. "I—uh—I can't remember off the top of my head. Perhaps. Or perhaps it will be on next year's budget."

"But you just said you love your people. Just think of all those needy citizens who, with your support, can get back on their feet. Become productive employees, homeowners," she grinned and finished with, "taxpayers. Don't you want to provide that kind of security for your people, Mr. Mayor?"

Mayor Tuputala's chortle grew into a full-on belly laugh, complete with his hands covering his stomach. "Are you planning on running for mayor, Ms. Alinari?"

"If I have to. But I think my skills are better served helping people one-on-one rather than by committee."

"There you are, Jameson." Shepard appeared at her elbow. He wore a huge smile and he practically bounced on his toes. "Excuse us, gentlemen, Mr. Mayor. Jameson, I've just met the new manager for Wilton's department store. She's very interested in hearing about your idea to partner with them. She wants to talk to you more."

"That's amazing." She turned to the men. "If you'll excuse me, please."

"Of course." Ronan dropped a sweet kiss to her cheek and Ethan gave her hip a squeeze before stepping away. "Good luck," he said with a smile.

As she matched Shepard's quick steps, he looked at her with a confused frown. "What was all of that about?"

"Just putting the mayor on notice and working on getting more shelters on better real estate."

"No. I meant the kiss. Are you dating Ronan Daniels?"

"Of course not." Searching for a murderer in no way constituted dating.

"You're dating Ethan Daniels?" he exclaimed.

"I'm not dating anybody." Geez, Shepard. Keep on task. "Now who is it specifically that we're looking for?"

"You're right." He shook his head as if clearing his mind. "Of course. How silly of me. Of course you're not dating one of the Daniels brothers."

Jameson stopped short. "Of course? What does that mean? What? You think one of the Daniels brothers wouldn't be interested in me?" Her head rolled on her neck. "You think I got nothing in common with two smart, hot, multimillionaire twins?" she asked with her best brawler accent. "Why you do me like that, Shep?"

Shepard closed his eyes and shook his head again. "I am so confused."

"Let me clarify. There is nothing going on between the twins and me. But it's because we are in a professional relationship. And I have no time to date. And they are—hoo, they have special…needs. I mean, we are from two different worlds, we communicate completely different. Like, way different." Shut up, James. Who was she trying to convince here? "The reason we are not a thing is not because I couldn't land one of them if I wanted to. Anyway, who is it that you wanted me to meet?"

"Right. Okay. Gotcha." His confused frown didn't ease. "I think. Anyway, right this way."

Shepard led her to a statuesque woman who had her dark hair swept up into a sleek bun and a gray designer suit that fit her body like a second skin. She stood elegantly on five-inch heels that Jameson knew if she wore them she would break her ankle in a nanosecond if she attempted to stroll across the floor.

"Jameson, let me introduce Raquel Munoz. Raquel, the illustrious leader of our organization, Jameson Alinari."

"Delighted." Raquel reached out for a handshake that was Jameson-approved. "Shepard here has told me a bit about your idea. As a woman who struggled to find suitable clothing for job interviews when I first got out of college, your idea has me intrigued."

"What I'd like is to offer scholarships for women to pay for an outfit on discount they can use to go on job interviews. Or have a set wardrobe available appropriate for the season that can be borrowed and/or purchased at a discount."

As Jameson delved deeper into her plan, her earlier meeting with the grocery store managers faded away. This was her area of expertise. She was in the zone. Nothing mattered more to her than the people who came through the shelter. However, despite being in her element, it was impossible to forget that Ethan and Ronan were in the vicinity with the sole purpose of looking out for her.

Over the crowd of attendees, she occasionally spotted the top of one of their heads, a sight that sent an odd thrill running through her body. And even though she couldn't fully see them or hear their voices, their presence was a constant hum surrounding her, engulfing her in a giant, purring hug.

The thing she found most disconcerting was that she

swore she could sense when one of them focused their attention on her. Although no words entered her mind, it was as if their awareness was a breeze buffeting her body. A tropical, gentle gust that swept over her shoulders and down her arms.

But even more impossible, she was starting to tell the difference between the two men as they did so. A phosphorescent brush of bubbles she could attribute to Ronan, while Ethan was more like cinnamon. Spicy, a little hot, and warmed you from the inside.

"I think I may be going insane," she muttered against the rim of the new drink she accepted from a passing waiter.

"Excuse me, dear?" Raquel asked her.

"What? Oh, I'm sorry. I zoned out there for a second." She rubbed at the spot between her eyes. "It's been a long week."

Raquel laughed and took a sip of wine. "Yes, it has. And when you're wearing five-inch heels and your spandex is cutting into your circulation, it feels longer. Actually, if you don't mind, I'm going to run to the ladies' room and give my tummy a brief break from the elastic cutting it in half."

"Certainly. No problem."

"I'll be right back. I'm interested in hearing more. And I'll want to schedule an appointment with you and my head of merchandising."

"Great." Jameson tempered the huge grin burning in her cheeks. "I look forward to it."

As Raquel swept away, Jameson resisted the urge to break out into dance in the middle of the ballroom, and instead shook with excitement as she squealed inside. This deal was going to be huge for the women she worked with.

I can't wait to tell Ethan and Ronan the good news.

What? What did she just say? Her heart skipped a beat. Weird. Shepard was the one she should want to share the news with first, not the brothers. Why was she thinking about them at all?

Dumb, girl. When are you *not* thinking about them?

She lifted her gaze, and as if she were being pulled by a magnetic force, she spotted Ethan across the room. He broke away from the conversation he was holding and met her gaze. Something within him softened, for his shoulders relaxed and the brooding scowl he always wore on his forehead smoothed out. The corner of his lips twitched and ever so slowly he smiled.

Unable to resist, she smiled back, enjoying the warm welcome of his expression and the way his grin seemed to make him appear more youthful, which was funny, because in no way did Ethan seem old. But it wasn't until seeing him at that moment, when he seemed not to have a care in the world, did she realize just how much stress he carried with him day to day.

"Well, well, well. Jameson Alinari. It appears you're the new flavor of the month."

"Mrs. Lance." Jameson blinked the stars from her eyes as she greeted the woman who joined her at the cocktail table. She had lost track, but Marjorie Lance was the third or fourth wife of Senator Lawrence Lance.

Jameson was not a fan of the senator. Ever since that time he had visited one of the Evergreen Women's Center day shelters during his re-election campaigns under the guise of wanting to learn about the people in his charge, he had been on her shit list. The visit ended up not being a humanitarian effort to help the community, but a photo-op only. A big, smarmy publicity stunt that left her feeling that her people had been used and exploited.

Shepard got a blistering earful and then some the moment the senator drove off in his limousine. After that, politicians weren't allowed near any of their shelters.

The latest Mrs. Lance was thirty years the senator's junior and was dressed more for a night on the red carpet of a Hollywood premier than a meeting for the local chamber of commerce. Her bubblegum pink dress with thin rhinestone straps barely kept the flouncy chiffon ensemble on her thin, athletic body. As the owner of a chain of tanning salons in the region, she clearly enjoyed showing off her wares. The hotel's air-conditioning added its own accessories to her outfit as the thin fabric did nothing to hide her puckered nipples.

Not knowing if the intended look of her choice of outfit was supposed to make other women feel intimidated or impressed, Jameson strove for no reaction at all and tapped the bottom of her glass. "I'm sorry, I missed what you said?"

Marjorie laughed and flung a long lock of her freshly dyed red hair over her shoulder. The huge rock of her engagement ring tangled in the strands. "I saw that look Ethan Daniels gave you. And the one his brother has been giving you all night long."

How long had she been watching them? Creepy much? "I'm not sure what you mean. Mr. and Mr. Daniels are new benefactors to the shelter. It's been a pleasure working with them on upgrading all of our systems."

"So that's what you're calling it." She shrugged. "Cut the crap, honey. You don't need to play coy with me. I have it on good authority from two of my friends that those Daniel boys love to share their women."

It was as if Jameson had fallen into the ocean. Her blood

ran cold and her fingertips felt like ice against her glass. What the hell was Marjorie Lance saying? "I'm sorry?"

Marjorie giggled again and patted Jameson's hand. "I know. You hear stories about sexy twins and think they only exist in pornos or *Penthouse* magazine. But those boys are the real thing. Here's something to keep in mind," she said in a tone that sounded more threatening than friendly. "Their little flings don't last forever. My friend Michelle said that they were done with her after one night. And another friend of ours, Stephanie, only lasted two weeks. Those boys go through women like kegs at a frat party. You might be an interesting diversion for now, but don't get too attached to them."

Through lips numb with confusion, Jameson managed to mutter, "I'm not sure what exactly you're implying. My relationship with the Danielses is purely professional."

"Ah." Her lips pursed together in a pout like one would give an innocent, foolish puppy dog. "You keep telling yourself that, sweetheart. But I saw how you looked at them, too. Don't feel stupid. I know your pain. Ronan and I had an encounter once. This was before I met Larry, of course. His kisses were hot and steamy, and man, can he fuck. Ethan was a killjoy, though, and made him leave as soon as we were done, which was weird. Ethan was quite the playboy once upon a time and he could party all night long." She rested her arm on the tabletop and leaned in close as if to impart a nugget of wisdom. "What I found out later on was that in order to get with one of them means you have to be with both of them." She sighed and shook her head. "I just don't think you're ready to play that game. You don't strike me as the kinky type."

"Maybe that's the difference between you and me, Mrs.

Lance. I don't see people as pawns in a game with the end goal of being a hookup. If you'll excuse me." Jameson stumbled away.

Marjorie called out one last parting shot. "If you plan to get more funding for your little homeless shelters by wooing those two, let me give you some advice. More cleavage and spread your legs. That's the only way any man will pay any attention to you."

For real? Was that for real? What the fuck just happened?

Sweat soaked through her clothes and the air became as stifling as a sauna. Her joints felt stiff and she felt as graceful as Frankenstein's monster as she lurched toward the exit of the ballroom.

A trip to the restroom to splash cold water on her face was not going to make her feel better. All she wanted was to be away. Away from people, away from the enclosure of four walls, just away.

Jameson? Ethan reached out to her. *Jameson, what's wrong?*

No, no, no. Having one of the twins around was the last thing she needed.

She blanked out her thoughts and continued to walk toward the hotel lobby. Shepard might have driven her there, but she could catch a cab ride home.

Why did what Marjorie Lance say bother her so much? Of course the twins had a social life before they met her. It was probably a pretty epic social life at that. And like she told Shepard earlier, she was not in a romantic relationship with either of the Daniels twins. Was she? And if so, which one?

For fuck's sake. She groaned and picked up her pace.

The brothers were…well… What were they to her, exactly? Business partners? Friends?

Potential lovers?

Oh no. Back that train up. She absolutely did not want to be tied to either one of them in that way.

Girl, why you lying like that?

Shut up, she told her innermost desires.

'Fess up, sis. I know you.

Okay. Fine. They were pretty great guys. Smart, kind, good-looking, and successful. If she wasn't her and they weren't them, then yeah, she'd be panting right after them like any red-blooded woman with a smidgen of a libido.

But she *was* her. Lived to work, righter of wrongs, not afraid to kick ass and take names, social justice warrior, Jameson Alinari. And they were them. Multimillionaires, world travelers, telepathic, *telepathic*, Ethan and Ronan Daniels. No shit were they them.

She had her own needs and an agenda to fulfill, and the twins had a special set of needs as well. Their paths might have crossed at this moment in time, but what about next month? Next year? Not to mention there were two of them and one of her. She liked them equally. Society would make her choose. Society—ugh. She hated doing what society wanted. But there was no way she could continue her work with both of them in her life. Could she? Should she? The entire situation was all too messed up to contemplate.

"Jameson, wait," Ethan called out, reaching her side before she reached the doorman to ask for a taxi. "What's wrong? What happened?"

"Nothing. I'm just really tired and ready to go home."

"You're upset. You feel upset. It's churning my stomach. What happened?"

"Knock it off, Ethan. I just want to go home."

"Where is Shepard?" he asked, glancing around, his lips tense.

"I don't know. But I'm sure he's busy. It's okay. I can get my own ride home."

Ethan touched her arm then tilted her chin up with his finger. His dark eyes swam with concern. "What did Marjorie Lance say to you?"

She huffed out a breath. "Nothing. Just regular stuff. Come to my tanning salons, I'm the senator's wife, I should be on the *Real Housewives*, blah blah blah."

His eyes narrowed. "I can go find out from Marjorie herself, but I'd rather hear it from you."

Gah! She clenched her teeth. Ethan anywhere near Marjorie was the last thing she wanted.

"Fine." She sucked in a breath and rolled her head from side to side as if she were loosening up for a fight. "Word on the street is you and your brother like to get freaky between the sheets and share your women. Marjorie was under the delusional assumption that I was the latest filling du jour in your twin sandwich. When I corrected her, she basically called me a liar and accused me of trying to seduce you to get my hands on your money. She also said that my attempt to seduce you would be useless because there is no way you two would be interested in me for anything more than a one-night stand. There. You happy now?"

"Fuckin' hell," Ethan muttered and shook his head, his eyes closed. "Jameson, I'm so sorry. She—uh, fuck. I'm sorry."

"Yeah. Me too." Bile burned the back of her throat. "Now good night, Ethan."

"Wait. Wait. Wait." He grabbed her elbow when she

spun on her heel. "Where are you going?"

"Home."

"Let me take you."

"No. I just want to be left alone."

"I don't think it's safe. I can have you home in no time."

She wrenched her arm away and barked, "Ethan, just back off."

"Jameson." He stepped back and raised his hands in surrender. "I understand your anger at what Marjorie said. But why are you mad at me?"

"I'm not. It's just—you..." She growled and dug her fingertips into her clutch, wishing she had the strength to tear the leather to shreds.

She wasn't angry at Ethan, not really. Hell, she wasn't sure if she was mad at all.

Marjorie was being vile. Fine. As if the two of them would ever find a reason to be in the same room again, like, ever. Who cared about the bitch? Not her. And so what if she didn't think Jameson was worthy of genuine affection from the brothers? She was worth any man's attention. In fact, any man would be fucking fortunate if she chose to accept them as a partner, if she was in the market for that kind of attention. She was a fucking goddess. Marjorie Lance could go and suck it where Jameson's love life was concerned.

And how could she be mad at Ronan for getting all kissy-face with that horrible woman once upon a time in a galaxy far, far away? That had nothing to do with her. He could kiss whoever he wanted, have sex too for that matter.

Ronan. Having sex. With someone else.

White-hot pain flared behind her ribs. Why did the mere thought of either of the brothers writhing naked in someone else's arms make her so fucking angry and hurt? It was stupid. All these thoughts and feelings she was having were stupid. Nothing was going to come of them. Nothing ever would.

"Wow," Ethan said, rocking back on his heels. "That's a lot to unpack."

The fingers of her right hand curled into a fist. "Dammit, Ethan."

He raised his hands again. "You're projecting. Loudly. I could be across town and still pick up on all that noise."

Tears of frustration burned her eyes. "You fucking suck."

A sad smile flirted on his lips. He slowly reached out and smoothed his thumb down her cheek and over her frown. "I know. We need to talk. Please. Let me take you home."

"We don't have anything to talk about," she whispered, swaying on her feet. Aching to fall the rest of the way to the comforting expanse of his chest.

"You can tell yourself that, but obviously it's not true."

As if on cue, Ted pulled up alongside them in the limo.

"How about a compromise. Can we at least talk in the car?" Ethan asked.

"Fine." She probably should just bite the bullet and hash out her complicated feelings for the twins once and for all. Get it all off her chest and sorted into neat boxes so she could crush the shit out of them and move on with her steady, focused life either with or without them.

Ethan opened the back door for her and she slid in. She started in surprise when he climbed in after her and shut the door, Ted pulling away from the curb.

"What about Ronan?"

"Ted will get him later. I think it would be best if just you and I talked for now."

"Oh."

Somehow the expansive backseat grew even more voluminous as the interior became more constricting. It had never been just her and one of the brothers before. When the three of them were together, whatever tension might have been growing between them was broken by one or the other of them diffusing the moment.

But now it was her and Ethan in the backseat. All alone. In the dark and quiet, floating on the smooth ride of the Lincoln rolling across the pavement.

"I guess I'll start," Ethan said. "Some of what Marjorie Lance said about Ronan and me is true."

Ah fuck, here we go.

CHAPTER NINE

"WHAT?" JAMESON SAID sharply and shrank back against the car seat. Good God, did she want to know what part Marjorie Lance was right about?

"It's a simple explanation that is unfortunately rather complicated." Ethan rubbed at his nose with agitation. "After Ronan and I developed our powers, dating became almost impossible. Being telepathic wasn't a problem that we anticipated until one of us became interested in a woman. Because our emotions are so intertwined, what one feels so does the other, so if Ronan was attracted to a woman, I felt his attraction to her, his desire. And if that person happened to be someone who I was ambivalent toward in a romantic sense, it became difficult for both of us to reconcile those feelings. And it was the same for Ronan." A wry grin tilted the corner of his mouth. "Take Marjorie, for instance. Her parents and ours were acquaintances, ran in the same social circle. She and I flirted, here and there when we were lots younger. Might've kissed once. Don't really remember. Life before super powers is kind of a blur."

Apparently, Marjorie remembered that part with clarity. She claimed Ethan was quite the playboy, or had he forgotten that as well?

"Not too long after the accident, we were at a party. The entire situation was dumb, really. We hadn't seen our friends since before the crash and we were trying to… I don't know... pretend that we weren't different." He blinked and looked at his hands clasped in his lap. "But we *were* different. I sat in the corner nursing a bottle of scotch, trying to quiet the voices in my head. Ronan was looking for physical activity to keep his focus and ran into Marjorie. They hooked up that night. And it was terrible. For me, anyway, because I could hear her giggles in my head even though I was across the house from them. It was one thing to suspect she was boring and insipid, but to hear her thoughts set my teeth on edge.

"After that, Ronan and I made a few failed attempts at dating individually, but the result was the same. So, we thought we might try dating the same girl. It wasn't an entirely horrible experience, to be truthful. But we could never be honest with the woman about why we want it to be the both of us. They assumed it's a kink, and we didn't trust them enough to tell them otherwise. Soon, dating became complicated, and the rumors about us grew and spread, sometimes to our clients. If we ever were with a woman, we knew we had to become more discreet and selective."

"Is that a fancy way of saying you hired a hooker to get your jollies?"

"Jesus, Jameson." He sat back with a huff. "Why do you always go right to the extreme about people?"

"Instinct." She shrugged. "Experience. Years of my gut feelings being right."

"Well, you're wrong about this. We just stopped dating altogether. We haven't been with a woman in quite some time."

She didn't want to ask, even with the words burning her tongue. Did she want to know? Yes. But it was not her place to ask.

"It's been about a year," Ethan answered anyway.

She scowled, partly because he probably read her mind. And also because his version of "quite some time" was a year, yet she hadn't been with a man in several. Not that she had been counting.

"Marjorie was wrong in saying that you're a flavor of the month. We both care about you very much, Jameson. *I* care about you."

Ethan reached for her hand and brought it to his lips to place gentle kisses on her knuckles. He then opened her fingers and placed another kiss in her palm. His lips were hot and soft, and his cheek was warm.

"Believe me, Jameson. You have us coming and going," he murmured against the skin of her inner wrist. "We don't know what to do with you."

"Good. I shouldn't be the only one who's totally lost."

"Lost?" He looked at her with surprise that faded to a slight smile. "Funny. I was thinking that I was finally found."

Well…hell. That was charming. Everything about Ethan was smooth and dreamy. The smoldering light in his gaze. The dark and cozy confines of the back of the car as they gently swayed to the motion of the vehicle. The way he drew her closer, cuddling her against his heat as he lowered his head and settled his lips on hers.

If her mouth wasn't otherwise occupied, she would have laughed out loud. For all the times Ethan had been hesitant to engage in any physical contact, he was all in now. His kiss was firm and powerful as his hands smoothed up and down her back with sure caresses before gripping her hair at the nape of her neck, holding her still to give and take as he desired.

Of course, she shouldn't be surprised. Ethan was intense about everything. Why would his kisses be any different? Why would she want it any other way?

In Ethan's arms she felt safe even as her heart beat so hard, it threatened to burst out of her chest. Both fevers and chills shook her to the bone, leaving her a quivering mess in the backseat of the limo.

"We're here," Ethan said when he finally allowed her to come up for a decent breath.

"Oh. Good." She sat up and pushed her hair off her sweaty forehead. As her eyes adjusted to the new lighting, confusion struck. "Um, where are we?"

"Home." He slid out of the car and held out his hand to her.

"No, it's not." The wood and glass palace with a decorative rock wall and waterfall near the front door was definitely not her home.

"It's my home."

She scooted away from the open door. "What are we doing here?"

"Our conversation wasn't finished, and if I took you to your home, then you would have to let me into the shelter. I know how protective you are of the women there, and how you probably wouldn't want anyone to know I was there."

Gah, how she hated when he was logical. "True. But you could've asked me first."

He straightened and placed his hand on the door. "You're right. I'm sorry. I can have Ted take you home right now. But I would like it if you came inside. There's something I want you to see."

"What, you have some sketches you want to show me? Or some freshly painted Dungeons and Dragons figurines?"

"I do, actually." He smiled. "But no. It's a place. A place where it can be just you and me. No outside world."

Right. Just her and Ethan. Alone.

She stared up at him and was certain of two things. One, if she said she wanted to go home, Ethan would kiss her on the head, shut the door, and she'd be off. And two, if she took his hand and went inside, there was a 99.9 percent chance things were going to get physical between them.

Hell, who was she kidding. There was 100 percent chance someone was going to get naked. And she wanted it. For all the excuses she came up with to convince herself otherwise, she wanted to be with Ethan so bad.

A fine tremor shook her hand as she allowed him to assist her out of the car. It delighted her to no end that Ethan's hand appeared to tremble just as much.

He ushered her up the front steps and through the grand double doors. In the stone floor entry, the water feature outside continued into the interior, with the small stream running through the floor and underneath a plate of glass toward the back of the house. The open concept of the first floor was designed in teakwoods and flagstones, while the furnishings were a mix of midcentury modern and contemporary pieces in leathers, wood, and chrome.

The far wall was nothing but floor-to-ceiling windows. At this time of the evening, the interior of the main living room reflected in the amber light of the lamps that flickered on as soon as they entered.

"Is this a Frank Lloyd Wright house?" she asked in awe.

"Frank Lloyd inspired. My dad was a big James Bond fan, and he thought this house looked like something Goldfinger would have owned. Let me give you a little tour," he said, taking her hand.

He showed her the office where he and Ethan did most of their work. Then he took her down the hall into the oversized gourmet kitchen.

"This is amazing," she exclaimed, running her fingers across the rim of the six-burner gas stove. The black quartz countertops were a thing of beauty. "My mother would love this room. Actually, she'd probably live in this room. She'd make her bed on that little banquette over there and never leave."

"I take it she's a cook?"

Jameson shrugged. "She's an Italian woman. She shows her love in carbs and olive oil."

"She sounds fun. I'd love to meet her one day."

"You can keep hoping," she said in a singsong tone. She barely agreed to this step, whatever it was. No one was ready for the meet-the-parents step yet.

Ethan smiled and tugged at her hand. "The best part of the first floor is this way."

Through the French doors and across the stone patio lay an outdoor oasis. Under a canopy of trees and glass was another living area, complete with fire pit, a grilling station, and a swimming pool that resembled a pond. Another waterfall trickled down and fed into the stream that flowed through the house.

"This is beautiful," Jameson marveled.

"This is our favorite part of the entire house. We can just relax in the quiet of nature, but with all the best comforts of man. When it's warmer we spend more time out here than we do inside."

"Too bad we have more cooler months than warm around here."

"That's why we have these." Ethan gestured to the tall

heaters that were set around the patio.

"You leave those on all day? Isn't that a waste of resources?"

"Of course not. I turned them on by remote when we arrived."

"Uh, that's a handy little gadget you've got there," she said.

"Technology is my game." Ethan removed his tie, setting it on the bar. He gestured to the kitchenette area. "Would you like something to drink? Wine? Soda?"

"A glass of wine would be nice." A little alcohol wouldn't hurt to settle her nerves. However, she couldn't pinpoint why she was so nervous. The moment she walked into the home she felt welcomed. Comforted.

Perhaps that was it. She was too comfortable, and Ethan was too welcoming. How was she supposed to take this day by day when it was all too easy to imagine spending all her time lounging poolside and drowning in kisses. A dangerous fantasy to indulge in at this point in her life. Best not to go there at all.

"How do you do that?" Ethan asked in wonder, handing her a glass. "You shut down your mind as if you were snapping your fingers. Sometimes it's so loud I swear I can hear the lock slide into place and the chains drawn across the door."

"Do I? Weird." She cradled the glass to her chest. "It's just a habit, I guess. When I was a kid and couldn't physically get away from a situation, I could always leave mentally."

"How do you do it? Block it out?"

"I don't know. I suppose I put up a wall. Imagine I'm wrapped in cotton batting and sealed up tight with duct tape and nothing can hurt me." Most of the time. "You do it enough times, it becomes like breathing. You just do it."

He led her to the sofa and took a seat beside her. "I envy you. When I first got my powers, I ran away to a private island out in the Bahamas to escape the noise in my head."

A private island. Of course that would be his go-to solution. "Ah…poor baby." She pouted and batted her lashes.

"I know. I live an incredibly charmed existence. Except for that whole parents dying in a plane crash thing."

"Fuck, Ethan, I'm sorry. That was right bitchy of me." She took a sip of the chilled wine, which did nothing to ease the burn of embarrassment in her throat. Way to step in it, Alinari.

"It's perception." He picked up her hand and placed a kiss on her fingers. She was getting to enjoy those little kisses. "Observation is not the same as knowledge. You have to talk with a person, really talk with them to see the truth of a situation."

"Where did you hear that?"

"Experience. Years of my gut feelings being right." He grinned as he repeated her words from earlier. "I'm sure you've met thousands of women who have gone through worse than we have."

"Probably."

"And what about you?" He pursed his lips as if he were trying to hold the words back and flailing. "Did you…did something …bad…happen to you in the past?"

Right. The "Have you been abused or assaulted yourself" question. One she had been asked many times in her line of work. In fact, most people assumed she had been abused, because why else would she want to be a champion for human decency?

Then there had been the occasions where the women in the shelters didn't think she understood what they were going through because she didn't wear her scars on the outside. Street cred was everything in her world. To some she was lacking; to the few others who knew the truth, she had plenty in spades.

"I guess 'bad' is relative," she replied. "I've been in situations that were not good. Seen things I'd rather not." Done things she shouldn't have had to but didn't regret.

She swirled the wine in her glass, watching the vortex as if she were staring into a time machine. Sharing details about her past was not something she did on the regular, if at all, really. Only a trusted few got the entire backstory.

A gulp of wine barely quenched her dry throat, and her tongue swept out to wet her lip. "I was about three when my dad left my mom on her own, unemployed and with no resources. We lived in the car for a while and bounced from shelter to shelter. I was in about second grade when we moved in with some other women my mom had made friends with in the shelter. Three adults and four kids crammed into a little two-bedroom apartment."

Even now she could smell the aroma of ramen noodles, Captain Crunch, and that fake baby powder smell of diapers.

"It worked out for a while, until one of the women decided to turn tricks in the apartment." She barely kept the venom out of her voice as she thought about the time that changed her life forever. "She always watched us little ones while the other moms were at work. That's probably where I learned to tune out the world. She would have us sit in the closet, no lights, while she entertained her johns."

Jameson learned at far too young of an age how to recognize the slap of pelvis against skin. To understand the intent behind a raised voice. She learned what the crack of the back of a hand against a cheek sounded like, and the hitch of a choked-off sob to keep the beating from getting worse.

Oddly enough, she had first learned to tune out her reality while in the shelter, ignoring the cries of the other children who couldn't adjust to their new environment and the weeping of their mothers who were at their wits' end.

But in that dark little closet was where she'd honed her skills. In the blackness she shut out the angry shouts and curses, the hushed breaths of the other kids by her side, the way Marcus would shake against her with his hand over his mouth, and Caitlin rocked with her head in her hands as they waited for the "date" to be over.

In the dark, nothing touched her. She floated in sensory deprivation until the light pierced her closed eyelids and she was brought back to the surface.

Except for that one night. That one where her mother's screams slammed through her wall and she lost the last thin thread of her innocence forever.

"Jameson." Ethan squeezed her fingers. "I'm so sorry."

She blinked and the bright bedroom light from her past was replaced by the amber glow of the patio and the soft gurgle of the waterfall.

"It's like you said. It's perception." She took a sip of wine. "I had it worse than some, better than others. Fortunately, I had an amazing mother who taught me to be strong, work hard, and loved me like no other."

Daily life without Maria Alinari was still an adjustment. It seemed as if it had been forever since she had walked into her apartment and the scent of garlic, tomatoes, and sizzling ham bubbled away from the kitchen. Jameson missed her mother terribly, and for more than her cooking, but she wouldn't trade her mother's happiness for anything. Maria had worked her ass off to save enough to relocate to Arizona. Now she was living her best life, painting glorious sunsets and taking daily swims in her condo complex's pool.

"You know, my mother's condo is pretty nice," Jameson said, then gestured at their surroundings. "But they don't have a setup like this."

"This was my mother's doing. She said if she had to play hostess to my father's business partners, she wanted to do so in a setting that brought her peace."

"I don't blame her. If this was my place, I'd throw parties every weekend in the summer."

"We did. At least my parents used to."

The loss in his eyes broke her heart. "You miss them. A lot. I mean, duh, you miss them because they were your parents, but it's still fresh."

"Sometimes." He put down his glass and stood, sidling closer to the heater where he held his hands out in front of the register. "The crash seems like a lifetime ago, but at times it's like yesterday. I guess that's part of the grieving process. It's also why we stayed in this house instead of moving somewhere new. With our powers, Ronan and I find it easier to stay close together. And being here keeps us close to our parents." The corners of his lips lifted into a grin. "This patio and pool were my mother's sanctuary. Now it's ours. It's almost as if she knew we'd need it."

"Thank you for sharing it with me."

Ethan's smile grew and gestured toward the water. "Want to take a dip?"

"You're funny. Number one, I don't have a swimsuit. Number two, it's cold. Number three, I don't have a swimsuit."

"You said that one already."

"Just reminding you and letting you know that I suspect that you're trying to get me naked."

Ethan shrugged. "I'm sure you have some sort of undergarments on underneath your dress."

"Mostly." The sheer bra she had on would become transparent the second she got in the water and wouldn't cover a damn thing.

"Jameson." Ethan stepped closer, close enough where she could feel his heat but remained far enough away to where she wasn't intimidated by his size. "Would I love to become more intimate with you? Absolutely. But I also want to spend time with you. Relax. Take a moonlight dip in the pool. I will follow your lead."

And whose lead would she be following? Her heart? Her head? Or all her erogenous zones that were screaming for her to get to it and strip down *now*! Take me! Take me!

Truth be told, she wanted to be intimate with him, too. She wanted to experience the strength of his embrace, lay her head on his chest and feel and hear the solid beat of his heart and the heat of his flesh. "Are you sure you don't have any neighbors who can peek over the fence?"

"Not unless they have a super telephoto lens. The nearest neighbors are six acres away."

Jameson sat on the couch and settled into the corner. She brought her glass of wine to her lips and looked over the rim. "You go first."

Ethan's eyes widened for a second and a flash of heat turned his gaze molten. There was no hesitation in his hands as he reached for the buttons of his shirt and unfastened them one by one.

He toed off his oxfords as he dropped the dress shirt and jacket to the patio. The bright white undershirt came off next, and she got her first glimpse of his lean torso.

"Are you a runner?" she asked, taking another slow sip of her wine as she admired his athletic frame.

"Stationary bicycle," he replied. "Then I can bike, no matter the weather."

Or he said something to that effect, because her hearing turned off as soon he reached for his belt. The slight rasp of leather pulling free from the buckle sent goose bumps over her arms. She also liked his display of urgency as he didn't bother to slip the belt free of his pants, he just went for the fly and dropped his trousers at his feet.

Some men might look silly standing there in black briefs and matching socks. But not Ethan. He could've been a marble statue of the perfect man, standing before her if it wasn't for the fine pelt of dark hair covering his chest and narrowing down to the waistband.

"I'm glad you like," he said with a smirk, then bent down to pull off his socks and tossed them in her direction.

He turned away, giving her plenty of time to admire his backside before he made a clean dive into the pool.

She waited for him to make some remark about how it was her turn to strip or how the water was fine, but he stayed silent, paddling from one end of the pool to the other and back again.

No, he didn't say a word to her, but by no means was he quiet.

There she lounged, alone on the sofa with her now-empty wine glass, experiencing everything Ethan was feeling in the water: the silky lapping of water over his arms as he broke through the surface. The lick of the current against his body with each stroke. The cool temperature of the air mixing with the warm water to invigorate his blood. Ethan fed everything he was feeling to her, including the hope that she would join him. And that when she did…

What the hell was she waiting for? Wasn't that why she agreed to come with him instead of having Ted take her home? To take their relationship from associates to something far, far, far more personal?

She set the wine glass on the side table and stood. Ethan never paused once in his strokes but continued to swim as she did a slight contortionist move to reach for the zipper of her dress. It didn't take long for her to be down to only her bra and panties.

She was more careful with her dress than Ethan had been with his clothes, draping the garment over one of the chairs.

The pool deck was cool and pebbly under her feet as she stepped to the edge of the water. She had been fourteen when she first learned how to swim because it had been a requirement in gym class. She wasn't one of those people who took naturally to the water. No one would call her Esther Williams or Michael Phelps, that was for certain. There would be no graceful dive from her.

Holding her nose, she jumped in, and promptly swallowed a mouthful of water as she gasped in surprise. Ethan's version of "warm" was way different than hers.

"You suck," she sputtered as she broke through the surface.

"Sorry," he said, sounding anything but. "It's warm to me."

With her best doggie-paddle/freestyle strokes, she swam from one end of the pool to the other more to warm her blood than for relaxation. Ethan swam in the opposite direction, the two of them circling each other around and around, coming closer with each revolution, creating a lazy whirlpool in the center of the water.

What was he waiting for? She was there. He was there. She was mostly naked. He was mostly naked. He was so close now that she didn't even need to straighten out her arms to touch him. Sexy swimming pool, gorgeous clear sky. Why didn't he have her pressed up against the side of the pool and ravishing her already?

"I'm waiting for you, Jameson," he said. "You need to be certain. And I need this to be your choice."

Wow. Right. Consent.

In the not so distant past, the guy would make his move, the girl would either accept or she'd decline and hope that the guy followed through with her wishes. A tango that should have been easy to play out, but thousands of years of societal pressures, self-esteem issues, and religious contradictions made the interaction entirely too complicated. For all her banner waving of being a strong independent woman, why was it that when it came to sex, she was a chickenshit at making the first move?

Suddenly Marjorie Lance's words came back to her. The knowledge that once upon a time Ethan was a playboy, experienced with the seduction of women while she never had a serious relationship in her life. Sex was a hunger sated with a trip to the club for an easy hookup so she could get back to work on more important things, like saving the world.

Would she ignite his world on fire, or would she embarrass herself with her lack of finesse and he'd end up finding her dull and unexciting? Or worse, she became disappointed in him, thinking he was this great lover when in reality he was below average?

Ethan stopped treading water and set his feet on the bottom of the pool, standing tall with the water hitting him at chest height. Clearly, he had no intention of going anywhere.

Jameson took a breath, then another, then swam toward him until her fingers brushed his torso. If she tried to stand, she'd likely drown, so she grabbed onto his shoulders and wrapped her legs around his waist.

The moment their skin made contact, Ethan took over. His arms banded around the back of her thighs. Lips and tongues collided as they feasted on each other's mouths in a leisurely pursuit of pleasure. Arms squeezed and her thighs clenched around his middle, trying to fuse them as one.

The softness of his lips was a delightful contrast to his hard, manly body. Oh, he was so hard everywhere. He felt so good. Hot in her arms with the coolness of the water lapping around them. The ridged length of his cock teased her, trapped behind the thin layers of their undergarments. The bulge rubbed against her clit, sending sparks racing through her veins.

Her hips swiveled as she ground against him. "Oh God. Oh God," she panted.

"Take it." He groaned against her neck and licked a hot path along her shoulder. "Take what you need."

Ethan's hands were firm on her backside as she bucked against him. If he was willing, she was going to take all that she wanted and then some. Hunger turned to starvation in a nanosecond, and she was ravenous. The ache inside her intensified. The press of his cock felt so fucking good.

She arched her back on a gasp, which Ethan used as an opportunity to snag one of her hard nipples between his lips. With the delicious press and release between her legs and the suction of his mouth through the lace, she hit the wall and barreled through, as a wave of orgasmic pleasure roared through her.

"Fuck, yeah," she groaned and bobbed in the surf as it slowly brought her back down from the heavens.

All the muscles in her neck relaxed and her head tipped back. The stars in the sky above her twinkled and burst in flashes of light so bright, she swore she could see every individual point on each star. Her breaths came hard and shuddered past her dry lips as her arms and legs turned to putty, falling loosely into the water.

But Ethan was there to keep her from drowning, cradling her close to his body as he murmured in her ear, "Fuck, you are magnificent when you come."

If she possessed any strength, she would have giggled at the spectacle of it all. Instead, the sound was more like a strangled hiss from her lips.

"Let's get you dried off a little before I get you more wet," he said and walked them over to the side of the pool. He helped place her hand on the bottom rung of the ladder and half pushed, half lifted her out of the water. Another set of warm hands grabbed her by the arms and lifted her the rest of the way.

She blinked in surprise and her eyes cleared to see Ronan holding her up with a big fluffy towel in his hand.

"He's right," he said. His eyes sparkled with desire and his cheeks were flushed. "You do look amazing when you come."

When the hell did Ronan return? Judging by his attire, long enough. His feet were bare, jacket was off, and his shirt was completely unbuttoned. And as if that wasn't proof enough that he was ready to rumble, the bulge pressing through the fabric of his jeans and towel against her belly was proof enough on its own.

Ethan climbed from the pool beside her, a smile playing on his lips. His cock was still hard and at the ready.

"Felt amazing too," she said, embracing her inner sex goddess who was quite the saucy minx.

"Want to feel more?"

She nodded and added an enthusiastic, "Oh, yeah," for emphasis then stood on her toes to press her mouth to Ronan's.

Fly or die, right?

Where Ethan's kisses where exploratory and searching, Ronan's were all-encompassing. He swept her up on a ride where her choices were to fall off or hang on for the fun.

He scooped her up into his arms and carried her across the patio. Setting her down at the end of a chaise lounge, he stepped back for Ethan to kneel in front of her on a stack of couch pillows.

"Lie back, sweetheart," Ethan said and pulled her panties down her legs. He then spread apart her knees, exposing her to his gaze.

As he bent to lower his head toward her sex, she stopped him with her hand on his head as her earlier confidence came to a staggering stop. "Oh, no. You don't have to. That's okay."

He looked at her questioningly. "What?"

"I know guys can be squeamish…down there. You don't have to."

Ethan's brow raised. "I have to. I need to. This guy isn't squeamish. And those other guys are fools."

"Let him have at it, wildcat," Ronan said. "He wants to."

Sure. Even with her inner goddess giving her an enthusiastic thumbs-up, she was supposed to ignore years of neuroses built by lovers of the past who had made cursory attempts at oral sex before rearing up and poking her with their penises, and just let Ethan do his thing. That constant *me-me-me* lovemaking scenario was why she was still single single single. Really, it was best not to have a guy go down her at all than go to through that disappointment.

At the first touch of Ethan's tongue against her skin she tensed, waiting for the "never mind," but then he groaned and took the whole of her pussy in his mouth.

"Holy shit," she exclaimed. Her hips bucked and she grabbed at his hair. Okay. Maybe he did like to eat pussy. He certainly was going at it like a champ.

Ronan started to undress by her side, and her attention shifted, focusing on trying to determine where he and his brother were different. To start, Ronan didn't have a tan line anywhere on his lean body, and he was bare skin from his shoulders to his toes. Obviously, a bigger fan of manscaping than his brother.

His cock wasn't too big, wasn't too small. And judging by the way Ronan's looked and Ethan's felt, she could tell both would fill her empty places just fine.

"Give me, give me," she said reaching out for Ronan's deliciously naked body.

"Not yet, wildcat. You just need to relax and enjoy." Ronan knelt by her side and pulled down the wet straps of her bra. He cupped her breasts into his palms and bent to take one of her hard nipples into his mouth at the same time his brother wrapped his lips around her clit.

She shot off the chair, but Ethan held on tight, refusing to let her get away as she succumbed to the most amazing sensation she ever experienced. The brothers played her as if she were a tribute version of "Freebird" or "Stairway to Heaven." Building her up to a rousing crescendo with epic guitar solos and a full orchestra before pulling her back from the edge at the last moment. Strumming the right strings as she moaned and whimpered to their movements.

She sent praises to the powers that be as she began that steep climb to the top for what felt like the millionth time. Were they going to let her come? Was she finally going to seek the relief she needed from the painful ache of desire Ethan created between her thighs?

"Take it, wildcat," Ronan urged. "Come for us."

With a flick of his tongue across her clit, Ethan shoved her over the edge. A scream tore from her throat as she fell, tumbling head over heels as the stars above her once again sharpened and swirled.

"That's our girl."

Whether that was said out loud or in her mind, she hadn't a clue. At that moment the only sound she recognized was the thump of her heart. Not even the ragged wheezing of her breath was identifiable as she had never been taken to such heights before in her life.

"No. Sleep," she mumbled and tried to slap at the determined hands lifting her up. Couldn't they see she was spent?

"Why sleep when there's more."

"More? No." Her head thrashed from side to side as they stroked and kissed her all over. "I couldn't. It's too much,"

"You can. Enjoy."

The sky swirled as they flipped her around so her knees hit the pillow placed on the pool deck and she was bent over the foot of the lounge chair. Behind her, Ethan's body was hot and slick against her sweaty backside, and she had barely caught her breath when she felt the broad head of his cock start to push inside her still-pulsating body.

She gripped the cushion of the lounge chair and tried to scoot forward. "Condom," she panted.

"Already thought of that," Ethan said with a rasp in his voice. Out of the corner of her eye she saw a flash of the shiny foil package that was ripped open and watched as it fluttered to the floor while he pushed inside her one more time.

"Oh, yeah," she groaned and held on tight to the chaise lounge as Ethan set a firm yet steady pace, plunging deep with long strokes over and over again.

The oral sex was great, but this was fucking amazing. Somehow Ethan made being impaled both exciting and comforting. Her eyes drifted shut and she gave herself over to the pleasure until she was jostled from her trance when Ronan straddled the lounge chair before her and sat with his thick cock standing enticingly in front of her.

Inner sex fiend fully unleashed, she grabbed onto the shaft with both hands and ran her tongue across the top. She eagerly swallowed him down as far she could go. With her mouth and both hands, she worked Ronan to a frenzy.

"Fuck," he groaned and jammed his hands into her hair, trying to slow her down, but she was having none of that, gobbling him down to the root.

She had been so wrong earlier about being with both brothers. This was the height of hedonistic sexuality.

Bookend between two gorgeous men as they filled her with their hard cocks. Each thought, each emotion rippled over her as the brothers shared their feelings. The slickness of her mouth, the squeeze of her pussy, the play of her muscles against their palms.

And she shared right back. The salty taste of Ronan, and Ethan's delicious fullness stretching inside her. The emotions ebbed and swirled as if she were in a hot cotton candy machine winding tighter and tighter with the sweetness until she burst, her cries muffled around Ronan's cock as she screamed with her climax.

"I'm going to come, I'm gonna come," Ronan groaned and pulled her away. "I want to come on you."

Ethan held her by the shoulders, never relenting in his thrusts as Ronan aimed his cock at her breasts and unloaded his thick creamy goodness all over her.

"Fuck, that's pretty," he groaned.

Ethan cupped her swollen breasts with one hand as the fingers of his other delved between the wet lips of her pussy. "Come with me. One more time, Jameson."

Was he insane? "I can't," she panted. She was going to drop dead from a heart attack. She just knew it.

"Yes, you can. Take it. Take all of it." Ethan sank his teeth into her neck, his fingers plucking her swollen clit until she lost the fight, falling into the swirling masses as her fourth orgasm of the night sucked her under. Ethan's groan in her ear followed as he lunged deep one last time and shattered against her with tremors of his own orgasm.

What a mess she must look. Sweat, cum, and everything else dripped off her as her muscles twitched and limbs shook. But never, never had she felt so satisfied in all her life.

The Daniels brothers were dangerous. If they asked her to give up her life and be their sex slave forever, at that moment, she'd agree. She'd agree in a heartbeat.

CHAPTER TEN

AFTER THE MENTAL and physical workout the boys had given her earlier, she should've been out cold.

She wasn't.

Far from it, actually.

The clock on Ethan's nightstand illuminated four in the morning. The blue numbers blended into odd shapes as her eyes refused to focus.

Over the last few days she had sensed there was going to be a shift in the relationship she had with the Daniels brothers. She fought it. Tried to ignore the connection. But there was no denying the spark that flared white-hot when the three of them were together.

If she had been honest with herself, she should've known it was only going to be a matter of time before she said, fuck it, and jump into the deep end. And did she jump. Boy howdy, she did a frickin' cannonball. But now she was dry, and sated. That shift was cemented, leaving her where exactly? What was she to them now? Girlfriend? Other?

Did she want more sex with them? Yes, please, may she have some more, sir.

However, mind-blowing sex only got one so far, no matter what the determination was on the relationship spectrum. At some point they—she—was going to have to decide if she was only in for casual sex or if she wanted more.

More. More…what?

Ugh, she was too messed up to even think about it.

The two men lying on either side of her in the dark did not appear to be having such an affliction on their minds. Ronan slept on his stomach, Ethan on his back with one arm slung above his head. They snored oh so softly, one then the other, as if they were sawing actual logs. Meanwhile, she was tossing and turning on their ultra-expensive mattress that wouldn't spill a glass of wine if disturbed.

"This is ridiculous," she muttered, then shimmied out over the top of the bedspread to the foot of the bed.

Sleep was not going to happen, and if she was going to be awake all night long, she might as well be at her own place where distance brought clarity. She hoped.

Where the hell were her clothes? Oof. Probably still out on the pool deck.

Well, she wasn't going to go skulking through the house naked. Fortunately, Ethan's room had massive floor-to-ceiling windows that allowed just enough light in to where she didn't need to risk stubbing her toe on a stray piece of furniture. Seriously, who had an entire living room set in their bedroom?

Apparently, it was the same person who had a settee and a full dresser in their closet. Did Ethan have some sort of energy deficiency that required him to take a rest every three feet?

"Rich people," she murmured, shaking her head and reaching for the closest dress shirt, slipping it over her arms.

Buttoning the shirt, she crept out of the bedroom and made her way down the long, long hallway and massive staircase to the patio.

"Whoop!" She bit back a squeal of surprise as the lights

automatically clicked on as she crossed the threshold.

Geez, why didn't they add trumpets and fanfare as well? How was a girl supposed to sneak out of the house if she kept setting off all the bells and whistles?

The temperature had dropped significantly during the night, and the pool deck was icy cold against her toes. At least the security lights made it easier for her to locate her clothing, but it was too chilly to stop to put them on. She scooped up her belongings and scampered back into the house, digging into her purse for her cell phone.

"In need of assistance, Ms. Alinari?" came a voice from behind her.

Jameson shrieked and dropped her shoes as she spun around. Ted stood in the hallway, fully dressed with his hands behind his back.

"I'm sorry, Ms. Alinari," he said, bending into a slight bow. "I did not mean to startle you."

"No, Ted." She placed her palm over her racing heart. "I'm sorry. I mean, I didn't mean to wake you."

"Not at all, miss." Ted knelt and picked up her shoes and purse. "I have been anticipating your need to return home. I was already awake."

"Right." Embarrassment burned hot from the top of her head to the tips of her toes. "Because that's what you do. You take girls home after a night of...recreation."

"Of course not." He waved his hands. "My job is to take care of the misters Danielses and those in their household. That includes you."

"Oh." She twisted the fabric of her dress with her fingers. "I just thought that maybe taking girls home was something you did often."

Ted grinned. "On the contrary. You are the first woman who has stayed overnight in a very, very long time."

A year ago long time? she wanted to ask.

Nope. Don't go there. Better to keep her mouth shut.

"That's good. I guess? I don't know." How much more awkward could she make the situation? "I'm floundering here, Ted. Floundering."

"So it seems. Would you like some tea to take with you for the ride home? To keep warm. There is quite a nip in the air tonight."

"That sounds great. Thank you."

She followed Ted into the kitchen, where he set a kettle on the stove then began to measure tea leaves. *Whoa.* No water in the microwave with a tea bag for this guy. He was going straight-up fancy.

"I didn't mean for you to go to so much trouble." She clutched her dress against her chest. "And I feel bad about keeping you up late. I can take a cab home. It'll be no problem."

"That I cannot allow. The brothers would have my head if I did not see you home safely."

"If they were really that concerned, they could take me home themselves."

"And I'm sure they would have, if they weren't so exhausted. Honestly, I can't remember how long it has been since one or the both of them were not awake at all hours of the evening. Let's let them rest. Sleep will do them good."

"They're always awake?" she asked taking a seat on one of the barstools. "Why?"

"Not always, but sometimes it feels that way. They're important businessmen who have other important men and women who rely on them. Then you add the stress of their powers. It's all rather taxing." His ultra-white grin turned sheepish. "Of course, the reason I know of their late-night habits is that I tend to keep odd hours myself."

"That does sound exhausting." She traced her fingers over the design in the marble countertop and bit her lip. "Do you like working for Ethan and Ronan?"

"Very much so. Considering what I did in the military, being a bodyguard is a welcome change of pace. I can still utilize my skills, and the chance of death is far less greater."

"Are the brothers' lives in peril that often?" she asked, aghast.

The extra seconds he took to bring forth an answer did not allay her concern. "Unfortunately, over the past two years, their lives have been at risk more often than they should."

The kettle began to whistle, halting her next question of what the hell had the brothers been up to that threatened their lives. Ted deftly picked up the handle on the kettle and poured the steaming water over the loose tea leaves waiting in the ceramic.

"That is why I'm glad they've met you," he added, to her surprise. "Milk?"

Milk? How could she think of adding milk to her tea after he dropped that little nugget? And *eww*. "No, thank you. And me? Why would you say that?"

"The three of you have a desire to do some good in this world, but you are also all prone to bouts of extremism. Perhaps together you can find balance and harmony as you tackle situations in your own unique way."

"You think so? What makes you say that?"

Ted poured the freshly brewed tea into a heated Thermos and tightened the lid before handing it to her. As she reached for the container, her startled gaze flew to him when he refused to let go.

The look in his eyes was as intense as the rest of his face was serene as he said, "It is my job to know everything about

Ronan and Ethan, Ms. Alinari. Everything. I am their eyes and ears when the noise in their heads becomes too great. It is my job to know what they're going to do before they do it. And to know what those in their inner circle and nearby circles are going to do before they do it. It is my job to know everything. Including information about you and your Crimson Angels."

Ted let go of the Thermos and she cradled the warm cylinder in her suddenly cold hands. Was this a threat of some sort? "And what of it?"

"Just as Ethan and Ronan have people who depend on them, you have people who depend on you. I understand the responsibility that comes with being a support for others. Ethan and you share the same drive for achievement, even if it comes at a stiff price. And Ronan is going to do everything in his power to keep both of you from falling off the edge. That is why I think you are good for the brothers. And why they are good for you." His lashes fluttered as he stepped back and placed his hands behind his back. "Do not be mistaken. You are free to make whatever choice you will. And it never hurts to take a step back to assess the situation. Even if it is just for one second."

"Uh…thank you?" Why did Ted's answer make her thoughts about the brothers clearer yet more foggy than before?

"I'll return you to your home now. You can dress while I bring the car around. It will be but a moment."

"Thank you, Ted."

Left alone in the massive kitchen, she fingered the collar of Ethan's shirt, suddenly not in a hurry to take it off. In fact, she wasn't in a hurry to leave at all.

And that was the most dangerous thought of all.

CHAPTER ELEVEN

"THANK YOU, TED," Jameson said as she opened the car door. "No need to get out."

"As you wish," he replied.

"Good night."

He gestured out the windshield to the lightening slate sky. "You mean good morning."

Oof. Fuck. It was going to be a long day.

"Funny," she said, blowing a strand of hair from her eyes. She pulled the ends of Ethan's shirt tighter around her. For some reason she couldn't bear to leave it behind after she had dressed. The fabric carried his cologne and felt like a hug against her tired body.

Ted waited until she had crossed the threshold to the shelter before driving off.

Why, oh why couldn't the chamber of commerce hold their meetings on a Friday? This Tuesday night bullshit was for the birds. At least as the boss she could take a few extra hours for a power nap before diving into work. Especially when the commute was a simple climb up the stairs.

"It's good to be the boss," she chuckled to herself as she inserted her key into the lock of her apartment.

Years of habit had her glancing at the floor where the glint of a pale pink strip of cellophane on the carpet stopped her short.

As far as security systems went, a thin piece of plastic

wedged between the door and frame was rather rudimentary, but it was silent and obviously did the trick. Someone had been in her apartment.

Suddenly it was as if she was surrounded by a vacuum. The rattle of the ventilation system, the hum of the lights, everything died away as training took over. She kicked her shoes to the side and pulled a Taser from her clutch. It was tiny and only carried a few volts, but it was meant to be a deterrent rather than cause serious harm.

As was true in the world at large, not everyone who entered the shelter was looking for a better life. Some of them were taking a reprieve before looking for their next hit. More than one person had made their way past the laundry room and into the private area to where the shelter's director resided. It wasn't the first time someone had broken into her apartment. Usually, Trini was good at keeping people away, but she wasn't perfect, hence the need for extra precautions.

Jameson drew a breath and then another before she slowly turned the doorknob to ease the door open a touch.

"He's going to pick Kimberly. I just know it."

"Which Kimberly? Kimberly A. or Kimberly S.?"

"Kimberly H. Seriously, chica? Have you not been watching? His eyes practically cross when he talks to Kimberly S., and Kimberly A. has the personality of a carefully cultivated Instagram account. All style, no substance."

Down to her right was the hallway to the two bedrooms and bath. The open kitchen was also on her right, with an island that separated the cooking space from the living room where five women were lounging on her modest couch and loveseat, eating popcorn and drinking wine as if they lived there. All except Ashley, who leaned against the back wall, her arms folded across from her ever-present notebook with a furious frown tugging on her lips.

The spike of adrenaline racing through Jameson's system crashed and she wilted where she stood, kicking the door the rest of the way in. "What the fuck, guys? Are you trying to give me a heart attack?"

"Where have you been?" Ash snapped.

"You're lucky I didn't shoot y'all."

"Where have you been?" Ashley repeated, over-enunciating each word.

"I told you. Last night was the chamber of commerce thing." Jameson put away her Taser and picked up her shoes from the hall before stepping into the apartment and closing the door behind her.

"That was last night," Ash shot back. "It's now after four in the morning. Where have you been?"

Trini gasped. "Oh my God. That's the dress I saw you leave in last night. And is that a man's shirt you're wearing? I'm sensing a walk of shame here," she sang.

The girls began to fire rapid questions as if they shared one mind.

"Who was it?" Ash asked. "Anyone we know?"

"Details, sis. Details."

"It was one of the twins, wasn't it?" Trini asked with a knowing smirk.

"Guys, guys, guys." Jameson pounded her fist on the kitchen counter. "Stick to the point—"

"Twins? You banging twins now, James? Right on." The girls began to talk over each other at a rapid-fire pace.

"Which one?"

"I bet it was both."

Jameson sighed. "Look, it's like this—"

"Both," the girls said in unison and high-fived each other. "Spill it."

"Well that's just great," Ash broken in with disdain. "What are you thinking? We're supposed to be saving lives and you tell us to stop, only to find out you're strolling around getting your clit flicked by some doublemint twins."

"That's enough," Jameson barked. "First off, do not doubt my focus on our mission. Second, don't you dare try to slut-shame me, Ashley. I am a grown-ass woman and if I want to jerk off every dick in the city whenever I feel like it, that is my prerogative. And finally, I told you, we have to keep a low profile. Some of our targets have turned up dead."

"It's not just our targets." Ash shrugged and shifted her weight. "Nina Gomez is dead."

"What?" Jameson asked. Her blood slowed to a stop and the other girls gasped in shock.

"Her husband was full of shit, just like we told her. Beat her up pretty good. She was barely able to send me a text with her location, and I still had to use the GPS to find her. She was dead by the time I got her to the hospital." Her mouth twisted as if the words tasted bitter and her arms tightened across her chest.

"Fuck." Jameson beat her fist on the counter again. "That son of a bitch."

"Cursing won't bring her back from the dead," Ash said with a slight sneer.

"I know that," Jameson growled and ran her palms over her face. "I'm processing."

"We need to get back onto the streets." Ash took a step forward. "We need more patrols. We need to get these women educated and moved to safety."

"I know. I know." A headache formed at the base of Jameson's neck. "But it's still risky with the police looking out for us."

"How do you know the police are looking for us?" Trini asked. "Like us specifically?"

Fuck. She swallowed against the lump in her throat. She was going to have to spill some info to keep her friends safe. The twins wouldn't probably be pissed, but her Angels meant everything to her.

"Look, Gerald Mulvaney didn't just go to the police after I roughed him up. He was later murdered. The police contacted me in order to get hold of Emily to question her. Then I heard on the news that somebody else was found murdered in a similar fashion as Mulvaney. If those two murders are connected, I don't want it getting back to us," Jameson answered. "I'm not doing time for someone else's crime."

She knew it would be clearer for them if she gave specifics and explained how the Daniels twins gave her the information, but with the way Ash had started pacing, she wanted to keep that tidbit to herself. No need to bring the brothers further into the conversation.

Lucinda raised her hand. "I vote for no jail time, too."

"Holy shit. Someone killed that son of a bitch? That's awesome," Trini giggled but quickly sobered. "And horrible. I vote for no jail time, too."

"So while we wait for incompetent law enforcement to pretend to do their jobs, we sit around and wait for more women to die?" Ash asked with a huff. "That's bullshit. They deserve better. Nina Gomez deserved better."

"No need to hit me with the guilt stick, Ash. I know."

Jameson bunched her fingers into fists and took a deep breath. She was tired and upset. Fighting with her sisters was not going to help anyone. "Look, it's not a permanent hiatus. Let's give the cops a few more days to find who murdered those creeps and then we can go back to kicking some ass. In the meantime, we can check in with our girls. Make sure all our ducks are accounted for and make a plan of action for when we can cut loose again. Jules and Bryn can still give out backpacks and shuttle people to the shelters. We can all pitch in there, too."

Ash's lips pursed in a resigned fashion. "Fine. I'll check in with the south end and see if there are any targets we need to keep an eye on."

Jameson grinned. "As if you don't already have a list in your back pocket."

"It can always use updating," she said with a shrug.

The tug of sleep pulled at Jameson's eyes. "Okay. Meet me back in the hole at eleven tonight. Now go. Let me sleep."

The girls grumbled but started to gather their things and make their way to the door.

"Hey." Jameson waved her hands at the bowls of popcorn and half-empty wine glasses cluttering her living room. "Aren't you going to put away your mess?"

"Nope," Lucinda answered after a beat, and Jules and Bryn followed her out with big smiles on their faces.

Ash stopped in front of her and eyed her up and down. "Are you in this for real? I don't want you to half-ass this."

"I don't half-ass anything. I know I might have seemed a little…off lately, but I'm as dedicated as ever. Don't forget whose idea this all was. How we dreamed up the Angels together. I'm in."

"Fly or die?" Ash asked, sounding hesitant.

"Fly or die," Jameson replied and held out her hand.

Ashley paused for a second then locked her thumb with Jameson's so their hands formed the shape of wings. They raised then lowered their clasped hands and finished with a fist bump.

"See you at eleven," Ash said, stressing the word "eleven."

"I'll be waiting for your lazy ass."

Ash nodded, the corner of her lips curled into the slightest grin. Then she left.

Soon it was just Jameson and Trini who lounged over the kitchen island, chin propped on her fist, gazing at her with a keen interest.

"Whatever you did last night looks good on you, mami," Trini said with a wink.

"Shut up." Jameson rolled her eyes.

"No, I mean it. I want the details."

"Never."

"Ooo. That means it was super good." Trini pointed at Jameson. "I will get you to the spill the tea. Just wait and see."

She wanted to spill. God, did she want somebody to talk to about the deets of the last week. Trini was her friend, her sister, but at this point her feelings about the twins were too new. Too raw. What if Trini pointed out all the reasons why she should run the other way?

Even worse, what if she agreed?

CHAPTER TWELVE

RONAN CRADLED HIS hot cup of tea closer to his chest and settled deeper into the chair as he watched his dozing brother reach out across the expanse of his giant mattress. As his fingers began to slap around in the vacant area, Ronan took a deep draw of the fragrant liquid and grinned.

Five...four...three...two...

Ethan sat up with a terrified gasp.

"Don't fret, brother," Ronan said and took another sip. "Ted took her home hours ago."

Ethan drew in several deep breaths, his confused gaze slowly clearing as he collapsed back on the pillows. "Hours ago? What time is it now?"

Ronan gestured toward the floor-to-ceiling windows. Through the gossamer curtains the lush green foliage sparkled in the sun. "Early enough, but late for you."

"Why did you let me sleep for so long?"

"Because you *were* sleeping." And heavens be, was it a peaceful rest. Ethan's mind had been so quiet, so blessedly, blissfully quiet. "You have not slept like that in a really long time."

"I guess it's because I haven't had a night like that in a really long time. Like, ever."

Understatement of the year. The night before was going to go down in history as the best experience Ronan ever had or ever would have in his life.

He handed Ethan his own cup of tea. "I have to tell you, I was delightfully surprised when I came home last night and found you two by the pool. I didn't think she was ready for that yet."

"I don't think she was either." Ethan frowned down into the steaming contents of his cup. "Her run-in with Marjorie Lance kind of propelled the conversation of intimacy farther along than I had planned."

The painful sting of humiliation made Ronan grimace. "Ah, Marjorie. Guess I'll be haunted about that one forever."

"Possibly." Ethan flashed him a sideways grin. "But it did start the conversation. And Jamison now understands what it means to be with us. Both of us."

"Obviously. And I hope you understand what it means to be with her."

Ethan's lashes lifted and their gazes collided over the rim of his cup. "What does that mean?"

Ronan relaxed deeper into his seat. Whether it be business or personal, this was what he did best. Maintain the loose threads and contain the chaos. If their relationship with Jameson was like a bowling ball, he would be the bumpers that kept the ball in the lane and out of the gutters. "That we will have to ease ourselves into her life. Our relationship will be scrutinized. And it's not just we are brothers. We're prominent business owners. It may bring forth unexpected questions and complications from those around us and who we do business with. We'll need to support each other as well as her."

"Of course. Without a doubt. Believe me, I'm trying to do things right by Jameson."

"I know. But I can sense your excitement. The need to

fit together with someone who may understand you. Balance you. Someone who is not me," he finished with a laugh. "Just don't let that need to connect push Jameson to go faster than she's comfortable."

"Don't be so obtuse. You're excited as well. I can feel it. You're practically giddy."

Giddy. Ha! *Ecstatic* was more like it. *Relieved* would also be a good word but might be seen as rather pedestrian and unromantic. Ethan deserved some happiness. Hell, so did he. And as long as they were emotionally tied for the rest of their lives, it was a relief to know that there was someone who understood them. Who was able to celebrate the two brothers together as well as what they provided on their own. Jameson was like that last piece of code that made the software work. She generally enjoyed being with both of them, and not once had she exhibited any awkwardness of her being closer to one brother over the other. Around Jameson he felt free, joyful. And in Ethan he sensed a lightness that his brother had not had in many years.

Ronan also understood his place in the relationship. Jameson and Ethan were like two kites in the wind, dipping and swirling in the tumultuous whirl of emotions as he watched their brilliant dance while holding on to their tethers. If they flew too high, he would bring them safely down. In fact, it was an honor to be a part of the trio.

"Now all we need is to make sure Jameson cannot be tied to any of these murders," Ethan said. "Then we can try to properly court her."

"*Court.*" Ronan snorted. "I think you've been watching too many episodes of *The Crown* with Ted lately. Anyway, I think those murders are something we're not going to have to worry about any longer."

Ethan stilled, his cup of tea at his lips. "Why do you say that?"

Ronan set his own cup on the table beside him and settled back, resting his clasped hands on his belly. "At the hotel last night. After you went in search of Jameson, a string of conversation drifted my way that I found very intriguing. It was a reporter from the *Tribune* asking Mayor Tuputala about the murders of Mulvaney and Fitzgerald. The reporter also mentioned a similar murder in Oregon. Same MO. Man spread out, beaten, and words carved onto his body. But this man was found to have been killed on Saturday."

Ethan scrambled across the bed toward his nightstand. "How come I didn't receive any alerts on my phone about another murder?"

"Your phone was pinging while you were asleep."

While Ethan frantically pulled up information on his phone, Ronan resumed sipping his tea, waiting for Ethan to come to the logical conclusion.

"This is great," his brother exclaimed. "I mean, it's not great that another man has been killed in such a horrific fashion, but if he was killed Saturday, we were with Jameson on Saturday. She has an airtight alibi. And I bet the garage of that nightclub has cameras that would confirm all of us being there."

"Exactly."

Ethan's smile melted, and his joy turned to something that looked like nausea. "When should we tell Jameson?"

Ah. That's what Ethan *said*, but Ronan picked up what his brother really wanted to ask, for it was a fear he also carried. "What you mean is now that we can prove without a doubt that she's not a murderer, you think Jameson will no longer want to spend time with us."

"No. Maybe. It's a concern."

"It is." He sighed. "And that is a risk we'll have to take. I want her. Don't you?"

"You know I do," Ethan sputtered with an incredulous glare.

"And all signs point to Jameson wanting us too. So let's show her how it can be. We'll invite her to dinner. Just dinner. No talk of murders, rapists, and all-around assholes. Just a nice dinner with the three of us to get to know each other better."

"That's a good idea." Ethan tapped the corner of his phone against his chin. "I haven't wanted something, someone, like this in a very long time. I don't want to lose her."

"We won't." Ronan stood with renewed sense of energy and hope. "There's nothing in our way now. All we have to do is show her how we will complement her, not overshadow her, not change her. You'll see. Everything will fall into place."

CHAPTER THIRTEEN

SO HOW DID a girl who was trying to avoid a murder rap and has freshly entered in a triad relationship with telepathic twins sort out her feelings? By having date night with said twins at their mega-mansion, of course!

Right. Probably not the wisest move for clearing one's head. But Ethan had asked so nicely, and Ronan promised to cook buttered shrimp with angel hair pasta and grilled artichoke hearts. The man was diabolical, tempting her with her favorite foods.

What sealed the deal was the promise of no talk of murders or Evolutioneers. Just a quiet evening of getting to know each other better. If they were going to have a relationship, they had to be able to spend one evening together without death and mayhem on the agenda, right? So far, everyone had held tight to that rule, and dinner had been an enchanting and sumptuous affair.

The sun was setting in a glorious display of oranges and purples and her belly was pleasantly full of pasta and the tastiest Viognier she'd ever sipped. The waterfall splashed melodically in the pool and the boys had placed her closest to the outdoor heater for warmth. The world at the moment was perfect.

So what was her problem? Why was there a little prickle of unease burning along her conscience? She was in Shangri-La. Life was beautiful.

For now.

Tonight, it was dinner. What about tomorrow? What about next week? What were they doing? Was this the start to a lifelong commitment or were they engaging in a brief fling to offset the stress of locating a murderer? And then there was the bigger question—would she still be able to do her work, if she were to align with them in a personal relationship?

"Breathe, wildcat. Breathe." Ronan settled his hand over hers. "You are doing *a lot* of thinking, and I'm too happy and relaxed to tune you out."

"Sorry. I'm… I'm not used to taking it easy," she finished lamely. "This is nice. I'm having a good time."

"Nice? Just nice?" Ronan exclaimed. "Did you hear that, brother? We're going to have to up our game."

Ethan set his napkin over his plate. "Let's tidy up and we'll light a bonfire and snuggle. We can count the stars as they come out."

"A fire sounds nice," she said. "But isn't there a burn ban?"

"It's a gas fireplace."

"Of course. You've thought of that already. Always so prepared." She rose from her seat. "I'm going to use your facilities real quick, if you don't mind."

"Go right ahead." Ronan stood as well. "It's Ethan's turn to do the dishes anyway."

"I can help when I'm done."

Ethan reared back. "Absolutely not. You're our guest. Take your time."

They cook *and* do dishes? Add a plus under the column labeled "potential forever."

She hurried inside and dashed to the door she thought

was the bathroom. The expansive space and willowy draperies were a dead giveaway that this was not the loo. Instead, she found herself in an artist's dream room.

"What is this?" she marveled aloud.

White dropcloths splattered with paint covered the floors, and several easels were strewn around the room. Along one wall were racks filled with tubes of acrylic and oil paints, and on the shelf were buckets of paintbrushes with their stiff bristles resembling abstract flower arrangements. Canvases of various sizes rested along the opposite wall and floor-to-ceiling curtains in white gossimer covered what looked like a giant window.

She wanted to explore more, but nature was calling bigtime, so she raced down the hall, opening each door until she found the bathroom and quickly took care of business.

Once she was finished, she crept back to the art room and slipped inside. Was she snooping? Yes. But she was dying to know more about the artist.

Well, whoever it was, they hadn't done any painting for a long time as a closer inspection revealed a layer of dust covering the pallets and canvases.

An unfinished painting sat on an easel closest to the draperies. Since Jameson knew squat about art, she hadn't a clue to what the style was, but there was something about it that appealed to her.

It was a portrait of a woman but painted with blues, purples, and yellows instead of life-like colors. The eyes were sultry, the mouth a full-on pout, but there was strength in the sexy expression. A warrior spirit that Jameson connected with on a level that made her smile and wish the entire portrait was finished, not just half the face.

Who was this woman? And what did she mean to the

artist?

Jameson pulled back the drapes a little, exposing the view out to the patio and waterfall. How wonderful must it be to pull back the curtains all the way and open the sliding glass doors to flood the room with sunlight.

The overhead lights clicked on, and she jumped with a shriek as if she'd been caught in a mousetrap.

"Hi," she said sheepishly to Ronan, who stood inside the doorway, and ran her palms down the length of her hair. "I, uh, got lost. It's a big house."

His grin widened. "It might be easier to snoop with the lights on."

"I wasn't snooping."

"And you lie to my face," he crowed.

She sighed and rolled her eyes. "Who's the artist?"

"Ethan."

"For real? Wow. I didn't know he painted. He seems more like the type who would observe and appreciate art, not create it. Whoa." She pointed to a corkboard hanging on the wall that had been hidden in the shadows until Ronan had turned on the lights. "Did you really base-jump off the Sydney Bridge?"

Pictures covered the corkboard, creating a collage that for most people would be lottery-winning levels of aspirations. Travels to sunny spots, adventures in foreign-looking countries, fancy cars, and scantily clad women. The smiling man with long, dark hair and a spark of mischief in his eyes was dressed in a jumpsuit with a parachute strapped to his back. He was the king of his world without a care, not even the threat of death from jumping out of a plane at ten thousand feet. Ronan had been quite the playboy.

"Wait a minute." She stepped closer to the photos and

touched one of the pictures taken in front of an airplane.

She turned to Ronan with surprise. "This isn't you. It's Ethan."

"Yep. Most of those photos are of Ethan."

"I don't understand. I mean, it looks like him, but at the same time it doesn't. I don't see a button-down shirt in any of these."

"I call this time 'Ethan BC.' Before the crash." He stuffed his hands in his pockets and tilted his head as he looked at the photos. Memories flashed in his dark eyes and his smiled turned sad. "Ethan was a very different person back then. Very gregarious. Loved art, and movement, and color, and reveled in everything that came with it. He even had a few successful gallery showings."

"And the crash changed all that? I mean, I know it was a traumatic experience, obviously. But why wouldn't he want to celebrate being alive and fuel his art even more?"

Ronan sighed and leaned against a low bookcase beside her. "Ethan carries guilt about how things ended with our parents. More specifically, with our father. It was no secret that my father wanted to pass the company on to both his sons, and I was all for it. I love the work and the people, plus I didn't have to start a business from scratch. Ethan, however, wanted nothing to do with working behind a desk inside an office building, and for some reason my father couldn't handle that. It was like he had this image in his head of passing down some great legacy to his sons like we were on some soap opera. Like nothing else mattered but having a giant photo hanging in the office of him sitting at his desk like a titan of industry with his sons flanking him dressed in matching suits."

"So it didn't matter to your father that you were ready

and willing to take over the business?" Did their father not think Ronan was good enough? How fucked up was that?

"I think it did and it didn't," Ronan replied with a shrug. "Having both of his sons on board was more important. It was a respect thing for him. How he built up this successful business for his family while he came from practically nothing. He worked hard for us, so he wanted us to show our gratitude by carrying on his legacy, not off surfing the waves or shitting our money away on paint and whimsy."

"He said that to Ethan?" she asked, outraged.

"Not exactly, but if you cobble together what he said over time, that's what I got from it."

"I can't even imagine my mother saying something like that to me. In fact, she tried to get me interested in careers that were different from hers. She said I had spent too much of my childhood worried about the system and how it affected us. But when she saw how passionate I was about my work, she was all for it."

"That was the thing. When our father thought Ethan's art was a hobby, he was fine. But when it became obvious that Ethan wanted no part of Daniels Software and turned this room into an art studio, he acted as though he was insulted. Like Ethan turned his back on his family. Unfortunately, that was how things ended between them."

Ronan's gaze turned inward, and he scratched absent-mindedly at his cheek. The way he spoke made her wonder if he had shared this story with anyone besides maybe Ted.

"We were on the way to Las Vegas for the Computer Electronics Show. My dad thought Ethan might be persuaded to take on more duties with the company if he worked the convention. Ethan thought he was going to have fun with his friends in Sin City. My mother thought the trip would be a way to bridge the gap that had grown between us all, and all I wanted was to create my own footprint in the industry. Then the plane went down in the Cascades and that… That was it," he finished, his voice breaking on the words.

Jameson didn't know if he realized it, but Ronan was projecting those terrifying moments to her. It had all happened so quickly. They hadn't even hit cruising altitude when the little pocket of turbulence they hit went from bumpy to the plane plummeting to the earth in the space of a breath. The lights flashed as he clung to the arms of his chair and met his brother's gaze across the cabin. The soft croon of his father's voice, trying to calm his mother, was barely audible over her wails.

This can't be it, was the final thought he shared with his brother before there was a bright flash of light. Then all went dark and silent.

"Jesus, Ronan. I'm so sorry." She pressed up against him and laid her hand on his cheek. Fine shivers shook his big body.

"Thank you, love." He turned his head to press a kiss to her palm. "And I'm sorry. I didn't mean to project."

"I'm glad you felt safe enough with me to do so." She leaned forward to nuzzle his chin. "And your dad was an ass for letting you think you weren't enough to take on the company."

"I never said that."

"But you felt it. I felt it for you."

"It wasn't—"

She placed her fingers over his lips. "Ronan. I understand. My dad abandoned me when I was little. I don't need him or his approval, and if I saw him today, I'd probably knee him in the nuts. But rejection hurts. After all this time. It still hurts."

Ronan gathered her closer. "Your dad missed out on an amazing woman."

"Your dad missed out on amazing sons."

"Jameson, Jameson, Jameson," he said with a sigh, his gaze turned liquid with hunger. "You are too much."

The kiss he laid on her suggested that "too much" was just what he wanted.

His hands on her back was as firm as his lips. Thoughts of sad times were over, and Ronan appeared ready to live for the moment as he supped on her lips as if she were a fine whiskey. Smoky, sultry, with a fire that burned slowly on its way to her belly.

He walked her back to a table covered in palettes of dried-up paint and lifted her on to the surface. His nimble fingers worked the zipper of her dress and pulled the garment down until the tops of her breasts were exposed.

"What about Ethan?" she asked once she was able to tear her lips away.

"What about Ethan?" His grin widened. "Do you only like having sex when it's all three of us?"

Maybe, but that wasn't the point. "Is this us having sex?"

"Wildcat." He threaded his leg between hers and ground his erection against her thigh. "We're having sex. Don't you recognize foreplay?"

"This is foreplay? I thought we were just making out."

"I plan on doing much more than make out. But seriously, Jameson." The look in his eyes grew intense. "Do you need Ethan here?"

At least that was what he asked. What she heard was, *Do you prefer my brother over me?* Or, *Can you only be with me if my brother is around?*

The answer to his questions was yes and no. Did she feel closer to Ethan? Sometimes. Just as at times she felt more in sync with Ronan. But was she attracted to them both?

Fuck yeah.

"I don't *need* him here. I… I just don't want to leave him out. Just like I wouldn't want to leave you out."

"You didn't seem to have that affliction the other night in the pool."

Heat blistered her cheeks. "That's because I didn't know the pool was going to happen until it happened."

"Uh-huh." Ronan's grin turned into a chuckle. "You're cute thinking that even if he's not physically here that he's not with us. Don't worry, wildcat. He's on his way."

His took her mouth again as his hands wandered over her body, stroking, undressing. The heat of his breath warmed the skin of her neck as he took teasing bites of her flesh.

Over his shoulder she saw Ethan enter the room. To her surprise, he didn't join them at the table, nor did he beckon them over when he sat on the couch opposite them. Instead, he sipped his wine as if he were watching the setting sun.

Ronan worked her nipple free from her bra, sucking it between his lips as his hand glided up the inside of her thigh. He quickly slipped her panties down and off her legs, then returned to slide his fingertips between the folds of her sex.

Unlike lovers from her past who went right for the clit like it was a magic button that would instantly turn her on for immediate penetration, Ronan took his time, easing the wetness spilling out of her pussy around and around until she was good and soaked.

"Are you enjoying this?" she asked Ethan, breathlessly. "Watching?"

"Very much." He sipped on his wine. "It's like watching a live version of my own X-rated movie."

"That's...kinda weird," she said with a giggle, both turned on and creeped out as Ronan laughed into her neck.

Ethan shrugged. "Maybe. But I like it."

His smile and the light in his eyes reminded her so much of the Ethan in the photos on the walls that she felt compelled to encourage that carefree attitude and put on the best show for him she could.

She writhed against Ronan's hand, panting and moaning as he worked his fingers in deep and worked her clit with his thumb. Heat rolled from her pussy to her chest, consuming her from the inside out in the most delightful burn.

"That's it, wildcat," Ronan whispered in her ear. "Make that pussy feel good."

It's you. It's all you, she said, unable to form a sentence.

It's you telling me what to do, he replied. *But not with words.*

"Oh my God," she gasped and gyrated her hips. "That's it. Right there. Don't stop. If you stop, I will rip your fucking head off."

She was going to die. She was going to die, she knew it. No way could her heart take anymore.

Then it was gone. All gone. Ronan stepped back with an evil chuckle, leaving her a weak heap on the table.

"I'm going to destroy you," she growled, sluggishly trying to grab at him. At least she was able to curl her fingers into claws. She was going to scratch the shit out of him, once she made contact.

"Save your energy, wildcat. We're building you up to make the drop that much sweeter." He took a condom from his pocket and rolled it down his hard length.

"That's the worst thing I've ever heard."

"Hey now," he tsked, and grabbed her wrist as she tried to finger her clit. "Wait for me."

"You're too slow."

"If you're not careful, I can go slower."

Her eyes narrowed. "Is that a threat?"

"A promise." He brushed the broad head of his cock against her opening, teasing her by pressing and retreating.

"Daniels. I will end you," she grunted as she shifted her hips for deeper penetration.

"No, you won't. You'll become too addicted to this to want to give it up."

And with that he eased all the way inside her.

Oh. That was good. So good. But still slow.

"My God, man. Hurry up." She kicked and bucked, hitting him in the sides with her heels to spur him faster. At least she made good on her promise to mark him and dug her fingernails into his back until he hissed.

Meanwhile, Ethan lounged on the sofa. He had opened his pants and his hard cock rested on his belly, throbbing and pulsing, making her mouth water.

When she bucked, he bucked. As she writhed, Ethan writhed. As her fingers dug in deeper into Ronan's back, Ethan's hands clamped down on the edge of the sofa.

Aren't you going to touch yourself? she asked him.

No. I'll come too soon. I want it to last.

You boys and your edging will be the death of me.

"You love it," Ronan said. His wicked fingers made a return trip to her clit, rubbing tantalizing circles over the swollen bud.

They were horrible, horrible men.

But she could be just as wicked.

She focused her gaze on Ethan's cock then imagined all ways she could stroke it and kiss it. How wet she'd make the length as she gobbled him down, working her tongue along the ridges.

Ethan's hips twisted as Ronan groaned against her, "You're a witch."

"Am I?"

She continued to feed them her fantasies of how she'd work Ethan over with her hands and mouth, and the way Ronan felt inside her, stretching her pussy as he thrust faster and faster. The way his fingers drove her insane until she was mindless with rapture. The spark of her imagination was just what she needed to tip herself over the precipice and into the bottomless well of pleasure.

"Fuck you," Ronan groaned again, and bit into her shoulder as he came deep and hard.

And this she shared too. The twitch of Ronan's cock and how her pussy fluttered and flexed, milking him for everything he had as she stared Ethan in the eye, daring him to come.

"Jameson..." Her name was a prayer on his lips as cum shot from his cock onto his belly.

Similar to the last time they had sex by the pool, this tableau was no less explicit, no less outrageous with its straight-out sexual hedonism.

And she loved it. She loved every second, every gasp, every drop of sweat and cum. She wanted to bathe in the debauchery until every cell in her body was permeated with their essence.

"That's our girl," Ethan mumbled with a chuckle, looking completely spent on the sofa. Ronan appeared no stronger as he crumpled slowly to sprawl out on the dropcloth-covered floor.

Her arms shook as she leaned back on the table, panting, wet, and gloriously satisfied. Ronan was right. She was growing addicted to them. And quickly.

"Well. That's a way to burn calories," she said, not ready to admit out loud how she wanted them to keep her forever.

She was supposed to be taking it easy in regard to the two of them. Waiting until the craziness of the murders had been cleared. At least that was what she promised Trini, in not so many words and without declaring specifics.

Oh my God. Trini.

Jameson bolted upright and instantly regretted it when the room swam. "What time is it?" she asked, holding her head.

"Almost ten," Ethan replied after checking his watch.

"Crap. I'm going to be late." She jumped from the table and looked around for her shoes. When did she lose those?

"Late for what?" Ronan struggled to his feet.

"I promised to meet the girls tonight." She half-walked, half-jumped as she slipped on the shoes she found under an easel and made her way to the table in the hall. "Where did my jacket go?"

"The girls?" Ethan asked, following. "You mean the Angels?"

"Some of them." Where were the closets in this place?

"What will you be doing?"

She looked over at him sharply. "Things."

Her heart rate rose along with her temperature as she continued to search for her jacket. The flapping of the top of her dress over her arms added to her agitation. Who did she have to fuck to find her jacket?

Ronan gestured for her to turn around. "Hold up, wildcat. Let me get your zipper."

She took the few seconds of standing still to catch her breath. There truly was no reason for the sudden case of claustrophobia, but damn it. Their barrage of questions was making her skin crawl. If she didn't get out of the house soon, she was going to lose it. Especially when Ethan stepped before her as Ronan crowded her from behind to do up her dress.

"Jameson," Ethan said, crossing his arms. "You promised no more vigilantism."

"And I'm not. There is other work to be done besides going after assholes." She wiggled out from between them. From the corner of her eye she spotted her jacket draped over an armchair in the living room and finally felt the breath ease.

She hated caring purses. The thought of not having her hands free in case she needed to defend herself made her twitchy. That meant she had to carry the essentials in her jacket. Without her jacket…she was fucked.

Ever the peacekeeper, Ronan stepped between them. "No need for tensions to get high. Jameson, you know we want you to be safe. As we've discussed, now is not the time for your nighttime shenanigans."

"Shenanigans? Are you fucking kidding me?" she exclaimed. "You say that like what I do is silly nonsense."

"That's not what I meant."

"Isn't it? And what's it to you?" Her voice rose. "You

two are talking to me like I'm a child. 'We've discussed.' What is that shit? Are you grounding me?"

"No."

"Yes," Ethan said at the same time as his brother.

She felt her eyes boggle. "No. No, no, no, no. Not cool. Not cool at all."

"Jameson. Just—"

"Ronan, if you're going to tell me to calm down, you can shut the fuck up right now." She strode toward the door. "Fuck you. And fuck you, and then the two of you can fuck off together. I'm out."

She didn't dare break stride as she marched out the front door and slammed it shut behind her. At least she would've slammed it if the wooden monstrosity weren't so fucking heavy.

But she was able to slam her car door shut and that was almost as satisfying, as was peeling off down their long driveway in a blaze of smoke and burned rubber.

The nerve of those two thinking they could tell her what to do. Nobody puts Baby in the corner. No one.

She hit the call button on the dash. It picked up in two rings.

"What up?" Ashley replied.

"Change of plans, sis," she said, pressing on the gas. "Get ready to fly or die. Grab your notebook. I need a mission tonight."

CHAPTER FOURTEEN

MOTHER NATURE WAS being her usual northwest Northwest flouncy self and went from a beautiful, sunny seventy degrees to a gray and chilly forty overnight, leaving Jameson and Ashley shivering in the rhododendrons.

"God, I hate this flower," Jameson grumbled and tried to press as close to the outside wall of the house as possible.

"Is it a flower or a bush?" Ash asked on a whisper.

"I don't care. It still stinks."

It always boggled her mind that the rhododendron was so popular. It was even the state flower, for pete's sake. It was a big, clunky bush for eleven months out of the year then blossomed for like a day. Then their colorful petals withered up into sad little corpses that stuck to everything and smelled like rotting vegetation mixed with mud in an odor that never failed to clog her sinuses.

"Are you sure this is the house?" she asked, desperately trying not to breathe through her nose. The pinch of her mask against her nose helped somewhat.

Ashley nodded. "My contact at the ER confirmed. The neighbor also confirmed Ahmed comes out for his evening smoke after eleven. Should be any moment now."

Their target, Ahmed Dara, came into view of the sliding glass door. Just beyond him in the kitchen was his wife, Myrna, who had been released from the hospital the day before.

That visit had been the third time Myrna had been to the emergency room in as many months, and the only reason she had gone at all was because a fainting spell dropped her in the middle of the parking lot at the grocery store.

It seemed Ahmed had a fondness for smacking his wife around. Charges were never brought against Ahmed because she was afraid he would retaliate and dish out more of his anger onto her or their eight-year-old daughter, who was currently by her mother's side, loading dishes in the dishwasher.

It was an excuse Jameson heard many times before, from women who were in relationships where the man viewed the women in their lives as property rather than human beings. To see these women believe they were worthless, to accept their lot and remain punching bags at their husband's whims, broke her heart. However, nothing was worse than the number of women she knew who ended up permanently disabled or killed when they tried to voice their own opinion and stand up for themselves.

Well, not anymore. The rules of the game were changing, and if they knocked some sense into this one's head, perhaps the cycle of abuse would stop with him.

"Jesus," Jameson whispered. "Don't these kids have a bedtime?"

Ashley grunted beside her and adjusted the thin hood of her jacket over her head as they watched the son, who appeared to be about eleven or twelve, run around the house from the open-concept living room into the kitchen. He carried a paper airplane in his hand as he raised the craft up and down, making airplane noises at the top of his lungs.

Dara was on his cell phone, pacing between the two areas with his back turned toward the women as they continued with their housekeeping. The little girl's eyes were droopy as she continued to shuffle plates into the wash racks. The poor thing was probably wishing for a comfy bed and a thick comforter.

"Varooooom!" Ahmed Jr. sailed past his sister, the plane still in his hand. He ran right into the corner of the kitchen counter with his forehead and spun around, smashing into the glass door, nose first. Falling to the floor with limbs flailing, he wailed, clasping onto his bloody nose.

At that, Dara roared and jammed his phone into his back pocket. Jameson did not understand what he was yelling as he stomped over to his daughter and pointed his finger in her face. He gestured back and forth between the girl and her brother, who was writhing on the floor as if he had suffered a severe decapitation. With another roar, Dara pulled his hand back and smacked his daughter across the cheek.

Jameson's eyes widened and red-hot flames streaked down her spine into her fingers, reaching for the knife strapped to her thigh. Beside her, Ash reached for her weapons belt.

"We'll kill the bastard," Ash growled, as she shifted to go on the attack.

"Wait." Jameson held her arm out, holding Ash back against the wall as she left her knife in its sheath. "Look. I want to kill him too, but we're not here to kill. No dead bodies."

"This asshole is not going learn with just a slap on the wrist, I can tell you that right now."

"I feel you, sis. Just take a breath. He'll get what's due."

Against her arm, Ashley vibrated with the same anger Jameson was forcing into a ball and crushing with all her restraint.

Breathe, breathe, breathe. She just had to be patient.

It felt as if an eternity had passed before Myrna took care of the crying boy and got the children squared away upstairs. The fact that the little girl hadn't uttered a peep after she was hit as the boy continued to wail told Jameson all she needed to know about how the girl was expected to behave.

Several quiet minutes later, the sliding door opened.

Jameson held her breath and waited as Dara stepped out onto the back patio, crossing the deck to stop at the top of the stairs that led down to a tiny patch of lawn. He pulled out a pipe and tobacco from the pouch he carried with him and began to fill the well.

With a quick nod at Ash, they stepped out from behind the bushes. One. Two. Three. Four. She slapped at her pockets and belt. Mask, whip, knife, phone.

"I'm so glad you can make it to class this evening, Mr. Dara," Jameson said.

Dara looked at them with a start, his lit match paused just above his pipe. They did make a striking pair, Jameson supposed. She was dressed in her corset and mask, while Ashley resembled a goth version of an *Assassin's Creed* character. "The fuck is this?" he mumbled around the mouthpiece.

"We know what you do to your family. How you beat them." Jameson lifted the handle of her whip. "We are here to inform you that such actions will stop immediately, or you will face the consequences."

Dara's eyes narrowed for a moment before the corner of

his mouth lifted and he began to chuckle. "You bitches are crazy. Get off my property."

"We thought you'd say that," Jameson said, trailing the length of the whip over her fingers. "We know lessons that are worth learning take a while to teach, so I will repeat. You will stop abusing your wife and daughter. If you continue to do so, harm will come to you. If you retaliate for this visit in any way toward your wife and daughter, you will face the consequences. Please don't make me show you a demonstration of how we work."

"Who the fuck *are* you?" He continued with the lighting of his pipe and gestured at them, the match still in his hand. The smoke made lazy circles in the night sky. "I am the king of my castle. Where I am from, it is tradition. Women are my property. Nobody tells me how to treat my property."

"Well, I have a tradition of beating the shit out of assholes like you," Ash said with a crack of her knuckles. "Let me share my tradition with you."

Ashley pulled back with her right fist and caught him directly in the temple, a talent that Jameson had seen many a man underestimate. The asshole went down easy. His pipe flying in the air and landing with a clatter on the deck.

She wasted no time and jumped on top of him, landing punch after punch to the man's face.

"How do you like my tradition?" she asked in a guttural voice. "Too much for you? Would you like me to stop? I'll stop when you stop."

Dara did nothing but lay there and twitch with each blow to the head as Ash unloaded years of combat training with her deadly, leather-covered knuckles, not appearing to be losing one bit of steam.

"You think women are weak? How about I make you

choke on my pussy," she roared, then jumped up to straddle Dara's head, smothering him between her legs.

"Whoa, whoa, whoa." Jameson grabbed Ash and yanked her back. That escalated quickly. "No dead bodies, remember, sis? Ease up. Ease up."

Ash broke free of her hold and jumped back on top of Dara. She leaned over, pressing her lips close to his ear as she whipped a blade from her boot. Pressing the tip of the blade against the man's Adam's apple, she growled, "This is your one and only warning. If you lay a hand on your wife and daughter again, I will cut off your dick and fuck you up the ass with it. The cycle of abuse stops with you. *We are watching you.* I will know if you even think about retaliating in any way. I will not hesitate to make an example of you and your stupidity, understand?"

The asshole whimpered, shaking where he lay.

"Understand?" Ash asked, pressing the blade deeper into his neck.

Dara whimpered louder and muttered a high-pitched, "Yes."

Ash reached into her side pocket then pushed her finger inside Ahmed's ear. "I've just placed a tracker in your ear canal. Good luck getting it out. There are also trackers in your vehicles, and I have cameras inside and outside your home. I will know every move you make. And do not think this will be my last visit here otherwise."

She stood and motioned to Jameson. The delightful sobs of Ahmed Dara weeping into the lawn followed their wake.

"Did you really put a tracker in his ear?" Jameson asked, slightly winded after running the few blocks to where she had parked her car.

"No. He doesn't know that. And I'd like to see what he

looks like after he tries digging it out."

"God, you are demented."

"Guilty," Ash replied with a grin. "Who's next?"

Jameson set the GPS for their next destination and pulled onto the road. She snuck a quick glance over at her friend, who was wiping the blood off her gloves with a wet wipe. "Ash… If I hadn't had been there, would you have killed that asshole?"

She shrugged. "Don't know. Maybe."

Oh. That was…comforting?

"You know, I've been wondering, are we taking it a little too far?"

"Taking what too far? That back there was nothing more than a boxing exercise."

"Honey, that was a full-on ass kicking," Jameson said incredulously. "There wasn't much finesse there."

Ash shrugged again. "He deserved it."

"No shit. Of course he did. But I keep wondering, what happens if we go too far and accidentally kill someone?"

"Don't worry, James." Ash reached over and patted her on the knee. "You're too smart for that. You're not going to kill anyone. Hey, what's going on over there?"

Jameson wanted to dive further into the "You won't go too far" comment and ask Ash for clarification, but she pulled over to the side of the road where Ash had pointed.

They were about two blocks away from one of the city's hotspots. The line behind the velvet rope snaked down the sidewalk, but where they had parked there were a few stragglers who were either coming or going from the establishment.

Near them were a trio of women dressed in what Jameson called the nightclub uniform of short skirts, backless tank tops, and massively tall stilettos. Seriously, just keep podiatrists and doctors in business with twisted ankles and back problems, girls.

Five young men surrounded them, all jostling for position to separate one girl from the other. The expressions on the girls' faces were a mix of concern and flattery as they tried to sidestep the male barricade without making it seem as if they were running away. Whatever instincts these girls had about not antagonizing the beast while trying to escape were probably spot-on.

"This will be good," Ash said as she reached for the handle of the door.

Jameson stopped her friend with a hand to the shoulder. "I got this, Mike Tyson. You just be the menacing silent presence behind me."

One. Two. Three. Four. She slapped at her pockets and belt.

As she approached the group, one of the men reached for the girl in the center. He wrapped his arm around her waist and hauled her in tight, smothering her with a big open-mouthed kiss as he groped her ass. His friends all hooted and high-fived each other as the girl in his arms struggled to escape.

"Let her go, you jerk," one of her friends said and was blocked by one of the goons from intercepting.

"She said get your hands off her, asshole," Jameson called out.

"Get off me, you creep," the girl said when she managed to free her lips.

"Aw, come on, baby. You been looking at me with those fuck-me eyes all night."

Jameson grabbed the whip attached to her belt and let

the end loose with a snap of her wrist, looping the length around the man's elbow and jerked, pulling him back. The poor girl, now suddenly free, landed on her ass on the sidewalk.

"Sounds like you need your ears checked, buddy. She said let her go," Jameson repeated in a cool, even tone, releasing him from her whip.

"What the fuck is this?" he asked, his lip curled. He shook the arm that she had pulled. "It's too late for Halloween, and frankly, bitch, you're too old to play dress-up."

"Girls, you can leave now," Jameson said.

The other assholes blocked their way.

"They're with us," the lead shitstain said, "and they're doing just fine. Even though you're like my grandmother's age, you can join us, if you want. I like it kinky."

Rage poured through Jameson's blood. It wasn't the digs at her age but the sheer arrogance of entitled white boys that sent fire dancing to her fingertips.

With a flick of her wrist, she snapped the end of her whip against his crotch. The asshole screamed and cupped his groin as he tipped to the side. Before he could collapse, she marched him backward with her hand on his chest until he collided against the wall.

"Apologize to these women," Jameson demanded.

"No way, bitch," the man garbled.

"Always the hard way with boys, isn't it?" She sighed, then hauled back and clocked him right in the face. Again and again she landed several blows. "Apologize."

The man shook his head, which only threw more gasoline on her anger.

"Quit being such an asshat." She punctuated each word

with another punch to his face. "Treat women with respect. The world owes you nothing, you fucktard."

She stepped back and watched with supreme satisfaction as he crumpled to the dirty sidewalk.

Man. What a workout. She turned, panting with the excertion, to see his friends staring at them with their mouths hanging open. Ash had stepped between them and Jameson, creating an impentertable line of defense.

"Apologize," Jameson growled at them, her voice even more guttural.

"Sorry. We're so sorry," the losers muttered toward the girls.

"Ladies," Ash said, adding sweetly, "Do you accept their apology?"

The girls just nodded, clearly dumbfounded about what they just witnessed.

"Then you should be on your way," she said with a flourish of her hand. "However, you jokers also owe an apology to my sister," she added, smacking her fist into her open palm.

"Sorry, miss. We're sorry," they stammered.

Jameson leaned over the leader to admire her fine handiwork as he struggled to a stand.

Holy fuck. A power like no other infused her being, sharpening her senses. Sure, she'd kicked ass before, but this was different. Maybe because her earlier targets were well researched, and this brand of justice was more primal. She was defeating evil with her bare hands. Now. Today.

She was invincible.

The kid was still breathing, and for the most part appeared all right, although he did wobble a little on his feet. Perhaps Ash was right, and Jameson would know how far she could go without killing anybody.

Unfortunately, this event made it clear that the past efforts of the Crimson Angels weren't enough to make an impact. They might have changed the world for a handful of people, but more needed to be done. As long as men went around acting as if women were their possessions, there'd always be a job to do. No rest for the wicked meant no rest for her.

"Let's go, sis," she said to Ash. "We have more work to do tonight."

CHAPTER FIFTEEN

"HOLD YOUR HORSES. I'm coming," Jameson grumbled as she gave the zipper on her hoodie a vicious yank up to her neck.

Whoever was pounding at her door had to be somewhat friendly, otherwise they wouldn't have gotten past Trini. But that didn't mean she was going to greet them with a smile. She had barely crawled into bed and her eyelids had been still fluttering to a close when the incessant knocking began.

She crept up to the door on tiptoes and peered into the peephole. A fish-eyed view showed identical frowns were on the other side.

"Fuck a duck," she groaned and opened the door. "What? Do you have any idea what time it is?"

"Do you?" Ethan asked and stormed past her. "Where the hell have you been? You didn't answer any of our messages."

"Oh, no. No, no, no." She tried to shake her head, but the effort with the lack of sleep made her dizzy. "We went over this last night. We don't do this. You don't get to barge into my space and start yelling at me. My time is my time and none of your business."

"Not this time, wildcat," Ronan replied. His lips were set in a firm line and the grooves around his mouth ran deep. "You've really stepped in it now. Where have you been?"

Ice-cold censure exploded from the brothers, robbing

her breath. She was used to Ethan futzing about everything, but to see Ronan without his carefree smirk and his hard expression made her second-guess whatever snarky comeback was about to pass her lips. It was also at that time she noticed Ethan was dressed in tan slacks and a blue Henley shirt instead of his usual suit and tie and Ronan's eyes were red and weary, his wavy hair swirling in odd directions.

"I was out with friends," she said with a dry throat.

"Who?"

Hey, she was entitled to her privacy. "I'm allowed to see my friends. Just because I fucked you two doesn't mean you're entitled to know my every move."

Ethan's nostrils flared. "Damn it, Jameson. This is important. Where were you?"

Nope. She was not going to play this game. She stomped to the kitchen and set the tea kettle to boil.

"Maybe I can shed some light." A familiar female voice preceded the friendly face of the woman entering her apartment. "Hey, girl."

"Alisia?" Jameson blinked hard. Okay. Maybe she had fallen asleep and this was all a weird dream. Otherwise, why would her friend be standing in her living room at o'God-thirty in the morning with Ethan and Ronan? "Why are you—why—What's going on?"

"I'm here to cordially invite you to meet the rest of the team," she replied, as chipper as she could be.

"The team? Meaning..."

"The Evolutioneers. Our boss would like to meet you," she said in a stilted tone before pasting a big, painful smile on her lips.

"Okay." Jameson pressed the heels of her hands into her

eyes. “I am way too fucking tired for this. Tell him thanks, but we can meet up another time.”

“No can do.” Ronan flopped onto the couch. “I told you, wildcat. You stepped in it good.”

“You went out last night,” Ethan said. The stricken look in his eyes made it appear as if he was the one who was wronged. “You went out and busted heads after you promised not to. Now the police are looking for you for murder.”

“Me? Murder?” She tried to rack her brain. Everyone she interacted with still had a pulse when she left them. “Who?”

“Why do you say that as if it could be more than one person?” he shouted. “And I see you didn’t deny you were out causing trouble.”

“I am neither confirming nor denying anything.”

Alisia stepped between them and held out her hands. “Guys. This is getting us nowhere. James, sweetie, you are not wanted for murder. Yet. However, there were reports last night throughout the greater metropolitan area of a group of women, all dressed in black, beating the shit out of various men. One of those men has died. As well as two other men earlier this week who appeared to have been killed in the same fashion. So while no one is saying you are directly responsible, based on your previous activities, you may have some insight. Perhaps even know who the killer might be.”

“Jameson, please.” Ethan came around the kitchen island and took her by the hand. His anger from a few moments before faded to concern. “I know how you feel when it comes to protecting those you feel are being tormented. It’s the exact same way I feel about you. I want to protect you. Make the bad guys go away so you're left with nothing but happiness. But what's happening out there is getting out of control. If you don't speak to Maestro, the police are going to come and talk to you themselves. I have a feeling it won't be as pleasant."

Was she really surprised the brothers were confronting her about her whereabouts the night before? No. Especially after how she had left things with them.

They had made it no secret about their desire to protect her, just as she had been quite vocal about her independence. They were going to clash, and hard, when it came to her involvement with the Crimson Angels. How much each were willing to bend on the matter was going to be the determining factor on their relationship.

But this latest development regarding the Evolutioneers was troubling. The police were now interested in her activities? Her personally? Yeah. That wasn't good. She thought she and Ashley had covered her tracks and kept their identities safe. But Alisia's appearance and a request to have an audience with the Evolutioneers was throwing her for a loop. Why-oh-why were they involved at all?

However... If an interrogation was to be in her future, a meeting with the Evolutioneers might be good practice. They weren't law enforcement, so anything she said could not be held against her. Right?

"So, when is this party to commence?" she asked, resigned to her fate.

"Now," Ethan replied. "Would you like to change before we go?"

"I'll at least freshen up."

He reached for her hand and placed a kiss on her knuckles. His dark gaze was warm and appreciative as he said, “Thank you.”

“Be right back,” she mumbled, rubbing her palm over the linger heat of his kiss on her fingers. She wasn’t quite ready to forgive him for their previous conversation. It was going to take a few more minutes and a cup or two of coffee before she was near personable status.

Alisia, bristling with all sorts of questions but not saying a word, followed her to her bedroom.

She gestured to her friend open arms. “Out with it.”

Her sister stood there in the doorway for a while with her mouth opening and closing. Finally, she admitted, “I have no idea where to begin.”

“Start with the obvious.”

“So, you and the Daniels brothers,” she exclaimed and flopped belly first on the bed. “How the hell did that happen?”

Jameson shrugged and reached for the jeans from the dresser drawer. “I don’t know. We’ve been working together on some…projects, and things just happened.”

“I’m not surprised you took a liking to them. They’re great guys. But both of them?” she exclaimed with all the scandal such news would garner.

Jameson groaned. “I know. There’s just something, a feeling, I have about them. And there’s this connection between us. I don’t mean with their powers, although their powers do play a huge role in their relationships. It’s almost as if they’re one person. So if you’re with one, you’re going to be with the other in some way, shape, or form.”

“I guess I didn’t think of it that way.” Alisia took a strand of hair in her fingers and began to swirl. “But I meant it. Both are great. And Ethan was beyond amazing helping to sort out the whole thing with my dad’s church. We’d still be there if it wasn't for his help. I'm glad you found them."

"Me too."

And she was. Despite their Neanderthal tendencies, they were decent human beings.

Jameson wrinkled her nose. "Isn't that twisted? The fact that I've found a decent guy to date is a cause for celebration? And by decent I mean kind and compassionate? That should be the norm for everyone, not the exception."

"I totally get you." Alisia laughed. "One day Ripley was with me as I was working on some research with Doc and I figured out one of the formulas. Ripley actually said to me, 'Wow. You're pretty smart.' As if he were delightfully surprised. Why would a demonstration of my intelligence be something that caught him off guard? My intelligence is surprising?"

"I've heard that one before too. It's so condescending in its backhanded way. Like, you finding me smart is supposed to be a compliment?"

"Exactly." Alisia flopped back down on the bed. "It's hard not to take it personally when he was trying to be nice. But I did slap his hand a little. Reminded him that I've always been smart. He's just really slow on the uptake."

You can chitchat in the car. We need to get going, Jameson.

We're coming, we're coming, she replied.

She tugged back on her hoodie. "The boys are getting anxious. I think Ethan is about a burst a vein if I take a second longer."

Alisia blinked, then looked around the room, even checking under the comforter. "Can you read their thoughts as easily as they can read yours?"

"I don't know. Sometimes it feels like there's an open

highway, while other times I need to put in a bit of effort to reach out to them."

She forced her mind to think about all the things she'd rather be doing at that moment and took an old receipt and a pen from her nightstand. Across the back of the paper she wrote: *It's getting harder for me to keep them out. Scary.*

Alisha read her note and asked, "Good scary or bad scary?"

Good question. Jameson shrugged. Truth be told, the jury on that was going to be out for a real long time.

"Guess I'm as ready as I'll ever be." She marched out into the hallway with her chin raised high. Time to start practicing that swagger she was going to need if she was going to walk into a room full of superheroes. "Let's get this show on the road. I have a nap with my name on it in a few hours that I will not miss."

Ted was waiting for them outside, standing next to a black SUV with all the doors open. Alisha jumped in the front passenger seat as Ronan slid into the back. Ethan motioned for her to follow his brother.

"How many cars do you own?" she asked.

"Enough," Ethan replied. "Where we're going, four-wheel drive is more appropriate, and a town car will draw too much attention."

Once everyone was strapped in, Ted took them out of the city and to the freeway, heading east toward the mountains. The ride was quiet. Scary quiet as everyone ruminated with their own thoughts.

Really, what else was there to talk about? Comments on the weather? Shooting the shit about their day at work yesterday?

It was on the tip of her tongue to throw out a topic, any

topic, whatever might break the silence. Especially when each mile down the road left her alone to consider the possible consequences of her actions.

Did she and Ash go too far the night before? At the time she had felt as if they hadn't gone far enough. In the light of day, and under the weight of the disapproving gazes of a certain pair of twin telepaths, perhaps vigilante justice hadn't been the way to go. But if someone didn't take a stand, how was change going to happen?

Doubts and more doubts began to weigh on her as they followed the ribbon of highway deeper into the mountain.

Ronan reached into the pocket behind the driver seat and pulled out a length of black fabric. Holding it in front of her he said, "This isn't meant to be kinky, but we can't let you see where you're going from here. Maestro is very protective of his location."

"Maestro? They're really taking the superhero, codenamed thing seriously, aren't they?"

"If you'd been through what they've been through, you'd be paranoid about your identity too."

"You do have a choice," Ethan said. "Bury your face under my arm and I'll hold you tight, or the blindfold."

"No offense, but I'll take the blindfold." She paused to chew on her lip. "But you can still hold me." It was comforting to know he still wished to show her affection, even though he thought she might be a criminal.

Ronan kissed her cheek, then tied the blindfold around her as she settled back against Ethan's chest and he put his arms around her.

Damn. Why hadn't she realized I-90 was so twisty? Perhaps she should've just stuck her nose under Ethan's armpit. The twists and turns of the mountain pass were starting to make her dizzy with the loss of her sight.

Just as she was about to lose what little contents she had in her stomach, the car slowed and turned off the smooth pavement and onto rockier terrain. They bumped and jostled for a few more minutes before the road smoothed out again. A while later, they came to a stop.

"Not just yet, wildcat." Ronan brushed his hands against hers to stop her from taking off her mask the moment Ted turned off the car. "We're not there yet."

"For real?"

"For real. Mostly for privacy. And I wouldn't discount that it's also a form of intimidation. Here, I'll help you out." Ethan took her arms to help guide her out of the car.

Okay, Alinari. Use your senses. There was a chill in the air, and the scent of damp earth, moss, and the overwhelming scent of evergreen trees stung her lungs as she drew in a breath. A few small birds twittered overhead. It was a cool morning. Misty. And she could feel the condensation begin to collect on her skin.

Okay. Well, first off, you're in the woods, obviously.

Ethan placed her hands on his shoulders while Ronan took her hips in his hands from behind. Was this for her safety, or because wherever they were leading was so narrow, they had to file in as a single line?

Great. Now she had images of them taking her straight into the mountain through a tiny fissure in the rock.

Of all the things in her life she had experienced, this was the freakiest. At least when she was little and made to sit in that closet, she knew what was on the other side of the door. The coats, and shoes, and the other children inside the closet with her were familiar. She had been blinded but she had not been without sight.

This was unknown territory. Literally. And she was reliant on people who might be walking her to her doom. Alisia would have her back, of that there was no doubt. The brothers, however, had a strong moral compass, and although they claimed to care for her, if a line was drawn between right and wrong, or they were faced with having to turn her over to the authorities, they might very well find themselves on opposite sides of the divide.

A series of beeps preceded the whoosh of a massive lock springing open. The floor beneath her feet was solid, but slightly uneven like rock, and their footsteps clicked as they marched down the hallway. Central air kicked in, sending shivers across the back of her neck.

A few more twists and turns later, they paused. Over the rush of blood in her ears, she heard more beeps and another whoosh and squeak of a door opening.

"Here you go, sweetheart." Ethan removed the blindfold.

Spots floated in her vision as darkness gave way to not-so-much darkness.

Holy...shit.

Did she walk onto a movie set? For real, one of the walls was covered with television screens and monitors of various sizes. Computers and laptops covered almost every flat surface, and a smart screen took up an entire wall. There were maps, lights, pictures of people flashing and scrolling across the screens.

"Are we in the Batcave?"

"Close enough," Ronan answered.

Somewhere along the journey they had lost Alisia, but some faces, both familiar and strange, had joined them.

There was a command central section of the room with

a long table in front of the largest screen. By the table stood Sheriff Lancaster. He was a solid block of a man with the prerequisite square jaw, crewcut blond hair and piercing blue eyes. From the hard line of his lips to the crisp pleats of his pants, everything about him was stern.

Beside him was a young woman in braids wearing a pair of black sunglasses that matched her black T-shirt and jeans.

Joining them was another man also dressed in the all-black and sunglassed ensemble worn by the Evolutioneers. His expression was almost as firm and menacing as the sheriff's, and with his pale skin he could have been made of marble.

The last person in the room was a hunky slab of a man. His blond shaggy hair almost brushed his broad shoulders, and the muscles stretched his T-shirt where he had his arms folded across his chest. Apparently hooking up with her best friend did the man some good. He appeared more content, although he was still as foreboding as the first time they had crossed paths.

"Beast man," Jameson said, popping a hand on her hip and giving Alisia's boyfriend a side-eyed glance.

He nodded in greeting. "Devil woman."

She smiled wide. That was right. She hadn't allowed the big bad shape-shifter to intimidate her then. No way was she going to be intimidated now.

"No disguise for you?"

He shrugged. "Why bother? You already know what I look like."

"True."

The tall dark stranger stepped forward and held out his hand. "Ms. Alinari. Thank you for joining us. My name is Maestro."

Huh. So this was the infamous Maestro. Kinda goth. Kinda Neo. He wasn't beefy, like Ripley, and based on all this swag, he had to be intelligent. And hella rich! But was that all he had to offer? Why did the others follow him?

She considered the hand he held out. The Evolutioneers were so secretive, the only reason she knew as much about them as she did was because of Alisia. Did he have powers too, or was his wealth his strength? And if he did have powers, what could those be?

It killed her to show any sign of weakness, but better safe than sorry.

She turned his handshake into a fist bump for minimum contact. "Thank you for having me. If I'd had more warning, I would have brought a bottle of wine or a cheese platter with me."

"Ms. Alinari," Sheriff Lancaster said. "I've asked you to be here to assist with a string of cases I believe to be connected. You've had interactions, even if by proxy, with a few of the victims. You may have some insight we're missing."

"Why here? If asked nicely, I could've come down to the station. Kidnapping was not required."

He raised his brow at the twins. "No, kidnapping was not required. Maestro and his team are acting as consultants. As you can imagine, their equipment is more updated than what has been provided by our generous taxpayers."

And if she hazarded a guess, police procedures could get a little blurry away from official oversight.

"In what capacity am I being questioned? The boys here made it seem as if I'm being considered a suspect. I'd like to have my lawyer present."

"You're not a suspect," he said, although she swore she

saw the word "yet" hovering in his eyes. "Just a potential witness."

"Without my lawyer present, you can ask your questions. Doesn't mean I'll answer."

"How about we start by taking a look at this video. Please, Network." He nodded at the blonde by his side who clicked a few keys on the keyboard. A video appeared on the glass wall.

The footage, taken at night, was dark and grainy, as most security cameras tended to record. But even with the dim light, Jameson easily recognized the location of the street and the people on the sidewalk.

Yep. There they were. Three girls trying to shake their male admirers and the main douche canoe reaching out for the tall blonde. Out of nowhere, two figures dressed in black appeared to save the day.

Truth be told, she looked pretty badass kicking the crap out of that loser. Even better than a hero out of an action movie. If she hadn't been flanked by the telepathic twins, she'd have enjoyed the video with greater gusto.

Fortunately, her face was covered in the video and mostly in shadow. There was no way anyone could identify her by that video alone.

Sheriff Lancaster turned toward her when the clip was over. "What do you think of that?"

She drew in a breath, carefully considering her words. "Looks like the guy had it coming."

The sheriff grunted. "Perhaps. As you can see, without positive identification from any of the witnesses, we can't tell who these women are."

Damn straight.

"And the light over the license plate was out, so the

plate wasn't readable."

"Uh," was all she said, careful to give nothing away.

Her team wasn't as financially solvent as the Evolutioneers, but they weren't without some type of tech. Trini wired the license plate light to turn off and on with a push of a button. Before she even left her car, she made sure the plates couldn't be easily seen and identified later.

"Network, next set of pics please," Lancaster continued with a heavy sigh, taking a seat next to Network. "Does this gentleman look familiar?"

Well, well, well. A set of pictures of Ahmed Dara came on the screen. The images of his face from various angles resembled a mug shot, but they were probably taken in a hospital. In the harsh light of a camera flash, the bruises and cuts on his face were bold and violent in color. Shit. Ashley did a number on his face.

She squinted at the screen and the picture of his profile. It looked as if his ear had been chewed off. Did that son of a bitch actually try to dig the "tracker" out of his ear? Ash was going to laugh her ass off.

Jameson shrugged, making sure her mind was as blank as her expression. "Is there a reason he should look familiar?"

"His name is Ahmed Dara. His wife and daughter have been in and out of the doctor's office with bruises and contusions for years. Abuse has been suspected, but the wife refuses to say anything negative." The hard purse of his lips gave away his feelings on that matter. "Last night, neighbors called the authorities about a commotion at the Dara house. Mr. Dara was in his backyard howling in pain, which in turn terrified his son, who began screaming his head off and ran outside. When police arrived, it looked like Mr. Dara was trying to dig his brain out through his ear. His story was that a couple of thieves, females dressed in black, broke in, roughed him up, and planted something in his ear."

"Jesus," Ripley said. "Why would someone do that?"

"We don't think that's how it went down. There was no sign of forced entry, and nothing was taken. Not even disturbed. The wife tried to corroborate her husband's story, but it didn't make sense at all when she tried to explain where she and the children were the entire time. I think he told her what to say. However, if two women did attack him, on the very same night as the altercation outside Jersey's Nightclub, it's possible they are somehow related."

With a nod from the sheriff, Network brought up another set of images. This time Jameson was more than familiar with the subject matter, and the sheriff probably already knew it.

"Good God," Ripley exclaimed. "What happened to him?"

"You're familiar with this man, right, Ms. Alinari?" the sheriff asked.

"Gerald Mulvaney. I spoke with Detective Sanchez about him last week."

Lancaster nodded and gestured for another set of pictures. A wood-framed bed, bare mattress, knocked-over lamps. She knew that room. These were of the crime scene of Travis Fitzherbert.

Jameson tried hard not to twitch. She stared at the photos for a while, then at Lancaster and shrugged. He gestured to another set of pictures.

Thank God. Someone she honestly didn't have a clue as to who it was. This gentleman had been laid out on the floor naked, his hands out on either side and the word "RAPIST" carved into his belly. The imagery was gruesome, which tempered her relief at not knowing who this man was.

"Next, please," Lancaster said, and another set of pictures came up.

And then another. Each one of a man murdered with "RAPIST" or "ABUSER" carved across their bodies somehow.

Ripley swallowed a curse and rubbed his hand over his face, shifting his body weight from one foot to the other. Maestro looked a little paler and even the Daniels brothers appeared to grow increasingly tense with each set.

Another set of photos appeared, and at those Jameson startled in surprise. "Wait. I know this man. I've never met him, but I've seen his face. How do I know him?"

"Jay Hopkins," Network answered. The slight sneer in her voice tipped Jameson off.

"Oh yeah. He's that guy in Idaho who kidnapped that fourteen-year-old, married her, and raped her. Even though he was convicted, the judge sentenced him only to time served from arrest to trial. He was released last week, right? What an asshole." Jameson then asked, "He was killed in Washington state?"

Lancaster shook his head. "No. Boise. But his body was found in a similar fashion. Tied up with 'RAPIST' carved across his abdomen. And he was left physically mutilated."

"Yeah. They cut off his dick." Network tried to stifle a snicker.

Jameson wasn't as polite. "That's awesome."

"That's a horrible thing to say," Maestro said with a look of disgust. "He might have been a bad guy, but that doesn't mean he needed to be mutilated."

"Says the man who literally pummeled another man

into the ground," Ripley muttered.

"Are you kidding?" Jameson exclaimed. "That's called justice was served. Justice that the law did not give to that poor girl. Imagine how mutilated her mind must be. Her soul. For the rest of her life. I think he got off easy."

"Jameson," Ethan said with a hint of warning.

"What? What are we doing here? You said you had questions for me, but so far all you've done is show me a bunch of jackasses who got what they deserved. You want to find out who did these 'crimes,' fine. But if you ask me, I think it was karma that bit them in the ass. And it was about damn time."

"Vigilantism is against the law," Lancaster barked. "This is vigilantism at its worst."

"Looks like someone is doing your job, Sheriff," she shot back, then waved her hands. "I know, I know. It's not you, it's the system. I know the statistics. Come on, say them with me. The percentage of sex crime cases in this country that go to trial is what again? That's right. Four percent. And how many of those end in a conviction? Right, three percent. And what about Portia Ackley?"

Lancaster sucked in his lips and looked away. His nostrils flared in time with her racing heart. Ah, was the little sheriff going to pout now? Did she strike a nerve?

"Fine. I'll ask," Ripley said when nothing further was forthcoming. "Who's Portia Ackley?"

"She was an officer."

"Detective," Lancaster interrupted. "And a damn good one."

"She worked the domestic violence unit before Detective Sanchez," Jameson continued, finding it difficult to talk about her friend after all these years. "How long was she in that unit? Eight years? Way longer than she needed to. But she was a warrior. Fought her cases hard. She had the highest conviction rate of anyone before or after her. Can you believe that? At barely four percent she had the highest conviction rate." Tears stung her eyes and her voice escalated as she aimed her frustration at the sheriff. "Eight years she worked herself into exhaustion time and time again, only for the criminals to get off on a technicality. It was only a matter of time before she decided to end her life."

"Ackley knew it was a tough job," Lancaster said with a rasp in his timber. "She could've transferred out after four years."

"As if that would've helped. That life never leaves you. You don't just walk away from domestic violence. It eats at your soul until there is nothing left."

"You think I don't know that?" the sheriff barked. "I know. Believe me. The shit I've seen…" His hand shook as he scrubbed angrily at his jaw. "Believe me. I know."

"I think you forget how others cope," she replied softly.

Portia Ackley's suicide had laid Jameson flat for a long, long time. It had been Ackley, who at the time was a patrol cop, who had arrived on the scene for one of the worst moments of Jameson's young life. Ackley who had kept in touch before, during, and after the case. And it had been Ackley who told her not to go into law enforcement. Who encouraged her to follow her mother's path and leave the hunting of criminals to her.

"Don't worry, little sister," she'd say. "Let me take care of finding the bad guys. You've had enough time spent in darkness. You fill your world with sunshine and lollipops."

So while Jameson soaked in as much brilliant light as she could muster, Ackley fell farther and farther into the dark. Fell so far, she was never able to crawl out.

"I understand," Jameson said, choking down years of frustration. "You've got a lot of responsibilities, and you can't be everywhere at once. But we live in a time where people are tired. Women are tired. And they're done waiting for that knight in a blue suit with a shiny badge to come help them."

"Still doesn't make it right." He shook his head and leaned forward in his seat. "You're frustrated. Everyone today is frustrated. There is a right way and a wrong way to seek justice. Vigilantism is not the answer," he directed the last part toward Maestro. "Ms. Alinari, I can understand how you may feel that these men got what was coming to them, but they were murdered. Murdered and mutilated. That's not right. There are other ways to combat assault and domestic violence." He folded his hands in his lap. "I know about you and your team, your Angels I've heard people call them, out at night getting people off the streets. You are doing right by finding those in need. Giving them shelter, providing a haven. We need more of that. More education on how to get out of or avoid harmful relationships. Awareness of the assistance that is available. Torture like this is not the way."

Jameson crossed her arms over her chest. "Right. Instead of making an example and punishing the bullies and the violators, you are putting the onus on the victims. It's always 'Here's how to avoid being harmed,' never 'Don't hurt people in the first place, asshole.' No one should have to take precaution from being harassed or abused. Stop the abusers."

"You may think these actions are noble, but whoever is doing it are criminals, and it is my job to put criminals away."

Jameson snorted. She knew the real deal. It was his job to *try* to bring the criminals to trial. Then it was up to a system that was corrupt to the very core to finish the job.

"I don't know what you want from me, Sheriff. I don't know who is committing these murders. It seems to me that they all have a connection to violence against women in some way shape or form, and I can tell you that every single woman who comes through my shelters has experienced that violence. My guess, each of these victims," she said, using air quotes, "has a list of enemies as long as my dick. Good luck trying to find them."

A flash of steel flared in his blue eyes. "Ms. Alinari—"

Lancaster's radio squawked on his shoulder.

"1042. Come in, 1042. Urgent."

"One minute. I'll call in. What extension?" he replied into the handset.

"6892."

"10-4." He stood and motioned at them all. "No one move. We're not done."

He may not have been done, but she was. After the night before, her energy reserves were depleted. As it was, it was taking everything within her to keep the twins out of her thoughts while paying attention to what the sheriff was saying.

The thread between her and those murders was short. Too short for comfort. If the sheriff was able to pin the fight outside the nightclub on her, it would be all too easy to link her to Mulvaney and then the rest of the murders.

Fuck. This was bad. How the hell was she going to get out of this one?

CHAPTER SIXTEEN

As Lancaster stepped away from the group to make his call, Ethan's presence loomed behind her like a heavy wool cloak. The heat of his palm grew closer as he reached for her shoulder, but she moved away from the touch.

Jameson. Please, he implored.

Not now. I can't believe I'm here. You think I killed those men.

I don't. We *don't. In fact, what the sheriff* didn't *tell you was that at least one of those men were murdered down in Portland the night we met to talk about Mulvaney. If worse comes to worst, you'll have us as an alibi.*

Wait, you knew that already? She turned to glare at him with wide eyes. *And you didn't tell me?*

We were going to, but then you wanted to have a nice dinner. No talk of death. We had great sex. And then you got mad and stormed off.

Ethan—

I know. I know. But look, we also know you're not entirely innocent. And you're not a lone wolf in your crusade.

You know nothing. *Just leave me alone.*

Not going to happen, wildcat, Ronan replied. *We care about you. That's not going to stop because you ask.*

She huffed out a breath. Was this what unconditional support from someone other than a family member felt like?

Her sisters in arms had always been there for her, but this energy was male and romantically charged. Totally different. How was she supposed to handle it?

Ethan approached her again on her right and tried to slip his hand along her lower back. She edged away from his touch. The only thing she wanted at that moment was to be left alone.

"Dude. Don't," she warned, making sure her tone could no way be misinterpreted.

"Please, Jameson," he said. "Don't be angry."

"You don't get to tell me how I feel. Especially when you were the ones who brought me here."

We had to. The sheriff didn't give us much choice once he suspected the Crimson Angels might be involved. You all are starting to develop a reputation. The image in that one video is murky enough that he can't officially charge you, but he's desperate for a lead and he's convinced you know something.

"I don't care," she said out loud as her knees threatened to buckle and her chest grew tight.

"I know. And that terrifies me," he admitted quietly in her ear. "The world as we know it is teetering on the edge of chaos every second. But there has to be another way to make things better. I wish you would let us help you find another way."

"I'm not asking for anything."

"I know you're not. But I wish you would."

Lancaster bit out a curse from the corner of the room that made them all turn in his direction. The rest of his conversation was muffled, but his gravelly tone was filled with frustration. He ended his call and stood with his shoulders in a tight line and his head lowered.

For several seconds there was only the sound of his

harsh breathing as he tried to rein in the emotions the phone call had caused. With a final deep breath, he turned toward the group. "Looks like we're going to have to postpone this conversation. Another body was found yesterday. They were posed in the same fashion as these other men. Forensics has started getting more data that is requiring my attention. Maestro, can you come with me? I'd like your input on a few things."

"Sure thing, Sheriff."

Lancaster turned toward the exit but paused with a last pointed look in her direction. "I'll be in touch, Ms. Alinari."

No shit, she wanted to say, but she flashed him a wave and a smile. "Looking forward to it, Sheriff."

If she had been alone, she would have crumpled to the floor as soon as the sheriff and Maestro left the room. She was spent, but in no way would she show weakness. Instead, she closed her eyes and wrapped her arms around her middle. Bring on the blindfold. Let's blow this pop stand.

"Are we going now?" she asked, ready to be done with the day and crawl back into bed for the foreseeable future.

"Hold tight," Ronan murmured next to her. His gaze was focused intently on Ripley, who jumped to Network's side as soon as Maestro and Lancaster left the room.

"Have it yet?" Ripley asked Network.

"I'm getting there," she replied. "Give me a moment."

Her fingers flew over the keyboard and several windows popped up on the screen then disappeared faster than Jameson's mind could register.

"Hold the phone," Jameson said in awe as she recognized some of the data. "Is that the police database?"

Everyone remained silent but flashed her massive grins.

"Here we go, here we go, here we go," Network crowed.

"And *bam*."

"Ah, Jesus," they all groaned and looked away from the screen.

Yeah. A bit of warning that a group of gruesome crime scene photos in all their Technicolor glory were going to be displayed on a ten-foot wall would've been helpful.

Ripley pointed to the screen. "Why does his face look familiar?"

"It's a congressman." Network used her mouse to highlight information on a police report. "Representative Wilson Dominguez."

"That's the asshat from the east side of the state who's trying to block gay marriage and proposed to take away the state's sanctuary status from those seeking asylum," Jameson said. "I hate that guy."

"Ah, yeah. That's it. I remember seeing his picture on billboards when Alisia and I were up at the church. Looks like he was found yesterday at a private room at a nail salon downtown. A nail salon?" Ripley asked in confusion.

"Not just any salon," Network brought up more information on the screen. "This one has been suspected of human trafficking. Bringing in girls on work visas, then taking away their passports so they're trapped and helpless."

"And this dude was found naked, tortured, and dead." Ripley shook his head. "What the fuck? And what was he doing in the city, anyway?"

Ethan snapped his fingers then pointed at two of the photos on one of the screens. "That's it. That man there, Salanger, and that one there. See here, they both work for the Department of Commerce. I bet they're here for the World Trade Organization summit next week. That's probably why Dominguez was in town as well. It's been twenty years since the riots of the last WTO summit were held in the city. The event is supposed to be a milestone in showing how far the world has come to become one marketplace."

"I remember seeing that on the news when I was a kid." Ripley's eyes glazed over with thoughts from the past. "Scared the shit out of me, seeing dumb assholes take advantage of the chaos and destroy innocent people's businesses. Places that my parents took me to on special trips to the city. Was never so glad to live out in the suburbs. Way, way, way out in the suburbs. Little did I know that was just a taste of what happens in other cities."

"That's also why the sheriff is eager to solve these murders," Ethan said. "Doesn't look good to have the eyes of the world looking down on him as politicians turn up mutilated."

"Did you read his mind, or is that conjecture?" Jameson asked.

"Just trying to put all the pieces together," he replied, not looking the least bit apologetic.

"What is this?" Network zoomed on a document. "Suspected cause of death is asphyxiation, but they can't yet determine how. Apparently, something was jammed down his throat."

"Something?" Ripley asked with a shudder. "After seeing those pictures, that sounds terrifying."

"Yeah," Network muttered. "Report says organic material. What the hell does that mean?"

"A uterus," the twins said in unison.

Ripley's eyes widened in horror as he gagged. "I'm sorry. But you said a uterus?"

"Yep," Ronan replied. His mouth worked as if he could

taste the acrid flavor of the words. "It was part of the call the sheriff just took. They're not 100 percent certain, but based on the shape, they think it's some sort of animal organ, more than likely the uterus from a pig or sheep."

"That is amazeballs," Jameson sputtered, unable to hold back her laughter.

Ripley hugged his belly. "That's just…that's just nasty. Where do people come up with this shit?"

"That is pretty badass," Network said with a little grin. She continued typing on the keyboard, looking for more information. "Can you imagine? Not only touching it but shoving it down someone's throat? Choke on this," she said with a sneer as she used her hand to imitate shoving something into a hole created with the fingers of her other hand.

Jameson's laughter turned into a gasp that burned her throat as a memory popped into her head.

Nooooo… It had to be a coincidence. It wasn't possible.

"Jameson? Are you okay?" Ethan asked, placing a steadying hand on her back as she wheezed. "What's not possible?"

She shook her head. "Nothing. It's just, what Network said reminded me of something I heard a friend say. It's like stupid crap men say. You know, like eat my dick, or suck it when they grab at their crotch."

Ethan and Ronan shared a look between them before Ethan pulled her gently against his side. "And why did that bother you so much?"

For a moment she pondered whether to speak the words out loud. On the one hand the notion was ridiculous. Probably meant nothing in the long run, and she was being silly. Then again, look at where she was. She was sitting smack-dab at the command center for Ridiculous City with telepathic twins, a shape-shifter, and a woman whom she suspected was part computer.

Jameson shook her head again and shrugged. She was probably freaking out for no reason. "I have a friend. One of her favorite comebacks is to tell people she doesn't like to choke on her pussy. Well now, here's a big-time abuser who was literally choked by a pussy. I just find that a strange coincidence."

"Maybe too much of a coincidence?" Ethan asked. "Is this friend one of your Crimson Angels?"

"Maybe." She took a step away from Ethan's closeness. His sudden interest pricked at her as if she grabbed a hold of a spiny cactus. "Maybe."

Ethan continued to press her. "Does this friend happen to have a grudge against accused pedophiles, rapists, and other bad guys?"

Was he fucking serious? "She's a friend of mine. Of course she does. Besides, as a female we all have a grudge against abusers, rapists, and other bad guys. So should the rest of humanity."

"Good point. But has your friend actually taken measures against those types of people?"

"By measures if you mean possibly knocking a head or two together, then yes," she drew out, exaggerating the sibilant.

"And would your friend have access to weapons, guns, training on how to torture people?"

Jameson rolled her eyes. "Again, with the internet and this country's horribly lax gun laws, everyone has access to those things."

"Is this your friend that you said was in the Army?"

Ronan asked. Sudden excitement buzzed through him as if he had touched a live wire.

"Yes, why…" She trailed off as the brothers surrounded Network to lean over her shoulder.

"What is her name?" Ronan asked. "Your friend?"

"I don't know what you're getting at." Sweat broke out over Jameson's lips and her ears became itchy.

"Wildcat, if your friend was in the Army, it's possible she knew Fitzherbert, or anyone else who has turned up dead recently."

"You two think she might be the killer."

He took her hand between his and flashed a kind smile. "We know you how much you protect your friends, Jameson. If she's innocent and gets wrapped up in all this like you, we can help protect her."

"Network can do a quick search. If everything checks out, then your friend has nothing to worry about," Ethan added.

Dammit. There he was, being all logical again.

This was ridiculous. There shouldn't be anything to worry about, period. Ash might get a little overzealous at times, the beatdown she laid on Ahmed Dara the night before notwithstanding, but she wouldn't do anything extreme.

For all the bravado she tried to muster, Jameson's stomach roiled, remembering the gleam in Ash's eyes as she landed punch after punch on Dara's face.

"Ashley," she said quietly, with a rasp in her voice. "Ashley Fairfield."

Network began to type. "How old is she? Do you know her birthday?"

Jameson shook her head. "She's about twenty-seven,

twenty-eight. I don't know her birthday, exactly. I think it's sometime in the spring. April, maybe. Some of us went to a baseball game to celebrate."

"Do you know where she was born?"

"Somewhere on the West Coast. Oregon, or northern California." Geez, she really didn't know her friend as well as she thought she did, huh?

"That'll give me something to work with. Not much. But something," Network said and continued to type.

The images on the screen moved and flashed faster as her fingers flew, which made Jameson wonder exactly how her powers worked. Was she controlling the information with the touch of her fingers, or was she more like the twins and could control the internet with her mind?

We have no idea how she does it, Ronan said. *We're just really glad she's on our team and doesn't work for some foreign government using our networks and databases against us.*

Do you think there are others? she asked. *Others who have powers like you all out there in the world, perhaps doing evil instead of good?*

Possibly. More than likely probable. And something I really don't want to think about, considering how difficult it is managing the few of us that we know of. Guess we'll jump that hurdle when we get to it.

True. Better to deal with the devil in front of you than that which is unknown and, hope to God, wasn't even real.

Network whooped and began typing faster, if that was even possible. "I found something. It's heavily redacted and behind a firewall. Give me a second."

It was as if a bag of snakes was let loose in Jameson's stomach. She crossed her arms over her waist in a vain attempt to quell her queasiness.

"Now this is interesting," Network muttered and began to throw a series of images on the giant screen before them, including a photograph. "Is this your friend Ashley?"

Jameson's mouth filled with bitter saliva as she snapped her teeth together. She wanted to say no, but there was no use in lying.

The funny thing was the girl in the photo was and yet wasn't her friend. Sure, the eyes were the same, same jawline, same skin and hair. But the girl in the photo who was dressed in her military finery posed with square shoulders and a proud lift to her chin. This was a girl who looked honored to wear the uniform and serve her country.

Somewhere, somehow that pride had changed, become twisted and dark. The Ashley that Jameson knew wore her pride like a battle scar. It was a badge earned with blood and sweat and of surviving hell. The steel in her spine was admirable while also tragic for what she had endured.

"Okay. So this is what I've got." Network broke through Jameson's maudlin thoughts and began to highlight images on the screen, including drafts of redacted documents and photos, including Travis Fitzherbert. "Apparently your friend Ashley was part of a group of four women in her unit who had filed sexual harassment charges against Fitzherbert. The charges ranged anywhere from verbal harassment to rape. The events themselves took place both in Afghanistan and at Fort Benning in Georgia. Their complaints were ignored until good ol' Trav harassed some local girls near their base in Afghanistan. One of the girls was the daughter of the clan chief they were working with to battle the insurgents. As you can imagine, the higher-ups put a stop to that immediately. Otherwise, their asses would've been left to hang out in the desert."

"He sounds like a real peach of a guy," Ronan spat.

"But check out this bullshit. Instead of punishing Fitzherbert, he was moved to another unit. Not only that, the girls who had filed the complaints were sent back home and discharged with false medical reasons to keep them quiet."

"So the Army covered their asses instead of taking out the dickwad who couldn't keep it in his pants. Great," Ripley muttered, and the muscles in his biceps and forearms twitched as if he wanted to pound his fists in the face of Fitzherbert personally.

Network snorted. "What? The military covering up a potentially embarrassing situation? So unheard of," she finished with a roll of her eyes. "But if Fitzherbert did assault your friend Ashley, it gives her one helluva motive to retaliate."

"Yeah." Jameson swallowed the bile burning in her throat. "I caught on to that."

"Any idea of where she is now?" Ethan placed his hand on her back. The weight and steadiness of his touch gave off waves of comfort.

"Sometimes she works at the sporting-goods store over on Plemons. Usually it's a swing shift, since we're out late sometimes and she works part time at a day shelter near the university."

"Do you know where she lives? Maybe we can check out her place while she's at work."

"We are not going to break in and enter my friend's home," Jameson exclaimed. "I will schedule a meeting with her where we can talk. Maybe she'll give up something. Maybe everything is fine, and she hasn't been anywhere near these dead guys. As long as there is a possibility that she's innocent, you will not break into her home."

"Fair enough," Ethan said. "But you're not meeting with her alone. If she does have something to do with these murders, she may feel cornered and lash out. Even though she is your friend," he added, seeing her gear up to argue. "You only know what you do about her based on what she told you. Who knows what secrets she may be hiding that are festering, waiting to find an outlet. I can't let you put yourself in danger."

"She won't hurt me."

"I don't know that. And we can't trust that she won't. Look, we don't have to physically be by your side, but you are not going alone."

"Think of when you have someone in your shelter that you know is returning to a potentially dangerous situation," Ronan said. "How many times did you wish they didn't go by themselves and had someone with them to watch their back?"

She snapped her teeth together and growled.

"I know, I know," he said with a smile. "Logical."

"Okay," she said with a sigh. No use in being stubborn when they were right. "Give me a minute to give her a call, see if she's home. We can do a quick run by her place, but that's it."

"Sounds like a plan," Ripley said. "We'll go with you."

"What? No," Jameson exclaimed. "We're keeping this simple. This is not one of your missions."

"Believe me. I've been doing this long enough to know that at any second the non-mission becomes a mission." He strode toward the door. "Let me see what kind of tech we have on hand to outfit us with. We can't all rely on telepathic powers for communication."

"It'll be fine," Network said with a grin, pushing her glasses higher on her nose. "Alisia and I can monitor things from back here. And it's like what everyone said earlier. Even if your friend has a connection with Fitz what's-his-name, that doesn't mean she was involved with his murder. For all we know, the killer might be one of the other girls who was in her unit. Oh!" Her eyes widened then she turned back to the keyboard. "I'll follow up on those leads too."

Ronan leaned over the woman's monitor as she worked. "Hey, Network. Think we can get Prism to give us any insights as to what will happen next?"

Networked snorted again without looking up from her screen. "You're funny. Of course she won't. The only thing she has said since Lancaster called for assistance was to bring her in," she nodded in Jameson's direction. "That was it."

"Give her my thanks," Jameson said, not the least bit thankful.

How much help would a psychic be anyway? At this point it felt as if Jameson's world was on the end of a lit fuse that was getting shorter by the second. Somehow, this case was going to blow open. And soon. When it did, Jameson had no doubt she was going to be burned.

CHAPTER SEVENTEEN

ETHAN GLANCED OVER at Ronan, who nodded at him once. Then he turned his attention to Network, who was typing furiously at her keyboard.

Addison, can you leave us alone for a few minutes to talk to Jameson?

She turned to glower at him over her shoulder. *You want me to leave you alone in* my *communications room?* Her incredulous tone carried across in her response.

Please. Just for a minute.

Network heaved a sigh then stood. "I'm going to, uh, help Ripley with something. I'll only be a few minutes. I could be back at any second," she finished with a pointed glare in his direction.

As soon as she left the room, he pulled over a chair. "Jameson, how are you holding up?"

"I'm not sure, to be honest."

Her coloring was paler than normal, and her shoulders shook with fine tremors. He didn't think she could cross her arms any more firmly over her chest before her bones snapped, she was so tense.

"Have a seat for a moment, please."

"I'm fine. Thank you," she said with a determined lift of her chin.

"I know. It's been a long morning already. And there's something we'd like to say."

"What's there to say? You two pretty much made your opinions clear last night. I don't think we have anything more to talk about."

Ethan groaned and rubbed his hand over his face. "We do."

"We're sorry," Ronan said, cutting to the heart of the matter. "We're sorry about last night and what we said. Of course you're free to hang out with whomever you want. And you're close to your friends, we know that. What we were trying to convey came out wrong. All wrong."

"We worry about you. As long as there's somebody running around slicing men open, and you could be implicated in those deaths, we're going to worry about you. But it was wrong for us to make demands on your time," Ethan finished.

Her gaze bounced back and forth between the two of them before she sighed and sank onto the chair. "I can understand why you may be concerned. That was some heavy shit the sheriff just laid on us."

Ronan pulled up a chair beside her. "And we did not want to kidnap you. We got a call from Maestro this morning. The sheriff had contacted him with the photos and the videos he just showed us. When the team saw the video outside of that nightclub, apparently Ripley made some offhanded comment of how the figure looked like Alisia's friend. When the sheriff asked him to be more specific, that's when your name was mentioned. Lancaster is desperate for a solid lead and jumped on your name immediately. That's when Alisia called us. She thought you might be more willing to come if you had a friendly face."

Jameson nodded and her gaze swept up to the monitors where pictures of the victims and her friend Ashley were still on display. Her gaze appeared to lose focus as she went to who knew where.

Ethan was dying to read her thoughts but didn't dare. Over the last twelve hours, her trust with them was already razor-thin. Nothing would make him cross that line.

So he waited. Ronan waited. Their patience stretched to the point that any morsel of contact made them shake in anticipation.

"I'm tired," she finally said with an exhaustion so far beyond her simple words. "I'm tired of being angry. And I am angry *all the time.* Just when I think this world is starting to pull itself together, some entitled man rears his ugly head and fucks up somebody's world because he can."

A hysterical chuckle eased past her lips as she continued to gaze into the unknown. The crackling sound made Ethan share a look with his brother. Their girl was in trouble.

"All I have to do is hear that voice," she continued. "That tone of entitlement and I see red. It's so weird. It's like a Pavlovian response. I hear it and my body goes into fight mode."

She gazed down at her hands and curled and uncurled her fists, slowly flexing her fingers.

"Last night," she whispered. "Last night wasn't meant to go down like that. But that ass was preying on those girls. Swinging his dick as if it were his right. When I slapped that smirk off that motherfucker's face…the power was incredible. I was making a difference. I saw it. I felt it. I never felt so in control." A tear slipped down her cheek. A tear she probably didn't notice and would deny with her last breath she ever shed. "And so out of control. I just want it to stop. I want the hurting to stop."

"We're working on it, wildcat. Somehow, we'll make a

difference. You, me, and Ethan. And the hurting will stop. I don't know when, but we'll get there." Ronan scooped her up in his arms and slid her into his lap, holding her as she shook.

Ethan watched the woman he'd come to love teetering on the edge of right and wrong, of good and evil. She fought for justice, but her methods were going to land her in jail or get her killed some day.

As she struggled to hold on, Ronan fed her strength and calmness while Ethan's senses fired and his mind calmed and readied for battle.

The irony of the situation was not lost on him. It appeared the more out of control Jameson became, the more in control he became of his powers. She was the yin to his yang. Together, they needed to find balance.

His gaze met Ronan's and he knew immediately they had the same mission. Protect Jameson at all costs. Even if it was from herself.

CHAPTER EIGHTEEN

WHY DID SHE let them talk her into this?

Because deep down you're a chickenshit who's afraid Ashley is involved in the murders and it's easier to rifle through her things than confront her in person?

Yeah. Maybe. It was a pretty good reason.

If she were to be questioned, she'd try to claim the boys bullied her into breaking into Ash's apartment, but deep down, she knew the truth. Knew it the minute they knocked on Ash's door and nothing but silence greeted them.

"We're here," Ethan had said. "We can be in and out, and if everything checks out, Ashley will never know."

"She'll know," Jameson told them. "She's just like me when it comes to her place. She'll know someone was inside."

"But we have super powers. And super gadgets. We can cover our tracks."

"She may come back any minute," Jameson pointed out. "Then what?"

Ronan tapped at the sunglasses perched on his nose. "She won't. Network logged into the security cameras where Ashley works, and I can see her there." He turned toward his brother. "By the way, these are awesome. How do we get in on this tech?"

"We kiss Maestro's ass. I'm digging this little guy, too." He placed a black disk with a little spike in the middle against the locks on the door. With a touch of a button, the disk whirled and unlocked the mechanism. "Man, she has a lot of locks."

"She's a paranoid girl." Jameson tilted her head and batted her lashes. "Hmm. I wonder why."

He pushed open the door with a flourish. "You worry too much."

"Do I?" She pointed at the little rectangle of cellophane that fluttered to the carpet just inside the doorway of the apartment. "See. I told you she'll know that somebody was here."

"Maybe she'll think it's the landlord?" Ronan suggested.

Ripley, having had shifted into the form of a German shepherd, gave a yip and stood in their path as Ethan made a move to enter. The tip of his wet black nose quivered as he took tentative steps inside the apartment, only to stop short. He gave a wag of his head and looked back and forth between them and into the room.

"Or she doesn't trust the landlord either. Network," Ethan said. The earpieces Ripley nicked from Maestro's supplies for all of them worked as both a speaker and microphone. "Can you do a scan for energy signatures? Ripley said he can sense something, like from a laser."

"Sure. Can you poke your head into the room for me?"

"Can I? Sure. Will I? Not until I know what that laser is attached to."

"Give me a minute. This won't be pretty, but it'll do the job."

A few seconds later, the world around them went eerily quiet. Dead quiet.

"What just happened?" Jameson asked as chills ran across her neck.

"I shut the power down to the building," Network answered. "I'd say you have about five minutes before someone at the utility company starts to poke around."

Jameson shuddered. "Her powers are fucking scary."

"I know, right?" Ronan agreed with an enthusiastic nod. "Guess we better make haste."

Ripley led the way into the apartment with his nose as the rest of them slowly followed. It was unnerving to realize how a person could become so used to the buzz of electricity until it was gone and the sounds of your footsteps and your breathing became magnified tenfold.

"Check that out." Ethan pointed around the room. "She's got security cameras. Good thing we cut the power before we entered."

Jameson stationed herself in a corner of the room while Ronan followed Ripley the dog, who wound a path from the front door to the sofa before moving on to the kitchen.

Everywhere Ripley indicated Ashley's scent was the strongest, Ethan searched the area. At least he was gentle, Jameson thought, giving little thanks to the effort even though they were breaking and entering into her friend's home.

"Want to lend a hand?" he asked her.

"No. Not really. I still don't like how this feels." She adjusted the fit of ther coat over her shoulders.

She couldn't shake the sensation that something was wrong. And by "wrong" she didn't mean only the breaking and entering part. There was a blade hanging above them all and it was holding on by one thin fiber. At any second, that sucker was going to fall and slice off all their heads.

Ethan was checking out the bookcase near the dining room table when Ripley trotted into the kitchen. He made a few circles in front of the sink and yipped with excitement.

Ronan kneeled. “Ripley says he smells gun oil from under the sink.”

Jameson joined him as he opened the cabinet doors and removed the bottles of cleaners and stacks of sponges to the side. With his fingertip, he located a groove in the bottom of the cabinet and lifted up, revealing a dark pit beneath.

Ronan took out his phone and turned on the flashlight. In the depths of the false bottom lay several rifles and handguns along with a couple of boxes of ammunition.

“Holy shit,” he exclaimed. “Check that out.”

Jameson shrugged. “So. What’s the big surprise?”

His eyes widened incredulously. “It’s a stash of weapons.”

“And? Where do you stash your weapons?”

“We don’t have a stash of weapons.”

“Sure,” she said with a roll of her eyes. “Where does Ted stash your weapons?”

He sucked in a breath to an answer before it caught in this chest and he blew it out. “I…”

“Mm-hmm.” She had him there. “Thought so.”

Ronan shook his head. “Fine. Where do *you* stash your weapons?”

She chortled. “Like I’m going to tell you.”

“Seriously, Jameson?” For some reason, sorrow and disbelief colored his eyes. “You have a stash of weapons in your home? Why?”

Now was her turn to look at him incredulously. She threw out her hands to encompass the world around them. “Because I’m a woman who lives on this planet, in this country, in this time period of the patriarchy. Of course I have weapons to protect myself.”

"Ah, wildcat." He reached out and brushed the backs of his fingers along her cheek. "I'm sorry you feel like that's what you have to do to feel safe."

She bit her tongue. Her need to protect herself by whatever means necessary wasn't something she felt like she had to. It was a necessity. No one was going to care about her or protect her better than herself.

In a million bazillion years, Ronan would never understand what it meant to not have the privilege of a cis white man. Empathize, maybe. But never understand.

"Hey guys," Ethan said from the dining area. "I found something."

"I'll put this back. Go ahead," Ronan said, setting the floorboards back to rights.

On the dining table Ethan had laid out sheets of paper that he had pulled from a binder.

"What is all this?" she asked.

"I'm not 100 percent certain yet, but if it is what I think it is, your friend Ashley is planning something big. Like multiple life sentences or the death penalty big."

"What?" She jumped to his side, scrambling to make sense of the photographs and maps Ethan had discovered.

"Who are these guys?" she asked, leafing through the eight-by-ten headshots. On the back was an itinerary of events for the next day.

"That would be the President of the United States," Ethan said as if that were obvious.

"I know that, dumbass. Who are these other guys?"

"Well, this one here is Stephen Proctor. He's the head of Ablution Outrigger International. And that is Senator Wally from Idaho."

"Ablution Outrigger. I've heard of them," she said.

"He's the jerk who cut his employees' pensions, laid off two hundred workers, and bought himself an island in the Caribbean, right?"

"Yep. And remember Congressman Pig Uterus from earlier today? Well, Proctor donated a couple million to Pig Uterus's and Wally's reelection campaign. Not too hard to see the connection as to why he might be in this folder."

"It's just a picture in a folder. Doesn't mean that they are connected, and Ash is involved," Jameson said, her voice growing softer with each word. Tears caught in the back of her throat as realization set in.

Ethan gave her a brief squeeze around the shoulder before he adjusted his sunglasses. "Network, are you having any luck in identifying some more of these men?"

"I could if you stop moving your head," Network replied in their earpieces. "I'm running a facial recognition scan now. This might take a while."

Ronan joined them at the table. "I recognize this guy. This is that state representative from Oklahoma. He was the one who was trying to get us to build a plant in Tulsa in an area that was all low-income housing. He wanted to try to recreate the housing bubble that happened here in the city and in New York. Offer big tax breaks to a company who will drop-in high-income tech jobs and replace low income housing with overpriced two-hundred-square-foot apartments. We told him no."

"I still don't get why she has these photos," Jameson said, picking up a piece of paper with a series of times on it.

Ronan read over her shoulder. "That looks like a schedule of the WTO meetings."

"Are all these men here for WTO?"

"I don't think so," Network said. On the lenses of their

glasses she highlighted a photo that was in the center of the group. "This guy is a professor at the University of Southern California."

"And he's here for WTO?" Ronan asked.

"No. But I did a search of his name and found news articles linking him to three rape allegations made against him by female students this last year. The university said their investigation concluded that the girls had made it all up to avoid having to take an exam."

"Ugh." Jameson gagged. Fuckers like that made her want to vomit.

Ethan flipped through a few more papers. "I think your friend is compiling a hit list. Network, can you ping these addresses for me. Just a couple of them." He pointed to a list of addresses located in different cities along the West Coast.

"Let's see… The first two are motels. Third one's a hotel. Fourth one's a campsite. Then another campsite."

"Yeah. Yeah, this is making sense." Ethan tapped his forefinger against his chin as his eyes danced with excitement. "She's gonna take out these three guys this week sometime during WTO. Then she's gonna head to, uh, what's the first address on the list? Spokane. Okay. Then head to Idaho where Sen. Wally is at and on down the line."

Jameson shook her spinning head. "That's crazy. That's…sounds…so fucking plausible."

She crossed to the couch and plopped down on the worn cushion with a heavy sigh. Dropping her head in her hands, she tried to suck in deep breaths to calm her racing heart.

As much as she believed her friend wouldn't become a serial killer, the little bit of evidence they discovered made it all too likely. And if she were to be honest, if she put herself in Ash's shoes with what she now knew about Ash's time in the Army, she'd be willing to take out a few losers herself.

Ronan joined her on the couch, rubbing his hand up and down her back in a soothing motion. "It's okay, wildcat. Look, these guys are still alive. Wait. Network, these guys are still alive, right?"

"I'm gonna guess so. I haven't run across any news reports that state otherwise."

He relaxed. "See. They're not dead yet. There's still time to stop her. Unfortunately, we can't do anything about the people she's already knocked off, but we can stop her from killing others."

"Allegedly. Possibly. We still do not have any conclusive evidence that she has killed anybody." She felt compelled to add, "Yet."

"That's right." He nodded, although his weak smile suggested it was all a matter of time. "And there is still a chance she hasn't been involved at all. But we can't ignore the fact that we have a strong suspicion she's about to be involved in something incredibly bloody. Let's find her and see what it's all about."

He was right. Right now, all they had were some pictures and a few details that the average person probably wouldn't be all that interested in. There could be a perfectly reasonable and logical explanation for Ash to have maps, photographs, and itineraries for these men. A perfectly logical explanation that did not involve plotting their deaths.

"You're right. There's still time." She got to her feet and pulled down the cuffs of her jacket with a decisive flick of her wrist. "I'll find her, talk to her, and if she is planning something dastardly, I will just talk her out of it and make her see reason."

"*We'll* talk her out of it," Ethan added, putting the photos and papers away where he found them. "We're not letting you go alone to meet up with a killer."

"Potential killer. And my good friend. She will never talk to me with you guys around."

Who knew how Ash would react when confronted about the items in her apartment that nobody was supposed to know about? If not handled delicately, the entire conversation was going to go over as well as a turd in the punchbowl. Lit on fire. With C-4. And having two hunky, telepathic twins by her side were not going to help the situation.

"We've been over this already, sweetheart. You're not going alone. We will find a way to be there, somehow, some way, to support you." Ethan reached for her arms and guided her to him into a loose hug. "We understand you know your friend better than we do and how best to talk to her. But you are not alone in this, Jameson. We will support you."

"I know you want to help. And I know you're worried about my safety. But trust me when I say having you there will make things more dangerous. Not that I'm saying they're going to be dangerous, but whatever danger is possible will be heightened if you guys are present." She pinched the bridge of her nose. "Look, the Crimson Angels are supposed to meet up tonight. You guys can take a sweep at where we're supposed to meet. You can be in the building, but you can't be in the room. Once the rest of the girls head out on their tasks, I'll pull Ash aside and see what she's up to. That's the best I can give you."

"How about we'll be in the room next door?" Ethan

asked.

"There is no next door to where we meet. Same floor, possibly. But you two cannot be seen."

"Three," Ronan added. "Ripley will be there too."

She glanced down at the dog. "Fine," she gritted between clenched teeth. "That's all."

CHAPTER NINETEEN

JAMESON SHOULD HAVE known that it wasn't going to be only the three of them.

Seriously, if this was how they operated, these people were going to make it difficult for the women's shelter to keep its anonymity.

She crawled into the back of the small delivery truck that was parked alongside the road about two blocks away from the shelter and glowered at the group of people huddled around the mini command center of computers.

"You people are insane," she said and slammed the back door shut, leaving the room in relative darkness lit only by the glow of computer screens and track lighting running underneath the countertop.

Ethan raised his hands in defense. "I know this looks bad, but it wasn't our call."

"It was mine," came a voice from the driver's seat.

The chair swiveled around, revealing Maestro decked out in all his black leather and sunglassed finery.

"Ah fuck," she muttered and hung her head.

His lips tightened. "There are a few things you need to know, Ms. Alinari. Number one, I'm a smart guy. I can tell when someone else has touched and used my equipment. Number two, my wife is psychic. She saw all of us here, so here we all are."

"Great. Fabulous," she said, sounding anything but

enthused. "And where is she at this time? She didn't see herself here?"

"Hell, no. There is no way I'm letting my pregnant wife anywhere near this situation. She's at home. Safe."

"As if she'd let him keep her away if she really wanted to be here," Ethan said to her under his breath. "I think she's more stubborn than you."

"Jameson, this is Doc." Ronan gestured to the woman seated between him and Ripley. She too was dressed all in black and wore sunglasses with a wool cap covering her hair.

"You're Alisia's friend." Doc smiled warmly and offered her hand. "It's so nice to finally meet you."

"That's right." Jameson shook her hand, impressed with the strength of her grip.

"Alisia thinks the world of you," Doc added.

"She's my sister. We've been through a lot of fires together, so she probably feels obligated to say nice things about me. But she does say nice things about you too, Doc, and ordinarily I'd be really thrilled to meet you, but I know you are a healer. If you're here, that means you all are expecting something terrible to go down."

"We're being cautious," Maestro replied. "A lot of people are turning up dead. And since we don't know what we're going to find, we want to be ready."

"And your psychic wife didn't tell you what's going to happen? Because let me tell you, that would be right handy to know at this point in time."

Everyone in the truck gave the same aggravated groan, but Maestro just smiled. "It doesn't work that way. If we know too much about what's going to happen in the future, inevitably somebody's gonna screw it up and change the course of the future, potentially creating something worse. She tells us just enough to be helpful."

"If you say so," Jameson said, highly doubtful.

"Trust me, wildcat." Ronan patted her on the shoulder. "It's better this way."

She didn't find their words that much of a comfort, but she did like the fact that Doc was present. From what Alisia had said about the doctor, the woman was a good ally to have in your corner. Fair, hardworking. If it came to choosing sides, Doc's allegiance to Alisia might work in her favor. At least they hadn't brought Lancaster with them. Unless…

Jamison nodded to the front of the truck. "You don't happen to have Lancaster riding shotgun, do ya?"

Maestro rubbed his finger along the side of his nose. "Lancaster does not know about this little operation. Not yet, anyway. At this moment, your friend Ashley is in possession of suspicious material. That's all." He sighed and relaxed in his seat. "I mean it, we all mean it, when we say that we hope your friend isn't involved. But right now, she's a potential lead. And if we find that she is somehow responsible, we have to put a stop to it and call in Lancaster. Does that sound fair to you?"

"It does. Thank you. But please know that *I* meant it when I said you all can't be present when I talk to her. If Ashley is…" Jameson swallowed hard and shook her head. It was still difficult to imagine her friend as a stone-cold killer. "I don't want her cornered or running scared."

"Understood. Right." Maestro clapped once. "Here's the plan. We'll set you up with a communication device but you should do most of your talking with us telepathically with the twins. That way your friends can't hear you talking to us via the mic. These will be backup in case something happens."

He meant in case Ashley got confrontational and tried to hurt her. An outcome Jameson in no way wanted to contemplate. But yay for being prepared?

Maestro continued as Jameson set the device into her ear. "Find out what Ashley is up to, and that is all. We'll be here on standby in case she does make a move against you or tries to run. Don't worry, we will contain her in the most reasonable fashion possible." The line of his jaw tightened as he added, "However, if she's packing any weapons and tries to use them, we're not going to be so gentle."

"Then let's hope that we are all mistaken about Ashley being involved, and we can laugh this whole thing off."

"Let's hope," he said.

"You'll do good," Ronan said, although she wasn't certain if he was talking to her or to himself. He futzed with the lapel of her jacket and smoothed his hands down the length of her arms as he gazed at her with worried eyes and a shaky smile. "It's just talking. And you know your friend better than we do. I'm sure it will be fine. We're just being extra cautious."

Cautious was an understatement, judging by the DEFCON 5 level of precaution Maestro appeared to be taking with their equipment and the orders he was giving Network back at base. Maybe Maestro's wife had let on more about the evening's events than he claimed.

Great. The hairs on the back of Jameson's neck stood on end. Now she was freaking herself out. God, she hoped she knew her friend as well as she thought she did.

"I'm sorry, wildcat." Ronan cupped her check in his palm. "I didn't mean to transfer my worry to you. Breathe with me a little bit. Please."

She wrapped her fingers around his wrist and breathed with him. In and out. In and out. For a second it seemed as if the entire truck took a minute to breathe with them until her heart rate slowed.

"Good luck." Ronan swept her up in a big hug, and his kiss lingered as if he were reluctant to let go. His fingers trailed down her corset-covered side. "By the way, you look hot in that outfit. Always thought so." His saucy wink that followed soothed the rest of the tension she carried.

"Kinky."

"Always," he said with a laugh.

Ethan took her hand and squeezed it tight. "Ripley and I are going to hide in the garage. Maestro will be behind the building, and Doc and Ronan will monitor things from the truck. We can be there in a second if you need us."

Maestro tapped on the screen that showed a street view around the truck. "Coast is clear. You're good to go."

Jameson opened the back door and Ethan and Ripley followed. He butted his cold German shepherd nose against her hand as if he too was offering his support.

"Thanks, beast man." She patted him on the top of the head.

Ethan tugged her to the side of the truck and out of view of the street. He wrapped her in a hug so tight she could barely breathe. "We're here for you, Jameson. Whatever you need, we are here for you. Maestro might be after a lead in those murders, but keeping you safe is my and Ronan's priority. And if keeping your friend safe makes you happy, then that will be a priority too."

Jamison hugged Ethan tight around the waist. "Thank you."

"Be safe." Ethan pressed a kiss to her lips, then another, and another. Each a little more desperate than the last.

"I'll be fine."

"I know," he said. "I don't think I'll ever stop worrying when it comes to you."

"You better." She fingered the open collar of his shirt. "Don't want you too exhausted for other activities."

His posture wilted as if a huge weight evaporated off his shoulders. "You're not angry at us anymore?"

"No. Not really." She ran her fingertips down his cheek, reluctant to break their connection. "After seeing those photos, I'd be worried if it were you or Ronan involved. But you've got to give me some credit too. I can take care of myself."

"I'll try. *We'll* try." He dipped his head and rested his forehead against hers. "Believe in us."

She did believe in them. In all fairness, they hadn't been wrong about what she had been up to. Sure, she had every right to do whatever she wanted, but they also had the right to be concerned for her well-being.

For all her trials and tribulations, this espionage thing was a new situation for her. But Ethan and Ronan had always been true to their word. Whatever she had needed emotionally, the two of them had provided in spades. She trusted them, crazy as it sounded. And she hoped like hell her trust was not misplaced.

"I suddenly feel as if I need a really long vacation. Somewhere tropical with twenty-four-hour bar service and suntan oil at the ready."

Ethan chuckled. "That sounds wonderful. First opportunity, we'll make that happen."

Of course they would. If she asked for the world, they'd

probably have it gift-wrapped and on her doorstep by the next morning.

"I better go. Stay hidden. I mean it," she warned.

Ethan gave a short nod and stayed by the truck as she took off around the corner. She rushed through the gate of the parking lot and jogged into the underground parking garage. Trini was waiting in the engineering room when Jameson arrived.

"What's up, home fries?" Trini greeted. She took a sip of her coffee. "You know that I know your boys stopped by your apartment this morning. Are you still the filling in that hunky twin sandwich?"

"Jesus, Trini. They are enjoyable to spend time with." She pointed to one of the coffees on the table. "Is this one for me?"

She swiped the drink anyway. It was good to have something to do with her hands.

"*Enjoyable.* Yes. That's the word I was thinking of." Trini snorted. "Come on, girl. Spill. I've never been in a three-way, and I've always wondered what it was like."

"It's..." Ah, hell. It was no surprise Trini was going to be ultra-curious about the twins and their sexual proclivities. The woman lived for gossip. The juicier the better.

Trini was her homegirl. They always had an open dialogue. If she didn't spill some tea, her friend was going to suspect something was up. However, Jameson was highly aware that their conversation was being broadcast to all and sundry out in the truck. In fact, she could feel the tingle of the brothers' laughter skating down her spine as she stood there, frantically searching for something to say.

Yeah, wildcat. What's it like?

"I...well... They—" Fuck. What was she going to say?

You can tell her that we've altered your world as you know it, Ethan said. *It doesn't hurt to always go with the truth.*

Shut up!

Two knocks followed by a pause then three more knocks interrupted them before Lucinda burst into the room. "What up, bitches?"

Thank the Lord.

Jameson wilted into a seat. "It's about time. Where have you been?"

"Where have I been?" Lucinda pressed her hand to her chest, affronted. "Bitch, please. Time waits for me."

"Hey, pals and gals," Bryn greeted as she strolled in hand in hand with Jules. "Two high schools are having prom tonight. Who's up for trolling the streets, making sure everyone gets home safe?"

Lucinda made a gagging sound. "I hated high school when I was in high school. No thanks."

"It's not the schools we have to watch," Bryn said. "It's the parking lot and the hotels. That's where boys tend to get the most handsy."

Jameson chuckled and eagerly grabbed onto the change in subject. "I could get in on that. Let's wait and see if we can get Ash to come along too."

"Ash isn't coming tonight," Trini said over the top of her coffee cup.

"What do you mean?"

Trini shrugged and took a sip. "She texted earlier and said she was busy."

"Busy doing what?" Alarm raced through her so quickly, sweat popped out on her forehead.

"I'm not her keeper," Trini groused with an agitated flip

of her wrist. "And this is funny, you know. You have the same expression she did the other night when you no-showed because you were getting Eiffel Towered by those twins."

Crap. Just what she needed. Ash going AWOL. Could the timing be any worse?

"Does anyone have any idea what Ash is up to?" she tried to ask as calmly as possible.

The other girls stared at her, blinking owlishly. "No clue," a few of them muttered.

"What's wrong?" Lucinda asked, jumping to her feet. The first-aid training she was so proud of kicked into gear. "You turned pale real quick."

"It's nothing, really." Jameson batted Lucinda's hands away from where she tried to place them on her face. "I'm fine. It's just... There's been a lot of focus in the news and online about vigilante justice against sexual assault perpetrators and such. The police have been contacting me more and more about the people in the shelter and I want them to keep away. Ash going rogue may not be a good thing."

"Gerald Mulvaney's murder. You think Ash may have something to do with it?" Jules asked.

"Did I say that?" Jameson squeaked then lowered her tone. "No. It's just that we don't know who is behind that murder. With the police more focused on the areas we patrol, the more danger we're in of being discovered for our more in-your-face humanitarian deeds. I just want to make sure we're all good and stay under the radar."

"I wouldn't be surprised if it was Ash going around whacking dudes," Trini said as casual as could be. "She's really good at kicking ass."

Jesus, Trini. Just let it fly with incriminating statements. Help your sister out and keep your trap shut.

"Look, let's just make sure that when we go out tonight that we're just extra cautious."

The girls nodded, and they agreed to check in with each other on the regular.

"Which high school are you going to patrol?" Bryn asked Jameson as they began to head out.

"I'll head to the south and see if I can get a hold of Ash," she replied. "Make sure she's okay."

"Cool, cool. See you later."

Jameson waved them away and waited until she was alone before reaching out to the twins.

Now what?

We're working on it, Ronan replied. *Network is tracing her phone number now and trying to get a location. Hopefully she still has it on her.*

Jameson met up with Ethan and Ripley behind the delivery truck.

"Find her yet?" Ethan asked the group inside.

"We found her phone," Network replied over their communication devices. "She's by the Sheraton downtown on Tenth Avenue."

"Why does the Sheraton ring a bell?" Ethan asked.

Ronan tapped on one of the computer monitors. "It was listed on those papers Ashley had at her apartment. Can we pull up a picture of that page?"

"Here you go." Network put up the file of information they had found at Ashley's house.

Ronan swiped through the documents on the touch screen until he found what he was looking for. "Right there. There's a function tonight at the Sheridan. The WTO opening reception."

"I don't suppose your friend has a part-time job at the Sheridan?" Doc asked Jameson.

"If she does, I've never heard her mention it."

On two of the monitors, Network hacked into the footage from security cameras around the hotel. "Looks like the police have already set up a security perimeter. Lots of cars, and it looks like they're checking people's credentials before allowing them to enter."

Ethan rubbed his hand over his face. "Guess we can try to book a room as guests to get into the hotel, if there are any available. But that won't get us into any of the public spaces for the event itself."

Doc giggled. "What? You mean the heads of one of the biggest software companies in the world didn't get an invite to WTO?"

Ronan rolled his eyes. "We declined the invitation. Neither of us have the energy to listen to hundreds of people's thoughts in multiple languages. We sent one of our vice-presidents in our place."

"Good thing you know somebody else who does have an invitation to this reception. Although I don't know why they invited him when his father tried to stage a military coup," Maestro said with a smirk.

"You know this someone?" Jameson asked.

The brothers broke into laughter as Maestro's grin widened.

CHAPTER TWENTY

"TED WILL BE here with the car in about ten minutes," Ronan said. "And he's bringing a coat and tie for you, Ethan."

Jameson's gaze shifted toward the front of the delivery truck and the rumbling movements of Maestro behind a partition.

"I thought it was weird when Prism told me to bring a change of clothes," he said from the other side of the curtain. "Now it makes sense. Still gives me the chills when she does that."

He stepped out, no longer dressed in his black super-spy outfit with long leather duster. Now he wore crisp pleated black slacks and a blue button-down shirt. He was still wearing a leather jacket, but this one was cut in a contemporary-style blazer.

Jameson rubbed at her temples, trying to ease the ache forming behind her eyes. "What exactly is the plan here?"

At this point she was beyond confused. The police perimeter around the hotel was so wide, they spent forever trying to find a parking space for the truck that was close enough for Ethan to be able to telepathically communicate with them, but where they didn't stick out. The last thing they needed was for the police, or anyone else for that matter, calling them in as transporting a suspected bomb. With all the haggling over "There's a spot," "No, over there," a formal plan was never discussed.

Ethan reached out and laid his warm palm on Jameson's knee, giving her a gentle squeeze. "Maestro, and me as his plus one, are going to the opening ceremonies reception. Ripley is going to scout the hotel for any signs of Ashley. You, Ronan, and Doc will hang out here and monitor feeds from the security cameras in the neighborhood and see if you spot her."

"And how does Maestro have an invitation to this reception?"

"I have my ways," he said, and adjusted the sunglasses on his nose.

"I still think I should go with you. Ashley is gonna run if you two goons rush up on her."

"I told you, Jameson. You'll make a better lookout in the truck. You will be able to see everything inside and outside," Ethan said.

"Besides, I can't have you as my plus one, as it will draw more attention if I show up with a woman not my wife. We do not need that type of media attention," Maestro added.

Jameson squinted at the tall, lanky man as her mind ruminated over the pieces of information she had learned about him since she'd had the pleasure of his company.

He was married. Pregnant wife. His real identity had to be influential enough to be on the guest list for WTO, because who was going to extend an invitation to a guy named Maestro? And what was that he had mentioned earlier? His father attempted to take over the country?

"Holy shit!" she exclaimed. "You're that rich inventor guy. Max Madden. My coworker Shepard talks about you a lot."

Doc slapped her hands on the countertop. "I told you

these disguises weren't really disguises."

Max shrugged. "They've been working for us so far. And Jameson here has had an unfair advantage being in our laps over the last two days."

"So, what is your super power again?" Jameson asked, leaning back in her chair. "You have tons of money and are super smart, like Batman?"

"Something like that," Max smirked.

"Hey, Maestro, our ride is here," Ethan said, gesturing to the screen depicting images outside of the truck. Ted rolled up behind them in the limo.

Ethan swiveled her chair around to face him. "I know you're stressed, Jameson. At best, your friend is nowhere in the vicinity and Max and I will spend an evening being subjugated to a boring event with free booze and political and economic hotshots swinging their egos around to see whose is the biggest."

"And at worst?" she dared to ask.

His lips tightened. "We find your friend and see if she looks as if she's going to cause some trouble. If that happens, we'll move her to a quiet and secluded location and wait for backup. No fuss, no muss. Everyone will stay safe."

Jameson drew in a breath and then another. Long and slow. Logical and reasonable Ethan was there to save the day because he was a logical and reasonable man. There was no reason not to put her trust in his hands.

Yep, no reason at all, except deep in her gut something was not sitting right. Maybe she too had a bit of the psychic powers going on, but she could not shake the feeling that they were racing down a hill, their legs scrambling faster and faster toward the bottom. Were their feet going to stumble, pitching them ass over end to a gully below, or would they smoothly leap the distance to safety? At the moment, she envisioned them in a sprawling, broken heap in the gully.

Sensing her inner turmoil, Ethan cupped her face in his hands and placed a gentle kiss on her lips. Touching his forehead to hers, he said nothing, thought nothing. He poured his care and affection to her as if he spoke out loud, but this was better. Warmer. More intimate, as if he tethered them together in an unbreakable bond.

She reached up and wrapped her fingers around his wrist, squeezing him back with all the fondness she felt inside.

Max scooted around them, heading for the back doors. "Let's get the show on the road, Daniels."

Ethan gave her another quick kiss and followed Max out the back of the truck. On the computer monitor they saw the two men move quickly into the back of the limo that pulled away from the curb with a silent motor that belied the strength and power of the limousine.

Ronan grabbed the back of her chair and pulled her to his side where he sat at the surveillance counter. Taking her hand in his he said, "We've got you, wildcat."

"I know. You always do." She squeezed his hand back and turned her attention to the computer monitors before them.

Maybe one day you'll believe it, he said.

I do.

His brow raised in disbelief.

I'm trying. You know I'm trying.

He lifted her hand kissed her knuckles. "I know."

"If you lovebirds are ready to pay attention," Ripley

interrupted them. "I'm going to patrol. Holler if you see anything."

And with that, he stripped off his pants, revealing his tan and muscular body.

Whoa. He couldn't warn a girl? Jesus, where was she supposed to look? The man was built like a golden brickhouse. Way to go, Alisia.

She barely had a chance to drink in his masculine loveliness before bones cracked and skin flexed.

"Eww," she shrieked and jumped back. "What is happening?"

"He's showing his beastly self." Ronan shook his head. "You don't have to show off."

Jameson blinked and the distorted man had turned into a fluffy, golden kitty cat. The little bundle of sweetness skipped over to her and wound his soft body between her feet with a purr.

"Aww. Oh my God." She bent down and stroked his silky fur. "He's so cute."

"Yeah. Too cute." Ronan stood and opened the truck door for Ripley. "You want someone to pick you up and adopt you?"

Snap, crackle, pop. A mangy orange tabby took the kitten's place. The stubby snout and condescending glare from his yellow eyes warned not to touch or else have your face scratched off.

"Better." Ronan set him out on the sidewalk and shut the door, leaving him alone with the ladies. "Who's ready to play a really difficult version of *Where's Waldo* where our target isn't wearing an easily identifiable red and white sweater?"

Jameson turned back to the wall of monitors and

promptly went cross-eyed. "What exactly are we looking at here?"

From her remote location, Network moved the cursor on the screens as she explained. "Well, kiddos, starting on your far left, this monitor you have the four traffic cameras around the hotel on the north, south, east, and west corners. I was able to sync into the security footage cameras of the hotel themselves, which are on these monitors here. The banquet room cameras are displaying on these screens, and the entrance to the lobby are on these screens."

In the hotel lobby, a few small groups of people huddled together as they meandered toward the hotel's banquet area. Jameson noticed that both local police officers and men in suits with square jaws were keeping a close eye on the area. They must be Feds or private security.

On another monitor to her right flashed pictures of people in the lobby on half of the screen as a rapid series of faces ran on the other side.

Jamison gestured to the screen. "What's going on here?"

"Network, are you running people through a facial recognition database?" Ronan asked.

"Yep," Network replied. "Looks like we have a cross-section of people in attendance. Most of them are government or law enforcement. I could check private company files for badges, but that would take forever to break into those programs. But it does look like we have gotten hits on a few politicians and executive bigwigs."

Doc tapped on the monitor. "I recognize him. That's a lobbyist from Sondheim Pharmaceuticals."

"Oh my goodness," Network exclaimed. One of the cameras zoomed in on a blond gentleman dressed in a navy blue suit with an open-collared white shirt. "Is that Leo? I swear, Maestro gets all the fun."

"Speaking of Maestro, where are boys now?" Ronan asked.

Another split monitor flared to life and an image from Maestro's sunglasses appeared on the screen.

"Won't Maestro wearing his sunglasses inside of the building draw attention?" Jameson asked.

"Transition lenses," Ronan answered. "They'll look like normal glasses from the outside but have the same monitors on the inside of the lens."

Nifty technology. If the news stories about him were true, he was super smart and had an incredibly huge income at his disposal. No wonder he had cool gadgets.

So far so good, Ethan projected his thoughts into their mind. *Everyone is just milling about. For such a high-profile event, security sucks. They scanned Max's photo ID and mine but barely glanced at our faces. Does anyone see our girl?*

Jameson scanned every security camera, and no one caught her eye. If Ashley was there, she could be anywhere. In one of the many hallways, the gym, the restaurant.

Out on the street, the police had closed the front of the hotel to street traffic and appeared to be funneling hotel guests through a side entrance. Reception attendees were escorted to the front, where they disappeared through the lobby up the escalators. From the corner of Jameson's eye she saw a town car pull up to the front of the hotel. The doorman opened the back door and a gentleman stepped out. Jameson took a second glance as she recognized him from a picture from Ashley's apartment.

He was a senator from New Mexico who was advocating stripping funding from the public school system. He also had been recently implicated in a human trafficking ring.

Undocumented immigrants in his state would be arrested on trumped-up charges yet disappear before arriving at any sort of legal facility. The last news report claimed an estimated three hundred people had gone unaccounted for.

His people were missing, yet there he was, looking tan and healthy with his perfectly styled hair and a smile of bright white veneers as he waved to the group of news cameras huddled behind a barricade.

Suddenly a crack tore through the racket and the senator dropped to the ground like a sack of bricks.

Everyone in the truck sat up three inches straighter with alarm.

"What the hell did we just see?" Jameson shouted.

"Ethan?" Ronan asked. "Did you see that?"

"What the fuck just happened?" Max asked them through his earpiece. "People started running in a million different directions, scared as hell."

"Collins just went down," Doc replied. "Senator Collins just went down out front. Was he shot?"

From the camera on Max's glasses they saw him making his way to the hotel entrance. The path was difficult as he and Ethan struggled like salmon swimming upstream of the crowd fleeing from the scene.

"Collins has been hit," Ethan replied, his voice strained. "Everyone around us is in panic mode and I can't sort through the thoughts fast enough. But I can hear cries for a medic."

Several police officers appeared in Max's view, stopping their progression. "Excuse us, sirs. There has been a medical emergency and we need you to go into the banquet room. Please go and wait for further instruction."

"Check this out," Network said. Another monitor in the

truck flickered and switched to the scene of the local television news broadcast.

Much the same as the traffic cameras in the area were showing them, the news was broadcasting the scene of the fleeing crowd in front of the hotel. Even with the camera operator's wobbling motion, the senator's car was in plain view. The passenger door he had started to exit from was open, and all they could see were his legs and a pool of dark substance dripping onto the ground and creeping across the asphalt.

Doc rose from her seat. "This is crazy. I have to go to see if I can give assistance."

Ronan stopped her. "You can't leave yet. If you appear out of the blue dressed as an Evolutioneer with none of your other team members present, it will look suspicious. Especially if you arrive so suddenly."

"He's right," Max added. "And Collins is dead. Ethan can't identify his train of thought. Has anyone seen anything on the cameras?"

Network rewound footage from all available cameras to thirty seconds before the shooting. They all looked at the monitors, their eyes searching the crowd for any movement of the shooter as the footage played over and over again in slow motion.

"I can't see anything," Jameson said. "The shot must've come from across the street. But it still doesn't make sense. If Ashley has been the one doing these murders, shooting someone in full view of everyone hasn't been her MO."

"You're right," Ethan said. He and Max were returning to the ballroom as security directed. "This isn't adding up. Fuck. And there's so much noise."

He staggered over to the side and put his hand over his

eyes, obscuring their view out his glasses. His breathing was labored over the earpieces.

"Ethan?" Max asked. "Are you okay?"

"So much noise. Ronan. I need. Help," he wheezed as if he were having an asthma attack.

"Do it," Ronan said and drew in a big breath. He reached out for Jameson's hand, taking it in his as if she were a lifeline.

"What's going on?" she asked, suddenly terrified.

"We're going to open the telepathic line between us all the way. Ethan's going to share everything he hears with me. We don't do it often because it's so much information, it wipes both of us out. But I have to help him take some of the noise away before he becomes incapacitated. Too much and it'll knock him out," Ronan answered.

That didn't sound good at all. "What can I do to help?"

"Just hang with me. That will be enough," he said with a tight smile. He took another breath and settled in his seat. "Okay. Bring it on, Ethan."

Ronan's fingers around her hand tightened, and his eyes widened as he gasped. They had a few hundred panicked people in that area with a million thoughts. The strain the brothers were under had to be incredible.

"There must be something I can do," Jameson said. "Can you share the noise with me? Like you did at Fitzherbert's house. Would that take the burden off you both?"

Ronan grunted, and the breath whistled in and out from between his lips. "I don't know. It's worth a shot."

Jameson shifted in her seat, finding a more comfortable position to relax and tried to slow the pounding of her heart. She closed her eyes and took down the last of her walls, opening herself up fully to Ronan. The wave of sound cascading into her mind knocked her back in her seat.

This wasn't like before where she was encompassed in a warm bubble and floated from person to person. This was a full-on plunge into category four rapids where she was tossed from thought to thought like a leaf in a hurricane.

"I'm good, I'm good," she said when Ronan squeezed her hand. "I'm just trying to get oriented."

Wow, people thought of the most random shit. She caught snippets for thoughts that ranged from outrage at not being allowed to leave the hotel to speculation on what would unicorn meat taste like. Who in the hell thinks about unicorn meat in an emergency?

"Holy shit. That's better," Ethan said. The earlier strain on his voice was gone. "Thank you. Thank you both."

"Thank Jameson," Ronan added. "Good job, wildcat."

"No problem." She slowly opened her eyes and gazed at the panel of monitors before her. "Now how do I drive this thing?"

Perhaps if she focused on each screen, she could pinpoint a sensible thought that matched the image.

Okay, there we go. She began to filter out the nonsensical thoughts and concentrated on information that was pertinent to the situation: What is going on? Was that a gunshot? What were the police doing?

Over and over the questions repeated until she picked up a familiar sound. She hadn't quite believed Ethan when he said that he could hear people's thoughts in their tone of voice, but clear as day a familiar alto complaining about bourgeoisie pigs came across her consciousness.

"Wait," she gasped. "I think I found something. Near the elevators. Check the elevators."

The monitors began to flip as Network displayed images

from all the cameras in the elevators. Jameson scoured the screens until she found what she was looking for. "Stop. Third monitor. Lower left. That's Ashley right there."

Instead of her usual black utility pants and hoodie, Ashley was dressed for business casual in slacks, a long, dark gray blazer, and a satchel that she wore across her body. If not for her signature ponytail, Jameson might've passed the woman by without a second glance.

She stood in the far back of the elevator car with her head down, and she was still. Still as a statue as the car trundled up and up the floors.

"Where? Where?" Max asked. The view from his glasses showed they were on the move.

"Car two."

"Who is in the elevator with her?" Doc asked. "She followed them in."

"Give me a second." The sound of Network typing furiously on a keyboard echoed in the van. "Got it. Fred Dorian. CEO of Blue Star Pharmaceuticals. And his personal assistant."

"Fred Dorian. That name sounds familiar." Jameson tapped her forehead then she snapped her fingers. "I know. I think he was the dean at the university when all those students were molested."

"And he was on that list at Ashley's place," Ronan pointed out.

Jameson placed her hand over her mouth as tears sprung to her eyes. This wasn't happening. This couldn't be happening.

The door to the elevator opened and Dorian and his companion stepped out into the hallway and out of frame of the camera. After a moment, Ashley followed. She reached under her collar and pulled a hood out and over her head.

"Thirteenth floor," Ronan said, tapping on the monitor for the display on the elevator that was visible. "They're on the thirteenth floor."

"We are on our way," Max replied, sounding slightly out of breath as the view from his glasses showed him and Ethan running up the stairs.

They reached the landing of the thirteenth floor and Max eased open the door. He and Ethan stepped out and crept down the long, carpeted hallway.

"Ethan wants to know what room Dorian is in," Ronan asked.

A few more clicks of the keyboard echoed in the truck. "He's in 1356."

The image on the monitors showed Max and Ethan both turning as one to the room at the end of the hall. The door was closed. The hallway was tomb silent.

Jameson's heart crept further up her throat with each step the men took down the hall. As they approached the end, Max held out his hand and the door to the hotel room slowly opened.

"How did that door open?" Jameson asked. Did she blink and miss something?

"Maestro's telekinetic," Ronan answered.

"No shit?"

"No shit," Doc confirmed.

Well. Of course he was. Smart, rich, why wouldn't he also have telekinetic powers?

Through the gap of the doorway, they could see a pair of legs splayed on the floor. The door opened a little bit farther, exposing the body of the man who had been with Dorian lying on the carpet, a bloodstain growing into the beige carpet.

"Fuck." Jameson doubled over in her chair. What did Ashley do? "Fuck, fuck, fuck."

As Max slowly entered the room, everyone in the van held their breath, which amplified the only sound coming over the speakers from the earpieces. It was a sound that made Jameson's blood run cold and her stomach twist.

A small living area was the entrance to the room with a separate bedroom to the right. The door was open, and through Max and Ethan's glasses, they saw the source of the sound.

Ash was working over Dorian as if she were training for a heavyweight fight. She landed blow after blow to his soft belly and face, making him grunt with each hit.

Finally, she picked him up by his belt and a grip on his shirt and body-slammed him onto the floor, facedown with her knee on his back as she began to bind his hands together with a zip tie.

"Stop right there," Max shouted. "You're surrounded."

Ashley looked up. Her expression, one of complete surprise, quickly melted as she took in the arrival of Max and Ethan.

"Oh yeah?" she asked. "By whom?" Then her eyes narrowed with a determination Jameson recognized.

"Maestro, look out," Jameson exclaimed the second Ashley sprang into action.

She barreled into his midsection, the two of them crashing into the wall in a flurry of limbs, while Ethan rushed to Dorian's side, pulling his body out of the way to give Max more room to maneuver. The view from the monitor became a jumbled blur as Max's glasses were knocked off his face and fell to the floor, the image turning upside down.

"She's going for her gun," Ethan shouted. And from his glasses they watched as Ashley pulled the gun from the holster hidden under her jacket. She trained the barrel on the men moving from side to side.

"Why doesn't Maestro use his powers to take her gun away?" Jameson asked.

Doc shook her head. "They're not in disguise. Dorian or someone else could identify him. Right now, for all anybody knows, they're just good Samaritans who heard the commotion in the hallway as they passed by."

"Easy, easy," Max said, holding up his hands. "No one else needs to get hurt here."

"You know nothing," she said with a snicker. She looked at the beleaguered CEO struggling to sit up, and her brow furrowed with bittersweet sorrow. "We were going to have so much fun. Pity."

She turned her gun on Dorian and *bang!* In the corner of the screen they saw Dorian's body jerk and slump to the side.

Holy shit. Jameson jumped to her feet. Holy shit. That was cold. That was so cold and matter-of-fact. This blatant brutality was a side of Ashley that Jameson never knew existed.

The bang of the gunshot was still echoing in the truck as Ashley ran out of the hotel room and Max and Ethan tried to tend to Dorian.

"Fuck it." Doc leapt from her chair and strapped a utility belt to her waist. "I'm on my way. I'll be there soon as I can."

"He's hit in the arm," Max replied. "I tried to deflect the bullet as much as possible, but she was quick, and these are close quarters."

Jameson followed Doc out of the back of the van.

"Where are you going?" Ronan asked her.

"Thinking. I need space to think. Figure out where she might do next. I just…need some air."

She could see the word "no" form on his lips. He didn't like having her out of his sight. She felt it, felt his need to keep her near. But after a moment he nodded.

"Be safe," he added.

"I will."

CHAPTER TWENTY-ONE

By the time Jameson jumped out of the back of the truck and hit the pavement, Doc was halfway down the street, racing toward the hotel.

What was happening? What the fuck was happening?

She drove her hands into her hair and pulled, using the pain to fight her frustration and help her to focus.

"Network?" she asked. "Is Ash still in the hotel?"

"Uh, possibly. The dot of the GPS on her phone is still there. Unless she ditched her phone, she should still be onsite."

"Right. Thanks."

Think. What was Ashley's next move? Better yet, if it were *her*, what would be her next move?

Okay, okay, okay, Ash's initial plan was probably to take out Sen. Collins, and while the police and National Guard or whoever arrived to deal with the chaos, ambush Fred Dorian in his room and wait out the time by torturing the CEO. Then she was going to probably leave him for dead and escape out the front lobby doors with the regular hotel guests after all the first responders left the scene.

Fairly solid plan. Still, she would have a backup in case she was trapped inside or discovered early, as she had been.

Jameson began to circle the block, or at least as much as she could with police starting to erect barricades at the intersections closest to the hotel.

One side of the hotel shared an alley with a building that had storefronts on the first floor and residential properties above it. As she rounded the corner, she noticed that people were being allowed to enter those businesses on the far end, away from the hotel. The alley itself was blocked from exiting or entering, but if somebody wanted to, they could go from the back of the building to the hotel through one of the side doors with a modicum of trouble. Especially since the officers stationed on the scene were keeping their backs to the alley.

Perhaps that was Ash's way of escaping the hotel. Leave out the back entrance to the building next door and walk out through the attached restaurant.

Doable. But risky. So was leaping from rooftop to rooftop. Most of the buildings on that side of the street were about the same height as the hotel's third-floor pool deck, but the gaps between them would be near impossible to cross.

The only other way out of the hotel while the police and SWAT teams were present would be…

Jameson looked up. Way, way, way up to the top of the hotel hovering twenty-six floors over the city. The sun had just set, and the black glass structure of the hotel blended into the skyline except for the soft glow of lights coming from some of the hotel rooms. It wasn't the tallest building in the city, but it definitely towered over everything else in the vicinity.

A vision of the photo of Ethan jumping off the Sydney Bridge coupled with a conversation she had had with Ashley a while back about her spending lots of time on Cougar Mountain flashed in her memory. Cougar Mountain was a popular spot for skydivers and paragliders.

"No way," she breathed.

Ash wouldn't. That was insane. Suicidal.

"Fuck. I've got to get into that hotel."

But how? There was no way the police were going to allow her to waltz past their barricades, especially dressed as she was in her corset, leather jacket, and with a whip on her hip.

Or would they?

To her left and right were nothing but restaurants and the odd high-end clothing and jewelry store. On the corner she spotted a drugstore. Excellent.

She ran inside and whooped with delight when she spotted the rack of sunglasses near the register. She spun the display around until she found a pair with black frames.

"Yes," she hissed, then caught a glimpse of herself in the mirror and grimaced. A messy ponytail was not going to cut it.

She quickly retied her ponytail and raced past the front counter, reaching for the emergency twenty-dollar bill from her pocket. She threw it at the cashier as she shouted, "Gotta go, gotta go. Thanks!"

Sure, she could have gone back to the truck and asked Ronan to score her a pair of official glasses, but then he'd try to stop her from going after Ash herself. Sweet man, but nothing was going to stop her.

She jammed the glasses on her face and strode right up to the line of police guarding the front entrance of the hotel as if she were stomping the runway. One of the officers turned to look her up and down. Confusion wrinkled his forehead.

"Hello there, Officer. I am with the Evolutioneers. Sheriff Lancaster called for backup," she announced with her best superhero bravado.

The young officer squinted at her. “Excuse me?”

“I’m here to help Doc. She just arrived a few minutes ago on Sheriff Lancaster’s orders. I’m one of the Evolutioneers. Now let me through.”

“I’m sorry, ma’am. But nobody is getting past.”

Ma’am? Oh no he didn’t.

She straightened and tried to appear as physically intimidating as her short stature would allow. “I know you’re trying to follow orders, but Sheriff Lancaster called me in specifically to assist in this situation.”

“How do I know you’re an Evolutioneer?” he asked giving her a sideways glance. “I don’t think I’ve ever seen you before.”

“You have no idea how many of us there are.” She pointed to the upper floor of the hotel. “Now I know that you have a very important man who’s been shot and is lying near death’s door as we speak. Step aside and allow me to save him.” She lifted her hand and slowly waggled her fingers. “Don’t make me use my powers on you. I take my life-saving duties very seriously.”

The officer’s eyes widened, and he pulled back the barricade. “I’ll let Sheriff Lancaster know you’re here.”

“You do that,” she said and dashed through the barricade and into the hotel. Hopefully it would take the man hours to find the very busy sheriff. If her hunch was right, she would only need minutes.

The lobby was full of law enforcement, hotel guests, and angry WTO attendees who either wanted to know what was going on or to leave the premises altogether. It was a loud and unruly bunch who fell into a startled hush as she strode through the doorway with all the swagger of Tony Stark.

"Evolutioneer here. On my way to assist," she announced with a wave as if she were a pageant queen.

The gaggle of people parted more smoothly than the Red Sea as she marched forward. Some waved at her and others grappled for their cameras for a picture as she passed. Holy shit. These people were actually buying it.

At the elevators there were two officers who were tracking hotel guests going in and out. "Excuse me, sirs. Official Evolutioneer business."

"Whoa." The jaw of the officer to her right dropped open. "Are you really? What's your power? Is the dog with you? Can he really turn into any animal?"

"Dude." His buddy slapped him on the arm. "Of course he can. Everyone knows that. Right?"

"Yeah. Sure." She shrugged and sidestepped them to enter the elevator. "He turns into all of them. All the animals. He has kennels of all sizes to accommodate him since he's so mangy, he can't sleep in the house. Now if you'll excuse me, gentlemen. Keep up the excellent work."

Lucky for her, it was early enough in the evening that the elevator did not require a room key to get to the upper floors. She hit the button for the top floor then collapsed against the railing as the lift carried her up. So much sweat ran down her back, her jacket was sticking to her skin.

Jameson, Ethan said. *What are you doing? Are you in the hotel?*

I'm following my gut. Now leave me to it. And with that, she walled off her thoughts to everything and everyone.

The passing floor numbers on the control panel acted like a countdown clock to the final showdown. She swayed on her feet and rolled her shoulders as if she were preparing for battle.

The door to the top floor opened, and she looked around for the signs pointing to the helicopter landing pad. A big red sign warned that access was granted by permission only, and alarms would sound if opened.

Jameson shook her head. That was dumb. By the time anyone responded to the alarm, whoever had trespassed would be long gone, or completed whatever it was they had gone up there to do.

She kicked at the pieces of glass already lying in the doorway. Or they could smash out the panes. Apparently, that had worked just as well.

There was no time to hesitate. Who knew how big of a lead Ashley had on her? Jameson pushed through the door at the top and raced across the flat expanse of the landing pad. On the other side was a dark outline of a person.

Immediately, Jameson reached for her whip then lashed out, wrapping the coil around the person's waist as they began to climb the short retention wall. She jerked her arm back and the figure tumbled to their butt. As they flailed for purchase, their hood fell back, revealing their face to the security lights.

"What the hell?" Ash sputtered then her eyes narrowed in recognition. "Jameson? What are you doing?"

"What am I doing? What am *I* doing? What the fuck are you doing?" She tightened her grip on the handle of the whip. "When did you start killing people? We don't kill."

"For fuck's sake." Ash struggled to her feet, with her arms still bound to her sides by the whip. Across her chest were the straps to a backpack. "How—why—how did you find me?"

"Those men. The ones who were mutilated. Like Gerald Mulvaney. That was you, wasn't it? Do you know how many people are trying to find the killer? There's, like, a bajillion agencies looking for the murderer. You're the reason the police are looking for the Crimson Angels. Why they're investigating me."

At least Ash had the grace to look ashamed as she averted her gaze. "I'm sorry, James. I didn't mean for you to get roped up in all of this."

"What are you thinking?"

She shook her arms free of the whip. "You seriously have to ask? What does it look like? I'm dispensing justice. I'm doing what everybody else is too scared shitless to do."

"But murder?"

"I'm making a statement. I'm striking the fear of God into the patriarchy. Every day they grow bolder, untouchable. No one is holding them accountable." She spread her arms wide. "*I'm* holding them accountable. The time has come and we as females in this society cannot wait any more."

"You're committing massive felonies. You'll be sent to prison. If you're lucky. We're talking death penalty–type stuff here, Ash."

"That's a risk I'm willing to take."

"Well, you shouldn't be," Jameson shouted, fighting rising hysteria.

Why was it that the longer they stood out in the wind, the more Ash seemed convinced she was on the side of right? The woman's confidence was making Jameson wonder if she was somehow in the wrong. Everything about this situation was wrong.

A streak of brown raced between them and fluttered to the ground by their feet. Jameson blinked in confusion as the bat placed the tip of its wings onto the ground before the fine crack of bones reached her ears. Tiny bat legs morphed into those of a dog, and in a few heartbeats, a German shepherd was at her side.

"Fuck," she bit out. "I told Ethan I was fine. Go away."

The dog tilted his head and gave her a doggy version of a shrug.

"I mean it. Back the fuck off, Therian." At least she remembered to use his codename. "Go stand in the corner." She stared him down until he trotted to the side. Although he sat on his haunches, his fur bristled as if ready to strike at a moment's notice.

"What is that?" Ashley asked, backing away. Uncertainty finally entered her eyes. "Is that one of those superhero freaks? What have you done?"

"I told you. Everyone is after the murderer. Even superhero freaks."

"Murderer? Murderer?" Her voice rose. "You say that like I'm some common killer. I am a liberator. And what about you, Jameson? As if your hands are clean. You're the girl who killed her mother's rapist. Or did you forget?"

The breath in Jameson's lungs froze as the world went still around her. Even the wind died down and all was silent except for the rush of blood in her veins.

Forget? Forget?! As if that moment in time would ever leave her.

The darkness of the closet. The sound of her mother's screams when she had come home early from work and one of her roommate's johns wanted more.

Never would she forget the weight of that man's body against her chest and arms when she rushed out of the closet and barreled into his side. The push when they went through the plate-glass window. Only her mother snatching her by the back of her shirt had kept Jameson from tumbling out their third-story window after him.

And that smell. That metallic bite hitting the back of her palate from the scent of blood that covered the jagged line of glass of the broken window. No, she would never forget.

"Fuck you," Jameson spat. Her skin burned red-hot. "How dare you equate an eight-year-old protecting her mother and your killing rampage. It's not the same."

Ashley raised her brow. "Is it not? You got justice. I'm out for justice."

"You're out for vengeance."

"As if you're not? Look at you." Ashley gestured to Jameson's outfit and the whip in her hand. "Why have we been doing what we've been doing the last two years? Why is there a Crimson Angels? Vengeance. Seeking retribution for those who can't. It's who we are. It's who I am. Up until this moment I thought it was who you were too."

"It is. I am. But there's a limit—"

"What's the limit? How many women need to die before somebody takes a stand?"

Jameson stumbled back as the truth of Ashley's statement slapped her in the face.

No one questioned her conviction. Never. Once she made a decision on a subject, she threw herself in, 100 percent. Balls to the wall. No regrets. And now Ashley was calling out her loyalty to the cause? Because she wasn't willing to commit murder?

Long ago, Jameson had made the commitment to do whatever it took to protect those in need. No matter the cost. Fly or die. Well, apparently there was a cost. Ash was willing to kill and be killed, while she drew lines in the sand.

Was Jameson not doing enough for sisterkind? How

many women *did* have to be hurt or killed before their voices were heard?

"Look, James, you do you. But I'm going to do me." Ash dropped into a fighting stance. "And if you think you're going to hand me over to the police, you have another thing coming."

"You're going to fight me now?" Jameson asked incredulously.

Ashley smirked. "Looks like it."

And with that she threw the first punch.

Jameson dodged to the left just as Ashley's right hook brushed past her cheek. In return, Jameson threw up her hands, shoving Ashley away.

Ripley's bark echoed in the night as Ash grabbed her by the lapels of her jacket and spun her around and around, grappling with her as if she were a sumo wrestler. In the dark Jameson could barely determine what was left or right as they swung across the landing pad.

She came to an abrupt halt as she slammed hip-first into the barricade, but Ashley's momentum continued to take her up and over the railing, leaving Jameson to gasp in horror as her hold on Ash's jacket slipped.

"No!" Jameson screamed and tightened her grip. Her vision blurred then slowly cleared, allowing her to see the precarious grip she had on Ashley's sleeve.

Ashley half-dangled, half-balanced on tiptoe on a thin lip of the building that formed the top of the windows of the floor below them. It was the only thing keeping her from falling the twenty-six stories.

"Hang on, Ash," Jameson tried to shout, but the railing dug into her pelvis. The weight of her friend and gravity was doing its damnedest to take her over the side too.

"I've got you," Ripley called out, and wrapped his strong arms around her middle. "Hang tight. I'll pull you both up."

"No," she shouted in a panic. "Not yet. My grip is sliding. Ash. Give me your other hand."

Despite being a hair's-breadth away from death, the glow of the city lights reflected the serenity shining in Ashley's eyes as she gazed up at her.

"You can let me go, James. It's all right," she said in a steady voice.

"Are you insane?" How the fuck could she be so calm at a time like this? "Give me your hand."

"Let me go."

Tears streamed down Jameson's cheeks. "I'm not gonna let you fall. Give me your fucking hand."

"I'm not going to fall. Let me go, James. It's okay. It's going to be okay."

Jameson leaned into Ripley, who had braced his big, tree trunk–like legs, and dug her backside into his gut, trying to muscle Ashley up enough for Ripley to grab onto her and pull her over.

"It's going to be okay, James," Ashley kept saying, as tranquil as could be. "Fly or die. Let go."

The muscles in her arms were on fire. She couldn't see for shit for the tears in her eyes. But over the pounding of her heart, she heard Ashley say it over and over again.

"It's going to be all right."

Jameson dared to crack open her eyes, her breath hitching hard in the back of her throat. Ashley's blue gaze was laser-sharp and focused.

"I love you, sis," she managed to say past her dry lips.

Ashley smiled. "I love you, too."

Pain exploded in her knuckles as she relaxed her fingers,

releasing her grip on Ashley's sleeve. Her friend didn't make a sound, not even a gasp, as she tumbled over the side of the building and into the night.

Jameson sank to her knees in a sobbing heap and watched through the railing, hoping she had made the right decision.

Footsteps pounded from behind her, then Ethan and Max met her at the railing.

"Holy shit," Max exclaimed. "Did she fall?"

"No. There." Ethan pointed into the distance. "I see a parachute."

"What?" She struggled to her feet. Her desperate gaze searched the area where Ethan pointed until she spotted the black parachute floating down Fifth Avenue. "Oh my God. Oh my God. She did it. She did it."

Ethan gathered her close to his chest. "Sweetheart, are you all right?"

"I don't know," she blubbered against his expensive suit jacket. Her knees shook so hard, they were about to give out at any moment. "I don't know anything."

"Should I go after her?" Ripley asked. "I can track her in my bat form."

"No," Max answered. "Our job was to conclusively link Ashley to the murders. We've done that. We'll give what we have to Lancaster and let him take over."

"Got it."

"Thank you," she said to Max. "I don't think I can do anymore tonight."

Her world had turned upside down, and there was still so much unknown. Did Ashley really get away? Were the police waiting for her to land at this very moment? What did that mean for her? Was she going to be considered an accessory to murder? Did it even matter anymore if she was?

"I want a drink," she managed to say as tremors continued to steal her breath. "I want a big drink. Lots of them."

Ethan ran his hand down the back of her hair. "We can do that. Let's get you inside and warm first. You're shivering so hard, I'm afraid you're going to come apart."

They turned to go back into the hotel but stopped short when they faced the wall of Sheriff Lancaster and two other officers blocking their path.

"Drinks are going to have to wait, Daniels," Sheriff Lancaster said. "Ms. Alinari and I need have a talk."

Oh, for fuck's sake. The light was green. Her last thread of control snapped.

"What? What?" she screamed at Lancaster. "What do you want?"

"I need to ask you about Ashley Fairfield. About what you two were arguing about before she jumped."

She staggered toward him. Her body refused to cooperate with her commands as her adrenaline crashed and exhaustion set in. "What the fuck do you think we were arguing about? She shot that man."

The sheriff sighed and rested his hands on his belt. "I need specifics."

"Why don't you ask her yourself?" She pointed down the street. "She's probably at Fifth and Pike right now. If you hurry, you may be able to catch her."

"We've already dispatched officers. Ms. Alinari, I don't think you realize how serious this is. Your friend just killed two people. Possibly more."

"You think I don't know that?" Hysterical laughter bubbled from her lips. "Yeah, she killed two people. And you know what? I don't blame her. Those men were pieces of shit. They deserved every horrible thing they got. And you know what else? Good for her. If I had half the balls she did, I'd be right there with her."

"Murder is against the law," he began.

Ugh. She was so sick of that lame old excuse.

"Yeah, and so is the bullshit those assholes did." She stumbled closer and jammed her finger into his chest. "You are the law. You are supposed to keep the bad things from happening and stop the bad man. It's your job to keep people safe. But you didn't." She kept thumping on his chest. "You didn't make them stop. You are supposed to fucking make them stop."

She rocked back on her feet and turned on the men standing behind her with their mouths open in shock. "And you, with your powers. Gah. I can't even begin. What good are your powers if you aren't using them to stop these assholes?"

She marched around Lancaster with her middle finger high in the air. "If you're going to arrest me, arrest me. Otherwise, I'm going to the bar. Peace out, motherfucker."

CHAPTER TWENTY-TWO

JAMESON STOPPED SHORT with one foot on the bottom stair and the other in the hallway leading to her apartment and stared in disbelief.

It had been a long day—hell, a long week—but surely she was too tired to imagine two gorgeous men waiting outside her apartment door.

She shook her head and the vision remained.

Okay. But surely, *surely,* she was too exhausted to imagine that they smelled of garlic and sausage.

"What is going on?" she asked, carefully sidling closer.

Ethan lifted the picnic basket he held in his hand. "We brought gifts."

"Orecchiette with sausage and broccolini." Ronan lifted the bottle in his hand. "And wine."

Her favorite. Oh, they were good.

And no fair that they showed up on her doorstep looking so hot. They were freshly shaved, with their hair styled and dressed for a night of fun in jeans, different-colored Henley shirts and suede jackets. If they hadn't confirmed she was awake, she would have sworn she was still imagining things, since Ethan wasn't in his usual suit and tie.

Upon closer inspection, she noticed the dark circles under their eyes and the fatigued smiles on their lips. They were still adorable, but stress obviously took a toll on them and they were probably just as wiped out as she was. But who wouldn't be, after the fiasco at the hotel?

The last time she saw the brothers was in the hotel's bar, where she had downed a few whiskey sours and told anyone who came near her to fuck off. They had wanted to argue. Judging by the tight line of their lips and the grim expression on their face, she knew they were worried about her, but they also understood that she was ready to fight for alone time and obeyed her request.

They obeyed too well, if they asked her. What she hadn't anticipated was that one day apart was going to turn into a week. To be fair, that wasn't all their doing. Some of that time had been spent with her in police custody answering questions about Ashley. Since there was no evidence tying Jameson directly to any of the murders, and it was her assistance that helped crack open the case, she was allowed to go free.

The long separation had made her worry that perhaps things between them had fallen apart. That her refusal to condemn Ashley for her actions had been too much for Ethan and Ronan and they had decided they wanted nothing to do with her.

If that was how they felt about her, then that was how they felt. She couldn't pretend to be someone she wasn't just as she wouldn't want them to pretend either.

Seeing them there now, though, ignited a flare of hope that perhaps there was a chance for a relationship between the three of them after all.

"Did you bring enough for all of us?" she asked quietly.

"Yep. And some for leftovers tomorrow," Ethan replied.

"Well, let's not let that get too cold, shall we?" She scooted past them to unlock her apartment door. "Thank you, by the way, for not breaking and entering. I know you have the abilities to do so."

Ethan laughed. "We considered it."

"But while the gesture might be considered romantic, we figured you would find it an invasion of privacy," Ronan finished.

"You would be correct."

The fellas set their offerings on the kitchen island, then Ethan escorted her over to the couch.

"Sit down. We'll take care of dinner." He bent and slipped her heels off her feet. Taking a seat on the coffee table across from her, he took her foot into his hands and began to manipulate her toes. "I'm sure you've had a long week. Stressful."

Stressful didn't cover the half of it. After several long days of interviews with law enforcement, she was now operating on sheer determination alone. Trini kept telling her to take a sick day, but she had responsibilities, and she wasn't going to let them slide because she was exhausted.

"Were the FBI tough on you?" he asked.

Her chuckle turned into a moan as Ethan hit a sensitive spot on her foot. A girl could quickly become addicted to this sort of attention. "The FBI were okay. To be honest, Lancaster was much worse."

The sheriff was apoplectic. Enraged to the point she thought he'd stroke out right in front of her. Ashley had gotten away. And despite the spectacle of what had occurred at the hotel, Lancaster had very little to show for it at the end of the day.

Ethan and Maestro had witnessed Ashley shooting Fred Dorian. And the CEO could positively identify her in the murder of his personal assistant. That case was solved. But without witnesses and a weapon, no one could link Ashley to the assassination of Sen. Collins, since it appeared that another gun had been used in his murder and the ballistics didn't match to the Dorian shooting. All the sheriff had was circumstantial evidence.

As for the other murders, there wasn't any conclusive evidence linking to Ashley. There was a whole lot of speculation, but unless they found her and she confessed, the police had nothing on her.

"Ashley hasn't contacted you at all?"

"No." She pulled her foot from Ethan's hand and brazenly handed him her left foot. "I wouldn't want her to. Alisia called me last night. Network has been following up on the list of locations that Ash had hidden. So far, there's been no sight of her in any of them."

Ethan nodded and continued with the massage. She felt his question hovering in the air. Would she turn her friend in if Ash did make contact? At the moment, she still wasn't certain.

Ronan joined them on the couch, carrying a satchel. "We have something else for you." From inside the bag he withdrew a big plastic binder and several notebooks.

"What is this?" She asked as he laid it on her lap. She gasped as she opened the cover and flipped through the pages. "Is this for real? This is Ashley's tome of terror. I don't understand."

"After Ashley parachuted from the hotel, we sent Ted to her apartment to retrieve her notes before the police got there."

She looked at them in confusion. "I still don't understand."

Ronan took her hand in his. "We heard you that night. On the roof."

"Oh." All the warmth left her body. That meant they also heard about her and her mother.

"And we heard Ashley too," Ethan added. "The pain. The anger. The frustration. She's not as good at shielding her thoughts as you are. She had been dealt so many blows. Suffered many humiliations. While we don't agree with her methods at all, in any capacity, we understand them. And we hurt for her like we hurt for you."

"We turned over the evidence that we had initially found that day from her apartment," Ronan said. "That wasn't everything she had. What's in your lap is everything. It's yours now. To do with what you wish. If you want to turn it into the police, it's your choice."

The items on her lap suddenly became ethereal. Magical. It was a map of revenge for all womankind.

Talk about being in possession of a double-edge sword. Did she turn her sister in to the police or watch with bated breath to see if the much-needed revolution against the patriarchy would ignite?

She set the binder on the table beside Ethan. Whatever path she chose would be a decision she could not take lightly, because once she made her choice, she was going to be all in.

"Thank you. Thank you for trusting me." She squeezed Ronan's hand and reached out for Ethan.

"We have something else we want to tell you," Ronan said.

"There's more? Dinner, wine, and a hit list. What more could a girl want?" She laughed.

"We love you," Ethan blurted out.

She and Ronan turned toward Ethan with their mouths agape.

"Whaa?" she asked.

"Sorry." Ronan tried to recover for his brother. "We didn't mean for it to come out like that, but I guess getting right to the point is better. Yes, we've fallen in love with you."

"Oh—I… Oh."

This was it. She hit the wall. This was the last little thing this week that broke her brain and she had absolutely no idea how to respond.

"I know this may come as a shock," Ethan said and took both of her hands in his. "But we love you. We love your intelligence."

"Your generosity," Ronan added.

"Your crazy sense of humor."

"Your passion. The way you encompass everything with your entire being."

"Even your temper." Ethan half grinned. "It's adorable. Although sometimes I wish it wasn't directed at us."

"We love you, Jameson." Ronan shrugged. "Simple as that. We love you."

"I, I…" Her lips went numb. "I…have deep feelings of…like for you too."

The boys looked at her then at each other then back to her again as their grins widened.

All right, she knew it. She was a chickenshit. She was terrified to say what was in her heart because at that moment she wasn't sure she could trust what was in her heart. Too much had gone down in the last few weeks. They had gone on, what, one normal date? And even that it had ended in an argument.

But she did care for them. Very, very much. Over the last few weeks when she had dared to imagine her future, they were by her side. And she was happy. So incredibly happy.

She grabbed Ethan by the front of his shirt and brought him down to his knees before she threw herself into his arms and smothered him in a kiss. A kiss filled with all the emotions she was afraid to speak out loud. A kiss filled with all the hopes and dreams that she was too terrified to admit.

She drew back and laid her palms on either side of Ethan's face. She pressed her forehead to his for a second before returning to his brother. Releasing Ethan, she slid her hands around Ronan's neck and pulled him closer and nuzzled his skin before taking his lips with the same gentle ferocity she did his twin.

Both brothers were there with her, supporting her and not pressuring her to say the words back. Of course, their patience made her love them all the more.

I love you, okay? I love you both, too.

When she ran out of breath she pulled away and rested her head against Ronan's chest. Their happiness engulfed her in the warmest and delightful embrace she had ever experienced.

"What now?" she asked. "Where do we go from here?"

Ethan came to sit beside her and wrapped his arm around her shoulders. "We can start by taking you on a date. A real date."

"And we'll work on the projects for the shelter that we promised," Ronan added.

"Oh, yeah. You did promise me lots of money."

"More than money, wildcat. We're going to help you save the world. Without resorting to murder. But make no mistake, we will save the world. We promise."

She nestled between their warm bodies, confident that

they were going to be true to their word. "Save the world. That sounds nice. But you are going to feed me first, right?"

Ethan trailed a string of kisses along her cheek. "Are you certain that it's food that you want first?" He slid his palm up the outside of her thigh as he nipped her earlobe.

Her hmmm of consideration turned into a gasp of desire as Ronan began to unbutton her blouse.

"I could be persuaded to wait," she said.

Turned out the brothers were very persuasive indeed. Not only did they prove that she was ravenous for their bodies, they also proved without a shadow of a doubt that reheated pasta with a bottle of wine in bed was even better served at two a.m.

About Anna Alexander

Award winning author Anna Alexander is the author of the Heroes of Saturn and the Sprawling A Ranch series. With Hugh Jackman's abs and Christopher Reeve's blue eyes as inspiration, she loves spinning tales of superheroes finding love. Anna also loves to give back and has served on the board for the Greater Seattle Romance Writers of America as chapter president and on the committee for the Emerald City Writers Conference. Anna is also a co-founder of the Seattle UnCon

Sign up to receive news about Anna's latest releases at http://eepurl.com/Q0tsz

Anna welcomes comments from readers.

Website

annaalexander.net

Facebook

facebook.com/pages/Anna-Alexander/282170065189471

Twitter

twitter.com/AnnaWriter

Newsletter

http://eepurl.com/Q0tsz

Also by Anna Alexander

The Evolutioneers Series

Genesis

Instinct

Vengeance

Cavern Series

A Night at The Cavern

Only at The Cavern

Heroes of Saturn Series

Hero Revealed

Hero Unleashed

Hero Unmasked

Hero Rising

Men of the Sprawling A Ranch Series

The Cowboy Way

The Marlboro Man

To Have Faith

Sweetest Kisses

Eight Seconds to Forever

Elite Metal Series

Bound by Steele

Adamantium's Roar

Vibranium's Truth

Learn about Anna's latest release by subscribing to her newsletter at

http://eepurl.com/Q0tsz

www.ingramcontent.com/pod-product-compliance
Lightning Source LLC
Chambersburg PA
CBHW021321250626
47155CB00002B/584

* 9 7 8 0 9 9 8 5 2 0 3 7 7 *